ONE GIANT LEAP

ALSO BY HEATHER KACZYNSKI

Dare Mighty Things

ONE GIANT LEAP

HEATHER KACZYNSKI

HARPER TEEN
An Imprint of HarperCollinsPublishers

HarperTeen is an imprint of HarperCollins Publishers.

One Giant Leap
Copyright © 2018 by Heather Kaczynski
All rights reserved. Printed in the United States of America.
No part of this book may be used or reproduced in any manner whatsoever without
written permission except in the case of brief quotations embodied in critical articles
and reviews. For information address HarperCollins Children's Books, a division of
HarperCollins Publishers, 195 Broadway, New York, NY 10007.
www.epicreads.com

Library of Congress Control Number: 2018945998
ISBN 978-0-06-247990-7

Typography by Sarah Nichole Kaufman
18 19 20 21 22   PC/LSCH   10 9 8 7 6 5 4 3 2 1
❖
First Edition

To my parents, John and Rebecca,
who made everything possible

Here men from the planet Earth
first set foot upon the moon. July 1969, A.D.
We came in peace for all mankind.
—INSCRIPTION OF THE LUNAR PLAQUE,
LEFT ON THE MOON DURING THE *APOLLO 11* MISSION

Our most basic common link is that we all inhabit this small planet.
We all breathe the same air. We all cherish our children's future.
And we are all mortal.
—JOHN F. KENNEDY

ONE GIANT LEAP

ONE

I OPENED MY eyes to the interior of a spaceship and couldn't remember how I'd gotten there.

Focus. Breathe. Where are you?

Four stainless steel pods stood around me like a futuristic Stonehenge. The space was circular, confined. The lights were too bright, sending spots and flares dancing before my vision.

Memories slowly trickled back to me—flashes of blueprints and schematics I'd studied and memorized a long time ago. But they were disjointed, like pieces to a puzzle I'd forgotten how to put together.

I was sprawled on the floor, the door to my empty pod hanging open. The metal grate of the floor had left an aching imprint on my cheek.

My helmet was lying on its side nearby. I had no memory of taking it off.

The habitation module. That's where we were. And those pods held my crewmates in hibernation.

The general idea of the why and how of my situation was still there in my mind. It was the details and the most recent memories that were gone.

Cautiously, I sat up, tensing my abdominals to force blood into my head so that I wouldn't lose consciousness again. A short wave of dizziness passed, and I felt moderately normal.

How long had I been unconscious? I touched my cheek gingerly; the feeling in my fingertips was blunted from the skintight suit I wore.

The module was silent but for the air circulation system. At least life-support systems seemed intact.

No engines burned. I couldn't detect any motion. No windows here to give me a clue as to where we were.

I couldn't have been here long. My crewmates were sleeping inside their pods, their vital-sign monitors still flashing the steady rhythms of heartbeats.

I'd been supposed to wake up first. First into the hibernation pod, first out. The theory had been that I would respond best out of anyone else in the crew to the hibernation, being the youngest and most physically fit.

That, at least, I could remember.

The most worrisome thing wasn't that I couldn't remember how I'd woken up on the floor. It was that I was *on the floor.*

Which meant some kind of gravity was in effect.

When I'd gone under, we'd been floating in zero-g. There shouldn't be gravity now. Unless.

Had we . . . *arrived?*

Facts trickled back into my reality. I was on board the first faster-than-light-capable ship built by human hands. I'd competed for the honor of being included in this crew. We were here to . . . I couldn't remember. Something important. Something *massive.* The enormity was still there, circling the edge of my consciousness, lost in the fog.

For a terrifying second, my own name eluded me. Then my lips formed the familiar sounds, muscle memory more than anything else.

"My name is Cassandra Gupta," I whispered out loud.

"Hello, Cassandra," said a pleasant disembodied voice.

I would've jumped, if my body were currently responding to my brain's commands. I'd never heard the voice aloud before, but I'd had it in my head long enough to recognize it.

"Sunny," I choked out, and a strange sort of relief flooded me. Sunny may have been little more than a very intelligent computer program, in charge of our vital signs and ship trajectory while the human crew was asleep, but at least I wasn't alone on this ship, stranded who-knows-where in the universe.

My voice, when I tried to speak above a whisper, was like something that had been dragged down a gravel driveway until it was an unrecognizable carcass. "Sunny—water?"

A panel retracted on the wall nearby, and I dragged my

lower body to it, my legs feeling as though they'd been asleep longer than I had. I reached up with one arm, hand scrabbling up the wall with some difficulty, to retrieve the pouch of post-hibernation fluids.

I unscrewed the top and let the liquid trickle slowly into my mouth, unsure that my muscles would remember how to swallow. Chilled and slightly salty orange-flavored liquid coated my throat. A few coughs and gags, and I started to feel a little more human. "Sunny," I said, this time a little clearer. "Status report?"

"Please clarify request."

"Uh, *crew* status report. Please," I added sheepishly.

"Activation sequences have automatically commenced. Pod release of Dr. Harper Copeland in one minute, forty-five seconds. Please stand by."

I should've realized—the pods of the other crew members were triggered to activate not long after mine. Just then, the pod nearest me began to beep, a red light flashing on the display. I swore, climbing to my feet and immediately crashing to my knees in my haste. Somehow I made it to the pod, using its edges to help me pull myself up.

Through the small window cut into the steel, the sleeping face of Dr. Harper Copeland was an eerie pale blue. The tube began to hum beneath my hands. I took a shaky step backward as the gel inside the tube was drained away, giving Dr. Copeland's face back some of its natural deep brown color.

Waking sequence complete, the pod door unlatched, and

Dr. Copeland's limp body fell against it. I opened the door and just barely caught her before she hit the deck.

My arms couldn't hold her weight long. I ended up kneeling on the deck, supporting her helmeted head while her eyelids fluttered. Before she completely regained consciousness, I unlatched her helmet and pulled it off.

Her eyes opened. She blinked a few times, then focused on my face with the laser intensity that I had grown accustomed to after weeks of being her student. Her mouth opened, nothing but a hoarse, voiceless rasp escaping.

I was ready with the electrolyte solution. She was like an infant, learning how to coordinate breathing and swallowing for the first time.

"Cassie," she said after she'd finished the pouch. There was a question in her eyes, a furrow in her brow. Maybe she was wondering the same thing I'd wondered: Why is there gravity? Where are we? But instead of asking her questions, she gestured weakly to the pod beside hers that held flight engineer Logan Shaw. "The others."

His pod was beeping.

One after another, the hibernation modules released my crewmates, and they tumbled into my arms. I laid them each in turn on the steel deck, removing their helmets and repeating assurances to each that they were not, in fact, dying.

The physical effects of the cryogenic hibernation had worn off relatively quickly for me. The pouch of electrolytes, water, and glucose had jump-started my system. Which was good, because the hibernation pods of *Odysseus* weren't meant to open under normal gravity conditions. We were supposed to be able to float out of them in zero gravity. We weren't meant to wake with the full pressure of gravity bearing down on our weakened bodies.

Instead, the four veteran astronauts of *Odysseus*—men and women who had taught me, who had spent their lives working to further human spaceflight, who had once been the pinnacle of human health—now lay limp and gasping at my feet like so many beached fish.

They were all upward of forty-five. They'd basically been in a coma, living off liquid nutrition and floating in goo, and they were wrecked. I mean, so was I, but compared to them I was an Olympic athlete.

Dr. Copeland recovered enough by the time Shaw's pod opened to sit up, leaning against the wall for support. Her eyes a little sunken, but still sharp, still calculating. She helped advise me on how to take care of them best she could. Her instructions came in between short, breathy gasps. Sunny filled in the gaps in Dr. Copeland's memory for me.

The rest of the crew members gagged on their pouches of electrolyte solution, hardly able to hold them in their hands. Our muscles had atrophied. Not as much as they would have without the electric stimulation nodes and pressure of the suits regulating our bodies during hibernation, but still enough that it would take time for us to fully recover.

By the time everyone else could stand on their own, my

lungs felt heavy, my muscles overtaxed. The cushy, padded interior of my empty hibernation module was beginning to look really inviting.

Dominic Bolshakov spoke a command to Sunny, and the pods retracted behind wall panels and were replaced with molded plastic, high-backed chairs. There was now slightly more breathing room in the cramped hibernation module.

We each crawled into one, conserving our strength. None of us had any kind of endurance.

Nervousness fluttered in my stomach as I searched each crew member's face. They all appeared just as I'd last seen them, sealing me in my HHM in orbit around Earth. Bolshakov's gray buzz cut had grown out somewhat, and his skin was ashen. Logan Shaw, with his friendly smile and skin pale white beneath his freckles, had a strange absence in his affect like a sleepwalker, and it took him seconds to respond when spoken to. Michele Jeong kept blinking her eyes slowly, squeezing them shut and then opening them wide as though she was having trouble with her vision.

The men had stubble where they'd once been clean-shaven— the cryogenic sleep had slowed, but not stopped, our metabolisms. I was pretty sure my braid hadn't been quite this long when I'd gone under.

We were all a little too thin. Wasted from living on nothing but liquid nutrients.

I closed my eyes. Unbidden, the face of a boy I used to know rose to my mind's eye, older and sadder than I'd remembered.

I shook off the apparition. He was nothing more than a dream I'd had while in hibernation. A dream that kept chasing me into reality. He wasn't important right now.

"Why . . . is there . . . gravity?" Shaw was looking at his hands, then at his feet, as though he'd expected them to be floating.

"We shouldn't have landed yet," said Jeong, her face still slack with sleep. She shook herself a little, then placed a hand on the bulkhead. "No vibrations. We're not even moving."

"Computer, report," Commander Bolshakov said. His voice was almost back to full strength but hadn't lost the hoarseness we all suffered from. "What is our location?"

The cool, computerized voice of Sunny came from the wall speaker. "Undesignated terrestrial satellite of exoplanet designated Kepler-186f."

There was a beat of silence.

"What did she just say?" Shaw asked.

Sunny helpfully repeated herself.

Kepler-186f. That was it. That had been our original destination. More details kept trickling in, heralded by tidbits of familiar data. My brain was waking fully, like a slow computer churning back to life.

NASA and SEE would not have sent us hurtling through space toward a moon that we had not even discovered, much less named.

"Is anyone else . . . having trouble with their memory?" Shaw asked. "We were supposed to land on 186f, weren't we? Not its moon."

Jeong and I nodded.

"The computer was programmed to take the best possible course of action for our trajectory while we were unconscious," Bolshakov reminded us. "There must have been some problem that diverted us to this moon. She is designed to make some decisions autonomously for the best interest of the crew; this isn't that unusual. Sunny, pull up the projected map of the Kepler-186 system."

A hologram of circling spheres appeared in the middle of the room. In the center was Kepler-186 itself, the red dwarf star of this system. Then the four planets we knew about, circling too close to their sun to be livable. The fifth, designated Kepler-186f, had been the first Earth-sized exoplanet discovered within the habitable zone of its star, way back in 2014.

"This is the map of the system as we knew it when we left," Bolshakov explained slowly. "Sunny, now display the adjusted solar map, accounting for any new data the scanners detected upon arrival." A handful of small celestial bodies, all undiscovered until now, clustered around Kepler-186f, circling in multiple orbits. "Sunny, highlight our current location."

The smallest circling orb—one of the moons of Kepler-186f—glowed a soft blue.

"Just to remind everyone, seeing as we're all a bit fuzzy, Kepler-186f was highlighted for its potential to harbor life. But that isn't the reason we came. We came because we were invited."

A cold sensation pooled in my stomach at Bolshakov's words. I did recall that now. We'd come here on good faith, following instructions sent to us across light-years, in a ship of alien design.

But there was something *else*. Something still prowling around the outer edges of my knowledge, like a predator in the dark. Something crucial I had forgotten and needed desperately to remember.

I felt like I should say something. But I had nothing to say, and we had so much else to do. This eerie feeling might only be a side effect of hibernation, a lingering sense of a nightmare that hadn't yet burned away like the morning mist.

"Is that why our landing was diverted?" Jeong asked in a whisper.

Silence fell over the five of us.

"I don't know what's going on here," Dr. Copeland admitted. "But we're five hundred light-years from home. We need to stick to the plan, as much as we're able."

Astronauts—with the exception of me, who'd only had a few months' worth of preparation for this mission—trained over and over again for every possibility. The plan was everything. There were backup plans upon backup plans. Every eventuality had been discussed, dissected, and diagrammed.

None of our plans had included landing on this moon.

"All right, then. Since we seem to have some missing spots in our memories, we'll have to rely on Sunny to keep us straight. Sunny, what's next on our protocol?" Bolshakov said.

"Wait. Shouldn't we run Sunny through a diagnostic check first, to make sure she wasn't damaged during flight?" Jeong asked.

Bolshakov asked Sunny to run a diagnostic on *Odysseus.* Everything was functioning optimally. That seemed to rule out a system malfunction being the reason for the diverted landing. Then, with a heavy sigh, he asked what we all wanted to know. "Sunny, what is the Mission Elapsed Time?"

Sunny's computerized voice was calm and unaffected. "MET is five months, twenty-five days, fourteen hours, and seventeen minutes."

We looked at each other in confusion. "That isn't right," Shaw said, furrowing his brow. "It can't be. It's not possible."

Kepler-186 was five hundred light-years from Earth.

The computer sat silent.

When Shaw spoke, his voice was so tightly controlled it was clear to me he was trying to rein in some deeper panic. "Sunny, please explain how we were able to land on a planet five hundred light-years away in only five Earth months."

"*Odysseus* is equipped with an Alcubierre drive capable of faster-than-light travel." That was all she said. Like it was that simple.

Odysseus was equipped with Alcubierre engines, which had only been hypothetical until this flight. These allowed us to distort the fabric of space-time in a small bubble around ourselves, moving through space-time without violating the laws of physics, and hopefully without a time-distortion effect that would see us return to Earth to find that hundreds of years had passed without us.

The engineers and scientists behind Project Adastra had run tests on these engines, of course. Computer models. But in reality, we didn't know the full capabilities of these engines until we turned them on. They were not of our own design. They'd been a gift from whomever it was that had wanted us to come here.

I was itching to move on. We were on an alien planet. We needed to focus on that. "The ship is in good condition and we're all safe. I think it's more important for us to focus not on the discrepancies in the plan but on accomplishing our mission now that we're here."

A corner of Bolshakov's mouth ticked upward, and a pleasant glow warmed my chest. "I agree, Gupta. Let us follow procedure."

The others took their cues from him. Only Shaw's face still looked a little pinched.

Bolshakov said, "Sunny, is this moon habitable?"

Sunny's dispassionate voice cut through the room. "The surface temperature and radiation levels are lethal to humans. There is no detectable amount of liquid water on the surface. No signs of carbon-based life, and no artificial structures seen by *Odysseus's* exterior cameras on approach."

A barren planet.

I took another long, slow breath, concentrating on the feeling of my ribs expanding, the muscles pulling taut. We had come all this way. We had been *invited* here. Why?

"View screen up," Bolshakov said.

The screen revealed itself from behind a panel in the bulkhead. We waited, but the field of black never changed.

"What's wrong with it?" Shaw asked.

Jeong wobbled to her feet like a newborn colt—so odd to see from a woman I knew was so physically strong—and checked the controls. "The cameras are functioning normally. Computer, explain."

Sunny's voice came unaffected from the console. "*Odysseus* is currently underground."

The five of us shared bewildered expressions.

Jeong narrowed her eyes. "Computer, show recorded footage of ship landing."

A dull yellow-and-gunmetal desert materialized on the screen—the surface of the moon, small enough that we could see the curve of the horizon even as it came closer, zooming toward us at rapid speed. The bare rock was a mess of rubble, sharp mountains and deep cracks in the bedrock, veins of exposed metals running through the dust. The surface had been pummeled by asteroids and radiation until there was not a square inch of ground left unbroken.

An alien sun, comparatively smaller than our own, was a soft peach light in the dusty gray sky, and then it was gone as the camera footage turned black.

But the clock was still running—we hadn't lost the feed.

"What the hell happened?" Copeland's voice was growing louder with frustration. "We're obviously underground. But how did we get here?"

"Sunny, play the footage again, please," I said.

Again, the broken surface of the world came into view and zoomed larger, the details becoming more high-def the closer we came. This time I kept my eyes on the ground. And just before the cameras went dark, I saw something change. "There! Sunny, pause the feed!"

I balanced on legs that felt like they'd run a marathon and pointed to the spot on the screen. "Right there. Do you see? Sunny, rewind and play back at half speed."

As the crew watched, a dark spot appeared on the screen, growing larger as we approached. A hatch. A metal hatch in the surface of the planet.

We'd been flown by autopilot through a hangar door and into an underground shelter.

"Computer," Shaw began, "how long have we been here, on the planet?"

"Twelve Earth hours have elapsed since landing."

There it was again—the itch in my memory. There was something hiding there. Something massive. As I tried to dig deeper into the secrets my brain was keeping from me, a real alarm began to blare.

"Proximity alert," Sunny said, her unruffled calm belying the danger of the siren.

Something was moving outside.

We looked at each other, then at our commander.

Bolshakov climbed to his feet, attempting to hide just what an effort it was. "Ladies and gentleman," he began, fitting his helmet back over his head. It closed with a small *whoosh* of air as it sealed to his suit. "We came here to do a job. Let us go and greet our hosts."

TWO

"COMMANDER?" SHAW ASKED, awaiting direction. A sheen of sweat had broken out on his forehead. This was the one situation none of us had been able to rehearse. Not even their years of experience could help them.

Bolshakov's face was haggard, but his eyes were alert and sharp. "We came all this way. We might as well go out and take a look." NASA had known what they were doing appointing Bolshakov; he radiated decisive strength. "Suit up."

"Commander?" Shaw repeated. He shot a look at Jeong, and then to me. Then, "Yes, sir."

I had already put my helmet back on. We'd stay in the same suits we'd hibernated in, the black, skintight suit I'd first worn while in training back on Earth. It was the newest technology, able to protect us from temperature, radiation, and pressure extremes without sacrificing mobility.

"Computer, exterior atmosphere reading? What are we walking into?"

Sunny rattled off some stats as I began checking my suit over to make sure there were no irregularities. Copeland came over to help, her expert eyes and hands double-checking me.

Jeong translated the numbers. "Seems like we're in a bubble of protected atmosphere. Might even be breathable."

"Even so, we're not going to risk contamination." Copeland helped me into my Portable Life-Support System, or PLS, a heavy backpack that hooked into my helmet, and stuck her own helmet over her head with one hand. "The rebreathers should be enough for a good long look."

"We're really going out there?" Shaw asked. His eyes jolted nervously to the rest of us. "Now? We're still weak. We have time to test if it's safe outside."

"What, you think we came all this way to sit around on the tarmac?" Copeland smirked, her voice coming muted and electronic through the helmet's speakers as she slipped her own PLS on. Then, more serious, she added, "Temperature and radiation readings are all in the clear. There's even oxygen and nitrogen in comparable levels to Earth's atmosphere. I'd say we were brought here for a reason, and that reason probably wasn't to kill us."

Shaw swallowed hard but nodded.

Copeland approached me. She displayed no fear or hesitation.

She tapped the side of my helmet with one finger. "Remember your digital camera. All the footage from our helmet cams will be sent to Sunny to create a backup on *Odysseus*. Just tell her when to start and stop recording."

I knew that. Or at least, I had at some point. It was in one of the million-page manuals they'd given us to read before launch. *Pull yourself together, Gupta!*

Shaw helped me buckle the straps on my oxygen tank. "Be careful," he said in a low voice. Logan Shaw had been my easygoing instructor of physics and engineering. He'd been the nicest of my teachers. And now he was worried.

"Shaw, you stay here in case there's trouble. Keep in radio contact. Gupta's connection to Sunny makes her our default communications operator. Relay any messages through her." Bolshakov grabbed his gear, and we checked each other's PLSs to make sure everything was functional.

We followed Bolshakov into the airlock, leaving Shaw in the command module.

The airlock door slid closed behind us, and while we waited for decompression, Bolshakov came in over the comm. "Anyone come up with something historical to say?"

Before anyone could respond, the exterior door opened.

"Sunny, please begin recording." I said it quietly, without clicking my radio on so the others could hear, and felt that presence again—that flicker of recognition of someone turning their attention to me. It'd felt like a bizarre morphine dream.

But now I was awake, and she was still there. "Sunny? You there?"

Yes, Cassie. A mobile copy of my program has been downloaded into your suitboard computer. I am creating a backup of the video you are recording and maintaining contact with Odysseus.

Sunny's omnipresence in my brain was almost a relief. I reached up and touched the side of my helmet, as if I could actually hear her. *It.* Sunny was just a computer program, not an actual person. It was hard to remember sometimes. "Thanks. Am I the only crew member you're communicating with?"

Yes, Cassie. I have adapted to your brain waves.

There would be no communication with Earth on this trip—not from so far away. We were on our own here entirely. If things went wrong, the only way anyone would know was by the records Sunny was saving on board.

I took a steadying breath.

Standing behind both Bolshakov and Copeland in the narrow opening, I saw little of what was outside the ship, only a slice of smooth metal wall. The ground was a red, dusty stone, rough but mostly level.

Bolshakov took the first step onto the ground. I caught the historic moment just in time. This was the third alien world to see human footprints. The very first outside of our own solar system.

And I was witnessing it.

One giant leap for mankind. Impossible not to think it.

Bolshakov turned and looked back at us, a rare smile crossing his features. "Come on, now. We have lingered long enough on the shores of the cosmic ocean."

A flutter of nervous glee escaped me, a huff of laughter halted by my helmet. Bolshakov was quoting Carl Sagan. Nothing about this moment could have been more perfect.

My heartbeat and the whir of the air were the only sounds that filled my ears.

Copeland took her first steps down.

Then it was my turn. I took a quick breath and jumped, landing harder than I'd expected to, with both feet in a puff of rust-colored dust. I'd expected less gravity on such a small moon.

I crunched the dirt beneath my boot experimentally, examining the tread my footprints left. Alien dirt, I marveled. Alien molecules on my boots.

I wanted to dance—to scream—to twirl around like the child within me who was accomplishing her wildest dream. I restrained myself to a secret grin, and thrilled in the trembling of my limbs.

Jeong was a bit more agile than I was in her landing, and she carefully avoided treading over my first footprints. I appreciated that.

For a moment, none of us moved.

"This is . . . not what I expected," Jeong said.

The walls were smooth, pale gray, curving far above our heads to form a sort of domed tube. Pale gray light seemed to emanate from the walls. There was no other explanation I could come up with, as I saw no light source, and yet there was enough light to see thirty feet down the corridor, at least.

It appeared there was only one way forward: the tube ahead was long enough that darkness shrouded wherever its destination led.

Something was strange about the walls of the cavern. Curious, I wandered closer. They were entirely seamless.

Up close, I could see just what had thrown me from afar: it didn't look solid. Corporeal, but with shifting and dipping patterns in the shadows along its surface. Like gentle ripples in water.

Copeland came up behind me, her confused expression matching my own. Bolshakov and Jeong waited and watched as Copeland reached out a hesitant hand. "If I didn't know better . . ." Her hand hovered over the surface of the wall. "It looks . . ."

Her fingers touched the material lightly, and the wall *bent* under them.

Copeland yanked her hand back, and then laughed. "My God. It gives way. Like rubber . . . or something biological. It feels like touching a dolphin."

Something else was happening, too. A soft yellow glow was growing at the spot where Copeland had touched. As if in recognition, as if she had awakened something.

My hand itched to touch it, but we didn't know what this was, what Copeland may have done, or activated. The light faded again to nothing, leaving no trace.

"My God," she said again, and we looked at each other. Silently we both decided to step away from the wall and rejoin the group.

We moved forward methodically, examining every shadowed niche.

"Gravity's a bit heavier," Jeong noted, her voice warm and confident in my helmet radio, as clear as if she were speaking directly into my ear. "I'd say 1.3 g. Strange for a small moon."

"Perhaps there is a dense core," Bolshakov responded, his voice tight. "Very intriguing."

We were all a bit on edge. *Something* had alerted the ship's proximity alarm, but there seemed to be nothing out here at all.

We took a few more cautious steps forward, staying in a tight group.

"Perhaps the alien civilization lives belowground to evade the surface radiation," Copeland mused.

It was a valid hypothesis. Problem was, there was no civilization to be seen.

I turned back around to see *Odysseus*, its white surface now dull and pitted with innumerable dents and scratches, no longer pristine. A huge gleaming piece of Earth in an alien landscape.

"Commander," Copeland said suddenly, her voice a note of warning.

I felt a chill of fear.

Something approached us, but the light was too dim to make it out. Something was disturbing the shadows up ahead.

Bolshakov raised an arm, signaling us to wait. Tingles of anticipation vibrated in my hands and legs.

He took a step forward. And then another.

Then he came to a sudden halt. I froze behind his outstretched arm.

There was . . . a person coming toward us. A man, by the shape and size.

He came closer.

I took a step back.

Bolshakov held his ground.

The man stopped. We waited, but it seemed now that he was waiting for *us* to cross the final distance ourselves.

Bolshakov stepped forward, and we each followed him from a few paces back. As we neared the figure, I realized there were others—more humanlike shapes, shadowed in the recesses of the large corridor. Waiting, watching.

Now I could tell the strangers were wearing suits not unlike ours, thin and body-conforming, black but laced with veins of iridescent colors, catching the dull light with each minute movement.

They were not wearing helmets. So when the lead figure stepped forward, into the warm circle of organic light in which we stood, his face was clearly visible.

He appeared to be a middle-aged man. Tall, with black hair graying at the temples in a way that made him look distinguished and wise. Thick neck, square jaw. The shoulders of a linebacker and the posture of a leader.

And I recognized him.

He was the "Georgian ambassador" I'd met at Marshall, in another life, five hundred light-years away.

Luka's father.

THREE

LUKA'S FATHER OPENED his arms low and spoke with the slow, gentle tone of one who approaches an animal he fears will bite him. "Welcome, ambassadors of Earth. We have been waiting for you. I am sorry that we have asked you to come such a very long way, but I fear we had no choice."

Everything came back to me in a dizzying rush, a tidal wave that threatened to knock me over. I took a stumbling backward step, remembering all that I had forgotten.

Luka had been on board *Odysseus* when I'd awoken. It had not been a hallucination. Now that I saw his father in front of me, I knew it had been real.

But I still didn't understand why.

"I am sorry to startle you," the man said. "We thought it best to be forthcoming."

No one on my side knew what to say. Until Copeland. "Who are you? Why do you look human?"

The ambassador gave a pained smile. "Nothing has a short answer, I'm afraid. Perhaps this may help." He turned back toward his people in the shadows and gestured. Out of the small crowd emerged a familiar face.

Everyone recognized Luka; I heard their small intakes of breath over the comm. Luka had trained with all of us—had been chosen over me to take this spot. Until he'd been sent home. Or so I'd thought.

Luka appeared unchanged from my memory. He hadn't shaved in a couple of days, and looked like maybe he hadn't slept in a couple of days, either. His hair was a little longer, a little messier.

He didn't betray that he saw me. His focus remained resolute on Commander Bolshakov.

We were pretending that our meeting aboard *Odysseus* had not happened, then.

"That's . . . that's not *Luka*," Jeong said over internal comm. "Is it?"

"Is someone impersonating him?" Copeland asked.

"I think it is Luka," I told them on private comm. "That man there? I met him on Earth. Before the competition. He's Luka's father, and the Georgian ambassador to the US. Or at least, that's how we were introduced."

"What the hell is going on here?" Copeland asked, this time on external comm so that the strangers could hear.

Ambassador Kereselidze's voice maintained its cautious

25

cadence. "There is no need to fear us. We have no weapons."

Bolshakov seemed unsure what to say. Recovering his confident posture, he finally settled on, "Nor do we. But you have the upper hand."

The ambassador looked at Luka, as if asking for his help. Luka took a few steps toward me, but stopped short when Bolshakov bristled and put his palm forward reflexively in the universal gesture for *stop right there.* "Something is going on here and I want to know what it is before you get any closer, son."

Luka's voice mimicked the placating tones of his father. "Bolshakov. You know me. You all do. We trained together. Please. You can trust me."

"But you're—you were on Earth. You were in the competition for Gupta's spot, for Christ's sake!" Copeland said.

Luka nodded. "Yes, this is true."

"You were a spy," Jeong said quietly, coming to the same conclusion I had.

Alarm flared in his features before retreating. For a moment he seemed to consider lying. "Yes. In a way. But it was a necessary precaution."

"You've had a long journey," said the ambassador. He swung his arm in a low arc, a gesture to follow him. "You are likely hungry and tired from the journey. There is much to discuss, but it will hold."

"Sir?" Copeland spoke over the private channel. "Should we get Shaw?"

"Don't mention Shaw," Bolshakov ordered. "We'll leave him for now." Returning to external comm, he told the ambassador: "Lead the way."

Bolshakov obviously didn't trust them, but he had made up his mind. He was the commander.

We followed him.

The ambassador, Luka, and a small handful of the others led us down a passageway and through a thick door. The room was smaller than the hangarlike space behind us, but it was still spacious. The walls inside this room were the same as outside the chamber, but now they were lit from within, emanating the same soft yellow glow as they had when Copeland had touched them. The effect was warm and comforting. Probably on purpose.

It was alien, but it was obvious some effort had been made to cater to humans. There were chairs around an oblong table, enough for each of us and Shaw. It seemed there wasn't much point keeping Shaw on *Odysseus* after all. They knew how many of us there were.

So they knew about our mission. Of course they did. It seemed they'd been part of it from the very beginning. Possibly even before Finley offered to send me to the competition. I could see at least part of the picture; the mechanisms that had been in place prior to Luka and his father meeting me at Marshall that day. It certainly hadn't been coincidence.

This chamber was so weirdly normal within the alien

environment. Even a bowl of bright red and green apples sat on the table. Six doors with high, rounded arches lined the back wall.

"Feel free to eat if you are hungry. You may take off your helmets if you wish; the atmosphere is adjusted to human physiology," Luka said.

I shared a look with the others.

No. We'd keep our helmets on, thank you very much.

The other aliens stood together in the far corner. Two females and three males, standing like statues. *No*, I corrected myself. *Like guards.*

The ambassador said they didn't have weapons. Not that they weren't armed. How would we recognize weapons even if we saw them?

My crewmates didn't hesitate in sliding into the chairs. The effects of the hibernation were still heavy with them. I had some strength left in my legs, so I stood. I thought one of us should.

The ambassador waited until we were settled. He smiled. "We are very glad you have come. My name is Otor. And you know that this is my son, Luka."

"I must confess, I don't understand why this meeting could not have been accomplished on Earth," Bolshakov said. "Seeing as we were all apparently there, together, at the same time." His voice held a hard edge.

I felt the same touch of annoyance. We'd risked our lives to come here, and why? It felt like we were puppets being pulled along by invisible strings.

"I will let my son explain. He has better command of your languages." Otor nodded to Luka, and he stepped forward.

Seeing him again like this, in such bizarre surroundings, was surreal. We'd been friends once. We'd left each other with the lingering possibility of being something more, though I hadn't spent much time thinking about what.

But things were different now. *He* was different. Even the way he carried himself had changed. He moved like Bolshakov, with the confidence of command, an ease that spoke of being in intimately familiar surroundings. His eyes looked prematurely aged, like he'd seen things he didn't want to have seen.

Had I ever really known him at all?

"So what are you?" Copeland leaned forward onto one elbow. "Because you're obviously not human."

Luka seemed to flinch for a second, but all too soon the mask was back. "No, this is true. We are refugees who came to Earth looking for a new home. You may call us megobari. It's a word we adopted when we took on human physiology." Then, at our confused faces, he explained further: "We could not, of course, continue to speak our own languages with human mouths and human ears."

His words—speaking about us like we were the aliens while he looked just like us—were disconcerting.

Luka addressed Bolshakov. "Commander, you asked why we could not have had this meeting on Earth. That is a fair point. The answer is that we did our homework. When we first arrived on Earth, we studied media with great interest, as you can imagine. Throughout your recent history, fictional aliens were, invariably, the enemy. Not to mention the centuries of actual history of mindless violence against your own people. It would have been foolish to believe *we* would be welcomed with open arms. We had seen time and again how you treat refugees of even your own kind," he said, this time meeting my eyes with a gaze that smoldered. The truth of it made my skin hot with shame. "We are few in number, and we had to protect ourselves. We decided to make first contact in a neutral place."

"This is a neutral place?" Copeland asked. "Seems like your people have the upper hand here."

He quickly directed his laser gaze onto her. "Who is it, do you think, that designed the ship that brought you here? We have made every effort to help you, to advance your technology, to guide you in the right direction. You are safe."

"So your people sent the message to NASA twenty years ago? You gave us the technology to get here?" Jeong said with a touch of incredulity.

Luka nodded.

"And you were the ones who gave us the blueprints for *Odysseus*? Why would you just hand over such powerful technology?" Jeong asked. "Our scientists have been studying those schematics for twenty years. As we speak, they could be advancing human civilization centuries ahead of schedule. I hate to say this, but we could have even used your own technology against you."

"An unlikely but calculated risk that we had to take," Luka

replied. "What we gave you was merely a primitive design. Orville and Wilbur's flying machines compared to a supersonic jet. You were surprised, I assume, to have arrived here within only six Earth months. In a ship of our fleet, with a practiced pilot, that journey takes only days."

We stared.

His father broke in. "My son simply means that we gave you the first page of a very long book. We know humans learn and adapt quickly. We have seen—and admired—your ingenuity. It was our hope that we could learn and adapt together, as friends, and not as enemies."

There was a beat of silence as the humans in the room tried to discern whether this was true.

For my part, I believed him. Their actions gave proof to their words. But maybe that was just something inside me unwilling to think Luka could be lying to me.

"How could you know that we would build the ship correctly?" Copeland asked.

"Or that we would build it at all?" Bolshakov added.

Otor and Luka shared a look between them.

"We . . ." Luka's eyes flashed on me, as if trying to gauge my reaction before he spoke. "We had insurance. We placed a few of our own among the ranks at NASA, to keep an eye on progress and ensure that our plan was coming along as it should."

"But what were you doing in NASA?" I asked, hating how thready and weak my voice sounded on the external speaker. It was one of the first times I'd actually spoken out loud, and my voice sounded too small for the room. "You, personally. Why were you sent home? Why were you in the selection process at all?"

"I was only involved to get to know the potential crew of Project Adastra. We wanted to discern who would be the most receptive to our meeting. Once I knew you were going to make it, Cassie, I dropped out. My job was finished."

Bolshakov stood up suddenly, his face red and angry. "Every step of the way. Every step, you manipulated us."

He could have taken the words out of my own mouth. I could read between the lines. If they had placed some of their own people in positions of power, perhaps they were not simply *observing* the selection process, but *influencing* it.

As if he sensed what was going on in my head, Luka's cool mask melted away to show the boy I had known on Earth. He addressed me directly, his voice softer. "Cassie, I'm sorry for all the deception and the manipulation. We believed we had little choice but to stack the odds in our favor. Yours was the first planet we discovered where we could breathe freely. We adapted as best we could to living as humans. We studied and learned your ways for years before making contact. The plan was always to reach out to you, once we were ready."

His mouth opened like he was going to keep on, but I shook my head to shut him up. I didn't want to hear any more. At least not here, surrounded by all these people. "So, your plan was? You brought us all this way to ask for permission to, what, live on Earth? When you already have been? For *years*?"

He didn't have an answer to that.

"You say you are refugees," Bolshakov said. "Was there . . . some sort of war?"

The way Luka's face became blank of emotion was almost chilling. He was betraying the amount of emotion beneath the surface by just how much he was attempting to hide it. "Yes."

Otor took over, a bit quickly. "My friends, my guests. This can all wait. I know your internal clocks need some time to adjust, but it is nearly midnight by ours. How about we rest for now, and reconvene in the morning?"

We looked at each other.

"Thoughts?" Bolshakov asked gruffly over internal comm.

"They're trying to be hospitable, commander," I said. "And their quarters are more spacious than ours on board *Odysseus*."

"We're no less at their mercy here than on the ship," Copeland said in a sideways sort of agreement with me.

"Sir, I think accepting their invitation would be polite, considering this is a mission of diplomacy," Jeong said.

"All agreed? Okay. Gupta, radio Shaw and tell him to come out and join us. We're spending the night under the roof of our new hosts."

We followed an escort into our sleeping quarters, each containing double bunks cut into the walls. There was enough space for each of us to get our own, including Shaw.

The megobari guide didn't speak, but gestured to the bunk— very clearly a bed, though the surface appeared to be something akin to soft silicone and there were no blankets or pillows. She then showed me a shallow, tubelike depression in the opposite wall. When she touched it, water rained from the top into a fine grate on the floor, in what was either a shower or a toilet. Or possibly both.

When I thanked her, she only smiled. Perhaps the rest of the megobari did not speak English well, but she appeared to understand me.

And then I was alone.

Well, except for Sunny.

I suddenly felt small, weak, and very young. "I'm glad you're here, Sunny."

Thank you, Cassie, came her warm chirp in my mind.

I knew she was without emotion—that she was a series of code with programmed responses—but it didn't matter. Her presence helped.

I settled best I could onto the bunk, keeping my helmet on so I could maintain connection with Sunny and the others. The surface of the bunk was white and solid, and I'd expected something more familiar, like a mattress. But instead it was more like the surface of a yoga mat: dense and malleable, denting around my body shape only slightly, bouncing back when pressed.

Just as I'd gotten as comfortable as I was likely to get, my internal comm clicked on, startling me awake. "Everyone settling in okay?"

"Yes, commander," I said, my voice joining with the rest.

"Try to catch some sleep. Set your suitboard computers to

wake you in six point five hours. Good night, everyone. And good work."

I closed my eyes, taking a long, deep breath. I made a mental note to wake in six hours, and to my surprise Sunny chirped a *Yes, Cassie* in my head.

My heartbeat gradually slowed. My limbs relaxed. We were safe, for the time being. Everything had gone as well as we could have possibly hoped so far. Ninety-five percent of my body was relaxed and relieved. My body was worn down and ready to sleep.

But my brain was absolutely wired.

How could I sleep? I was on an *alien planet*. With actual aliens outside my door. I'd spent six months asleep. Now I wanted to learn all I could about this place we'd finally reached.

Luka had slipped away without saying anything to me. I assumed he and the other megobari were off sleeping somewhere else. We weren't prisoners; I should be able to look around a little bit on my own. Not far, just enough to sate my curiosity.

I eased out of the bed, wondering if sound traveled far in these cavernlike spaces. Outside in the antechamber, the lights had dimmed—the ceiling was now dark, and the only light was a ring just above the floor, enough to illuminate the circumference of the room. There were still apples on the table, but my stomach wasn't ready to handle solids.

The room was empty. I crept across the floor to the exit;

the door slid open silently at my touch. No megobari in the darkened passage, either. Nobody standing guard. That was reassuring.

I walked with measured steps down the hall, wondering at what this place was. Who had lived here and why did they live underground? It seemed an infinite maze of passages, like the underground tunnels of an ant colony. Except it was neat and orderly and calming, with the soft white walls dimmed for simulated night.

Every so often I'd pass a door with nothing marking it but a softly glowing rectangle of color. I couldn't see any sort of writing—not that I'd understand the language, but it only made me more curious. Were the rooms color coded for certain purposes? What did they mean? I wasn't about to start walking into random chambers—that was both foolish and rude, like snooping around your friend's house at a sleepover but with a degree more risk involved.

"Looking for something?"

I whirled, heart racing.

Luka stood some feet behind me, just outside a door I'd passed. "I'm sorry," I said automatically, even though I wasn't breaking any established rules. "I couldn't sleep." His face was unreadable. "What about you?"

"I heard you."

"How? I couldn't hear you."

"You are still wearing your helmet."

I resisted a smile. "I can go back to my room. If you don't want me wandering."

He shrugged a shoulder. "I'd probably be doing the same thing, if our positions were reversed. There's just not much here to look at."

"Oh," I said, dejected.

"But I could walk with you, if you'd like. Show you what there is to see."

I took a slow inhale. There was a small part of me that didn't trust him. Didn't *want* to trust him, at least. The memory of waking on the ship, weak and disoriented, seeing his face—it had come back to me in watery images. The surprise of him being here, being *alien*, had almost worn off. He still looked so normal, so human.

But now there was a part of him that was closed off. A whole world of him that I didn't know.

What else was there that I didn't know?

"Thanks," I said, and we fell into step uneasily. Whatever or whoever he was, he was offering knowledge, and that's what I wanted most. "So what is this place?"

"It was a research base. Scientists lived and worked here."

Past tense. "What were they studying?"

He shrugged again. "Sorry. I'm not actually sure. There were a few research outposts on this moon."

"Are there more megobari here, then?"

He glanced at me out of the corner of his eye and rubbed briefly at his chin. "No. It's just us."

"What happened to the scientists?"

"All the outposts were abandoned in the war," he said vaguely.

His tone and posture had gone stiff. I guessed this was a forbidden topic.

"Why did you guys bring us to this place, then?"

"It was safe. Hidden. There are still some resources and working technology here to maintain the atmosphere. We thought it'd be a good place to talk."

Talk. We were talking now, but not really saying anything. There was still a lot of talk hanging over our heads, a lot that had to wait until tomorrow.

He turned down a corridor on the left, and I followed him. "Are we going anywhere in particular?"

"Not really. Not much to see here beyond old labs. There's a small hangar with a fleet of research vessels. Tomorrow, my father wants to take everyone down to see our home planet."

"Luka, why didn't we land on your home planet?"

This time he didn't even answer me.

Maybe I shouldn't have asked. There was a reason they had come to Earth and lived in hiding, after all. But I was tired of being kept in the dark. We'd been drawn light-years from home and they still were holding things back from us.

Luka seemed tense, not himself—even annoyed, which annoyed me. An annoyance that kept building. All that time we'd spent together on Earth: studying together in the café, jogging on the track in the middle of the night, hiking through mud and mosquitoes, sleeping side by side under a tarp draped across tree branches. Using all my strength to wrench him out of a rain-swollen creek. Hearing his steady voice over the radio feed me instructions while my oxygen-starved brain struggled to focus, to save us all. And that memory I had done well to block, of his warm embrace in a dark courtyard, of him telling me to remember why I'd come here in the first place.

All that time, he'd never, ever told me who he really was.

All the wrong words were tumbling around my head. Frustration escaped me in a small growling sound.

He stopped. "Cassie, are you all right?"

I didn't answer.

He tried again, his voice melting into something so familiar it made me ache. "Cassie." His voice reached out to me, like a hand on a shoulder, but he didn't try to touch me.

I turned my eyes to him. And then, impulsively, I pulled off my helmet. I didn't want this recorded or remembered, and I didn't want to be accidentally overheard. The air of the chamber touched my skin for the first time, fresh and damp and cool. "You just left."

His eyebrows furrowed.

I let my emotions spew out in a thoughtless rush. "In Houston. You dropped out, you *knew* what you were doing, and you . . . didn't even say a word to me. You could have said something. You . . . *kissed* me. You used me. And then you just left." I gripped the edge of my helmet with gloved fingers, hard, until it hurt. I didn't know what point I was trying to make. What had hurt me more? That we had been friends and he'd deceived me? That I'd gone outside my comfort zone and kissed him back and he'd used me? Or that after all of that, he'd left without even saying good-bye. "Everything we went through and I never knew who you really were."

He watched me steadily, unsurprised and weary. He might've guessed I'd respond this way. Maybe even expected it. "I couldn't tell you, Cassie."

"You could have *tried*."

His eyes had never looked so sad. "I am sorry. I never meant to hurt you, Cassie."

"Stop saying my name like that. And stop apologizing, it isn't helping." An unexpected well of emotion rose in my throat, and I swallowed it down. *Get ahold of yourself.* "Okay, so, I understand you couldn't tell me you were an alien. God. I get that, okay? But then, if you knew you were dropping out, if you knew . . . then why did you . . . ?"

He got my meaning. To his credit, he met my eyes, as if trying to give force to his words. "I never deceived you about anything other than my identity. And I never wished to use you. I . . ." His eyes went to the ceiling, as though he might find an answer from above. "I was sincere. And . . . impulsive. And I am sorry for hurting you."

"You're sorry."

"It's all that I have."

I shook my head, took in a breath, and let it out slowly. "You're a different person to me now. Okay? So whatever . . . happened, back on Earth, that's not how it is now. Understand?"

He ducked his head in a nod, eyes still on me. "I understand," he said, voice solemn.

This wasn't how I'd wanted this to go. I'd wanted to make things right again. If not *normal*—because normal was out the window—then at least okay between us. I struggled for a neutral topic to switch to and came up empty. My breath was coming hard, and I was dangerously close to raw emotions.

It was Luka who spoke next. "I won't ask forgiveness from you, Cassie. You have a right to withhold it if you wish, and I have asked enough of you already. But I hope that we can work together going forward."

Why did he have to be so damn reasonable all the time? I sighed, the anger in me still fizzling, not having found a satisfying outlet. "Yeah, sure. Of course."

I walked back to my room alone.

FOUR

I SLEPT FITFULLY, chased by dreams. Sunny nudged me out of sleep at the appointed time, and when I opened my eyes it was like I hadn't slept at all.

The same delegation of megobari met us in the antechamber. We ate a breakfast of prepackaged NASA food from *Odysseus* with a side of fresh fruit—making me wonder how fast the megobari actually could travel through space.

It still seemed ridiculous to me the megobari had been on Earth at the same time as us, watched us as we launched, and then apparently *passed* us on the way here. Had they stayed on Earth until recently or had they been here the whole time? What had they been doing while we were asleep?

I added all that to the list of questions I wished I'd asked

Luka last night. I probably wasn't going to get another chance to talk to him alone again.

That morning the mood was a little lighter. My crew with their helmets lying on the table, breaking figurative bread with our hosts. One of the megobari, an older woman with deep brown skin, laughed at Shaw's jokes, while another conversed with Bolshakov in a language that sounded Russian, but was incomprehensible to me.

Still, it was mostly quiet, as the megobari by and large didn't seem to speak English.

I ate my rehydratable granola in silence, watching Otor attempt to translate a conversation between a megobari woman and Dr. Copeland. All the megobari seemed indistinguishable from humans. Other than their unique space suits, there were no telling differences between them and us. To an outside observer, we might appear to be the same species. The megobari were all quite tall and broadly built, most of them with dark hair and eyes, and shades of skin from light tan to dark. I wondered if this was part of their disguise. Did they adopt the features of the humans who lived wherever they first landed?

Luka was the only one among them with blond hair. I couldn't help wondering which of their genetics blended to create him, and how it all worked.

Otor cleared his throat and stood. "My friends—as I hope we shall be friends—I hope you have eaten well and recovered somewhat from your journey. I would like to invite you to come aboard our ship and take a short trip with us to our home planet, where I can give a full explanation as to why we require your help."

Bolshakov sat back in his chair, an apple core and empty food packets sitting in front of him, drinking coffee out of a silver pouch with a straw.

"Gupta, do you have any objections to us working with these megobari?" Bolshakov asked, tripping only slightly on the unfamiliar word.

Why did he start with me? "No," I said. "No objections."

"Anyone else?" Bolshakov paused, and at the silence, continued: "I think we have a duty to gather all the information we can before we return to Earth. We gladly accept your offer."

Otor nodded, pleased. "We can be ready to leave in one half hour."

As we boarded the megobari ship, Shaw quipped under his breath, "If anyone mentions something about a cookbook, *run.*"

That sparked a jolt of nervous laughter out of me and Jeong. Hopefully, the megobari had never seen any old *Twilight Zone* reruns, and weren't claiming to want to "serve man."

The megobari ship was minimalist and beautiful. Off-white, smooth lines, curved openings—I felt like I was inside an egg. The human crew followed the megobari crew up the ramp to some sort of control center that could have been a bridge, with two levels.

We stood at the top of the higher level looking down, with a half wall of a rail as a separation. The colors here changed slightly to break up the expanse, with the lower half more gray and the top half a little more yellow. I had no idea what the rest of the ship contained, but from the outside it was at least twice the size of *Odysseus*. It seemed every megobari we'd yet seen was coming with us, and that only amounted to about twenty-five individuals. Luka was the only young person among them. The rest all appeared to be at least in their midthirties.

The ship itself appeared to be constructed of a material similar to the chamber walls. When no one was looking, I touched a fingertip to it, feeling the same thing Copeland had reported: it wasn't rigid. It gave way, just a fraction, under pressure—like some incredibly strong, pliable silicone.

They didn't seem to use computers in the way that we did. Instead, it was like the entire ship was an interactive screen. It pulsed periodically with color, greens and purples and reds. Some raced down the walls like messages, sent from place to place. Others floated, lazy, undulating like jellyfish before dissipating completely. Could patterns of color be a form of written language? I watched, entranced.

I leaned over the railing a little. The lower level was an explosion of color: pop-pop-pop of yellows and reds, firing like bullets; streams of blue lines cutting through purple clouds. It seemed like some kind of psychedelic mind trip, but after only a few seconds I recognized patterns. Maybe it was a language I could learn.

Luka came down the corridor, still wearing the same black space suit with the strange shifting blue veins running throughout, this time carrying a helmet under his arm. He stopped in front of me and smiled without showing teeth, a polite thing. "How do you like the ship?"

"It's incredible. One day—when we have more time—I want to know everything about it."

His smile dropped away, but he indulged my curiosity. "It's called *Exodus*. It's the same one my family used to escape the war. They hid it on Earth before I was born." He looked away from me. "I had never even been to space before now. Not so different from you, yes?"

He glanced at me, unsure, trying to smile. So I tried, too. "Your original destination, Kepler-186f, was our home world. But it is not safe to land there, thus we redirected your ship to land here instead. But we wish for you to see it."

Apparently the megobari had found a way to simulate gravity on their ships. It was a nice convenience, except for those of us with reduced muscle stamina. Luka noticed how I'd grabbed hold of the rail to support myself and immediately realized their error. He enlisted some of his fellow crew to pull down some jump seats for us along the back wall of the bridge area. They'd obviously been installed after the megobari had changed their forms; the materials were distinctly more earth-like and human-proportioned. We each collapsed into the seats gratefully and buckled into the five-point harnesses. Once I was settled, Luka returned to his father's side.

I felt only a gentle pull as the ship lifted horizontally off the ground and into orbit. Either the internal artificial gravity or the weak gravity of the smaller moon made it much easier than our liftoff from Earth. It was like a lazy river ride in comparison.

The top half of the chamber turned translucent, a dome of distant stars, and I gasped out loud. We suddenly had a 360-degree view of space, almost as if we were floating freely within it. The constellations around us were all different from what I was used to; I recognized nothing by sight at this orientation.

In the distance loomed the planet Kepler-186f, seeming a lot closer than it was due to its massive size. It was a deep copper color, pockmarked with craters, and even from here I could tell there was no water, no clouds, no atmosphere. A dead thing.

The translucent screen narrowed its focus until the planet filled our vision. The entire world was dry and dusty, with no signs of life ever having existed on it. Even from this distance, it was obvious it was barren. Lacking even the beauty of a desert, because in deserts, there was life. It looked like the surface of Earth's moon. I couldn't take my eyes away, trying to envision what it could have been like.

Until, suddenly, I didn't have to. I blinked, and the bare rock above was alive. Sunlight refracted off a blue-gray ocean covering about half the world. White clouds swirled above a lush continent that covered the eastern hemisphere, and lights shined from the narrow slice of nightside that we could see, revealing pockets of cities and civilization. Smaller bodies of water, the ridges of twisting rivers, mountain ranges, deserts, and thick forests of bronze vegetation were all in sharp focus. What was this?

"This is how we wish to remember our home," Otor explained, as if answering my question. "Before war and destruction took it away."

All the megobari who were not piloting the ship had gathered on the bridge, standing around and in front of us. Luka stood beside his father, their backs to the pilots below, facing human and megobari crews alike.

A respectful silence had taken over the megobari, and we watched attentively as Otor spoke. "We can no longer touch the soil of the world that gave birth to our people." Otor's voice rattled out of his helmet radio, but it was clear and strong and sad. I felt suddenly like I was at a funeral. "But we come here so that it may be remembered, both as it was and as it is. We mourn the loss of home. All the beauty that remains only in memory."

For a second, the image on-screen wasn't an alien species' dead planet; it was Earth. Earth as I'd seen it last, green and glittering blue, marbled with clouds. Alive with the only color in a vast darkness.

I saw the color drain away from my home—the water vaporize and the grass scorch and the soil sweep out like dust into the void. Saw life vaporize in an instant.

I blinked. The megobarian planet hung before me. An illusion, a memory.

"My human friends. We did not ask you to come so far from home and face such dangers for nothing. We invited you here to simply ask for your help. We called you away from Earth because we believed it was no longer safe for us to speak there.

That Earth may soon be in danger."

Deadly silence pervaded the bridge.

"You're going to have to explain that one a little more," Copeland said, her voice dry and hard.

Luka stepped forward, taking over. Kepler-186f is irradiated and barren of life. But it once was home. Years ago, an alien species we call the vrag invaded us without warning or explanation. My people fought back, even managed to wipe out most of the enemy. But our planet, and even our colonies on various moons, were lost."

He said it so casually, it almost belied the pain within the words.

"One contingent of vrag escaped using a stolen megobari ship. What was left of the megobari scattered into the galaxy, fearing that to stay together would draw the attention of the enemy. The vrag have hunted us ever since."

Otor gazed at his son sadly. And I realized that now, all the megobari were looking at *us*. I felt dread trickle through my body. "There are only a few thousand of us left, spread out on a few hundred ships. We split ways so that we may expand our search for a new planet that could sustain us. And so that we may be more likely to avoid detection by the vrag, who are able to use our technology against us. We traveled many years and lost many of our family. We thought perhaps we would never find another home like the one that had been taken from us." His large hand covered his eyes.

"Until we found Earth," Luka finished, his gaze finding mine.

Tears warmed the backs of my eyes. I blinked them away.

Otor's voice was beseeching. "Earth was not perfect, but it was our best hope. We studied you for a long time before even attempting to land. We thought—we hoped—we could communicate with you. Ask for help. For alliance. A home, in exchange for technology."

"My father developed a genetic virus," Luka said. "To change our DNA. He inserted enough human genetic material into our own that it would make us appear in all outward respects as human. Permanently. He believed that was the only way we could communicate with you and be accepted. A third of our remaining crew died while perfecting the procedure. But they kept trying because enough of us believed in the hope of Earth, and they were so tired of running."

Otor grimaced at the reminder. His wrinkled skin became gray and bloodless. "We had so looked forward to this meeting. All the work spent to come to this point—the years of study and the sacrifices made. Everything had come to fruition, and the vrag had disappeared into the galaxy. Only for us to discover on the eve of our departure that the vrag had found us."

Beside me, Jeong sat up straighter.

"Shit," Copeland muttered on my other side.

"The vrag are ruthless, intelligent animals," Luka took over. His father looked like he might be sick. "They reproduce at astounding rates, act as one mind, and cannot be reasoned with. We cannot even communicate with them. They are swift, violent, and vast in number. Their only weakness now is that they are confined to a single ship, as they lack the physical capability to build their own."

Otor put a heavy hand on Luka's shoulder and turned his gray gaze to us. "They destroyed our world. And they will destroy yours, if we do not stop them."

FIVE

"WHAT THE HELL are you talking about?" Shaw demanded.

"There is a hope," Otor said. "A weapon. That is why we brought you here. This moon was at one time a research facility. It was abandoned before the weapon could be put to use against the vrag. But if it is still here, it may be our best hope."

I felt sick. This wasn't what I wanted to do. I suddenly wanted to go back. Back to when space was a grand adventure of scientific achievement and we'd return to Earth as heroes for the ages. Not as the four horsemen of the apocalypse.

Earth. I pictured it as I'd seen it last, a fragile, beautiful blue marble hanging in dark space. Alone, unprotected, and so far away.

Were the vrag there now?

Would it even still be there when we returned?

"How do you know about this weapon?" Bolshakov asked. To his credit, he sounded like he was taking this news much better than I was. "And why have you only now returned to retrieve it?"

Luka turned to his father for the answer.

"None of us dared before now. We feared leading the vrag directly to it. One of our deep-space probes alerted us to the nearing presence of the vrag. We knew they were approaching Earth. This was our only chance."

I may have been fighting the aftereffects of interplanetary travel, but I didn't miss that Otor didn't answer how he knew about the weapon to begin with.

"Where is it? Do you know?" I asked.

"We have drones searching for it now. I believe we may soon uncover the vault in which it was stored. Once we recover it, we ask that you return to Earth with us immediately, so that we may have it in place before the vrag arrive."

"It would take only days to return to Earth in this ship," Luka explained quickly, seeing the uncomprehending faces of my crew. "You would not need to return to stasis."

"Are you truly asking our permission?" Bolshakov asked wryly. "I feel as though you will do this regardless."

"No, in fact, we will not," Otor responded evenly. "You are free to return to your ship and your planet alone. If you do not wish further contact with us, we will not return with you. The last thing we wish is to be an invading alien species."

Copeland leaned over me to speak to Bolshakov, sotto voce: "They will only grant us the use of the weapon if we agree to let them stay on Earth. Otherwise, we're on our own."

I startled, but she was right, of course. That was the offer. They'd help us repel the vrag only if they got to share in the reward.

"It is our sincerest wish that no other species lose their homes to the vrag," Otor said diplomatically. "But we will not force alliance where it is not desired."

Jeong shook her head. "They're making us an offer we can't refuse."

I stared at Luka, and he leveled a hard gaze right back at me. We were on two sides of a divide now. And neither of us was the decision maker here.

When Bolshakov spoke, I turned to look at him instead. "Otor, my friend, surely you know that the decision to ally with your kind does not fall to me alone. We are only five out of seven billion. Even if I wish to give you what you ask, there is no guarantee those in charge back home will honor our agreement."

Otor nodded like this was a reasonable and expected problem. "Questions of the future can remain in the future. I know you cannot promise what I ask, commander. All I ask, at this moment, between your crew and mine, is if we have an agreement. Our help, for yours."

In that moment, the illusion of life on the planet above blinked out, and the cold reality of barren rock returned. There was not a speck on that rock that was not blasted away from meteors or radiation. We watched the feed of the dead world until it passed from view, obscured as we left it behind to float alone in the void.

"I agree," I said quietly.

After a moment's hesitation, I heard Copeland murmur her agreement. Then Jeong. Finally, Shaw.

Bolshakov unbuckled his harness and strode across the bridge, megobari eyes following him as he passed, until he stood in front of Otor. He held out his hand and Otor immediately grasped it with both of his own. "I am not known for my eloquence, Mr. Kereselidze. But if you'd allow me the liberty, there are some words I think are appropriate for this occasion. 'Give me your tired, your poor, your huddled masses yearning to breathe free.'"

At the familiar words, knowing what they stood for, my chest began to warm, like a rising fire in a cold hearth. I added my voice to Bolshakov's and soon, we were all speaking these famous words as one incantation. "'Send these, the homeless, tempest-tost to me. I lift my lamp beside the golden door.'"

Otor's voice softened as he gripped Bolshakov's arm in a firm embrace, his eyes shining. "We have run for a very long time. And now, perhaps finally, we have found a place that may welcome us home. Let us have gratitude."

The megobari closed their eyes.

I bowed my head and made a promise. *If Earth is still alive, I will not let her die.*

◑ ● ◐

Our return journey to the moon base would take longer, as we were now detouring to pick up the weapon. Since we were in a stable orbit above the moon, Otor deemed it safe for us to get out of our harnesses and perhaps have a small lunch while the drone finished its work.

And after the revelations of the morning, I needed time to assess what it all meant for us and for the mission.

There weren't many places to go to have privacy. I broke away from the rest of the human crew and found an alcove somewhere off the bridge—not exactly a room, but a place where I couldn't see anyone else. Small as it was, I needed to be alone to sort through everything that had just happened.

I sat against the bulkhead and breathed.

Weapons and war. Why did it always come down to this? Wasn't there a single species in the galaxy that had never heard of the concept?

We weren't soldiers. It shouldn't be our jobs to decide whether to bring an alien weapon of unknown power back home with us. I had no idea what was right. I knew only what *felt* right to my untrained gut.

Almost all my life, I'd made logical decisions—followed my brain, not my heart, as people like to say. Was this the logical choice? I hadn't had the time, much less the mental capacity, to decide whether this was the right thing to do.

Quiet footsteps approached, and I closed my eyes, hoping somehow they'd pass by without stopping.

No such luck.

He didn't say anything at first, but I knew it was Luka by his cautious steps. How did I know him so well and yet not at all?

It was too hard to open my eyes, to face him and the realities I'd seen of his past. He must've known, all along, that we'd come here, to this point. That I'd learn his truth and recoil from it. Knowing whatever relationship we had, even friendship, would be at risk of collapsing under the weight of this enormous secret.

He'd endured trauma beyond my imagining. At the very least, I could make my own peace with him. "I'm sorry. About . . . everything."

I heard him lean against the wall, his boots shuffling against the floor near my knee. "It happened before I was born. But . . . thank you."

If I blinked my eyes, I was afraid tears might spill from them. "Where do we go from here, Luka?"

"We go home," he said simply.

I willed the emotion away. "You know what I mean."

He nodded, still facing the ceiling. "It's up to you."

"I'm tired of things being up to me."

He shook his head ruefully. "An unfortunate consequence of life, I've found." He tried to soften his stance to something casual, shifting to lean an arm against the bulkhead. The wall glowed a soft white at his touch, as though awaiting an order. He noticed this and took his hand off it, shaking his head ruefully. "I forget myself here."

"They respond to touch?" I asked, though I'd already noticed this.

"Yes. It's how we communicate with the ship's computer. A touch can send a message, issue an order to the ship, or allow for the download of information, all in an instant of intention. It works best, of course, with our original physiology, but with our implants and modifications in our suits, we can maintain functionality of the ship." He displayed the palm of his gloved hand to me, showing the glowing aqua-blue fibers interwoven into the black and concentrated in his fingertips.

"That's incredible."

He smiled, just a little. "There is much we could share with you."

My eyelids closed on their own. My bones ached. Fatigue washed over me like incessant waves. How long had it been since I had really, truly slept?

Cassie, it has been thirteen hours since you awoke from hibernation.

Oh, that was going to be hard to get used to.

"You are tired," Luka said, apologetic. "I'll leave you. We will soon pick up the weapon, but we can do that without needing to disembark. You won't be missing anything. There is little to see now but darkness and ruin."

I was sorely tempted. I peered around the corner and down the hall, where Shaw had already dropped his chin to his chest and was dozing in his jump seat. "Little to see? Luka, even the *walls* are interesting."

As if on cue, a kaleidoscope of blue and purple bloomed on the wall in front of us, catching Luka's attention.

"What does it mean?" I asked, growing concerned by his confusion.

"It's likely nothing," he said, eyes following the swirls of color as they moved and faded. "Radar interference on our projected flight path. Perhaps some space debris or dust confusing the sensors. The pilots will adjust our trajectory to avoid it."

"I can't believe this makes sense to you. How do you understand it?"

"It's my native language," he said, eyes teasing.

"How do you get by on Earth when you are able to read shapes and colors as words?"

"Do you not also see shapes and colors as language? A red hexagon means stop. A yellow triangle means caution. A circle with a line through its apex means off or on. You also use this alphabet."

He had me there. "See, *this* is why I can't sleep."

For the first time since I'd awoken, his grin was warm and unguarded. I felt something—something like the old way I might have once felt. It was a flash of the old Luka. Or maybe just the true version of himself. "What else do you want to know? To sate your curiosity? I'll try to answer anything I'm able."

There was a swirling maelstrom of questions, and yet my mind could not pick out a single one. I settled on the obvious, the here and now. I hesitated to ask, but he had just offered to answer anything. "How did your father know about the weapon?"

He slid down the wall to sit beside me. I appreciated that he left a measurable distance of space between us. He sighed, lips pressed tight together. "He does not tell me, but I can guess. My father is—and was—a scientist. I can only assume he worked on this project during the war. His secret location here might have been why he was able to escape."

I suppressed a chill and filed that information away for later. *Otor knows more about this weapon than he is telling us.*

"What . . ." I stopped, sensing this was a bad idea, but his eyebrows lifted expectantly, encouraging me. "What happened to . . . to your mother?"

At the change in his face, I immediately regretted asking. "No, sorry—never mind. I don't need to know."

He shook his head. "It's all right. I am . . . strangely relieved to be able to tell you."

That made me blink. He'd always been mysterious, quiet, a little closed off. I'd assumed that was his natural inclination. But maybe he'd been struggling with secrets for a long time.

"I was the first of my people born post-transition. As you might imagine, it was very . . . difficult. She couldn't go to a hospital, of course. My family didn't know all the things that could go wrong, and didn't have access to medicine. No one knew how the genetic treatment would affect her condition. They could not save her. After that, my family decided it was safer not to risk having any more children."

"Luka, I'm so sorry."

His eyes found mine, and he gave me a little smile. "I do not remember her."

This had been a bad idea. I switched to another topic, saying the first thing that popped into my head. "This moon base seems pretty well intact. Why weren't you guys able to just, you know . . . stay here?"

He gave me a sidelong glance that told me I had misstepped. "This moon is not a home, Cassie. We cannot live in tunnels without sunshine any more than humans can, orbiting the graveyard of our species. Yes, there is a pocket of air and some water still left in reserve. But we would be trapped, and vulnerable to the vrag, should they return."

For a second I had a flash of humanity living that way: scattered, broken, living like galactic refugees on inhospitable planets, hiding underground. To live with only a handful of my own people on foreign worlds, surrounded at all times by hostile species. "I'm sorry. That was thoughtless."

His hand went through his hair in frustration, and now I saw why his hair had been in disarray. He was shaking his head, like all this had been a mistake. "I wish it did not have to be like this. Believe me. I wish this meeting could have been about how our two peoples could reach new heights together. Perhaps one day, we can have that conversation." He offered me a smile that soon faltered. "Cassie . . . the only thing I was ever dishonest with you about was my identity. Everything else—*everything*—was the truth."

I smiled sadly, but couldn't meet his eyes. Anger had drained from me. What was the point of it? After having seen his decimated home planet with my own eyes, how could I fault his people for what they did? Their worst sin had been disguising themselves, and that had been in self-preservation only. Had they hurt anyone? Stolen anything? No. They'd only been surviving. Would I have done any different?

I was too tired to maintain the energy of being angry. I was depleted of it. Instead, I was hollow and wounded and afraid.

"I only came to check on you. If you need anything, please let me know. I'll give you your privacy." He gave me a smile in parting, and I was relieved that he did not require anything else from me.

SIX

I RETURNED TO the bridge sometime later, rejoining my crew. They each looked about as tired as I felt, but Copeland and Jeong lit up at the revelation that the entire ship was a computer interface that we could manipulate. Our suits were not the best equipped to communicate with the computer, to give it wordless orders the way the megobari did so effortlessly, but the material of our suits still allowed blooms of color to explode from our fingertips at a single touch. It was fascinating and strange, like playing a children's game—and we were the children, comprehending nothing.

As Luka had said, there had been some kind of debris field and the ride was getting a little bumpy. We buckled into our jump seats and Copeland and Jeong continued to amuse themselves by sending dots of color back and forth over Shaw's head, who still slept. I'd never seen the two of them like this before, grinning ear to ear and laughing like little girls when one of them managed to change their blue dots to purple, or draw a circle, or shatter their spots of color against the indent of Shaw's helmet on the wall. It was the thrill of discovery, the joy in learning something beautiful and new. An entire alien civilization to be explored and known. Deep down I felt it, too. The thrum of excitement, of a whole new world opening up for us all.

It was almost enough to drown out the shadow that came with it: the steep price we might pay for this knowledge.

Luka came to stand beside me. "The shuttle drone has returned and the weapon has been stowed," he said, bracing his hand on the wall above my head. "Now we will return to the base, transfer your supplies from *Odysseus* to *Exodus*, and then we can all return to Earth."

Orange sparks, sharp and insistent, suddenly lit the bridge with the urgency of drumbeats. Luka startled upright, tensing.

"What is it?" I asked.

His face paled as he scanned the runes.

Then the ship rocked violently, throwing him into me, and the world exploded into fire.

I was thrown sideways into my harness, tearing the breath out of me. The serene bridge was suddenly madness. The megobari crew who were not strapped into their posts were thrown to the ground like toy soldiers. Small fires had erupted out from consoles near the pilots. Otor had tumbled down the corridor, a tangle of awkward limbs. The walls still pulsed with warning, now joined with an odd and fearful wailing of alarms.

Luka managed to stay upright, though the bridge was still lurching to one side, and ran to help his father. He helped him get to his feet, and then the ship rocked again, and both tumbled into the bulkhead.

Beside me, my crewmates were unstrapping themselves. Bolshakov succeeded first, and ran to aid Luka, slipping Otor's limp arm around his wide shoulders to help him stand.

I was scrambling to get out of my harness when Shaw shouted at me. "Cassie, stay here!"

My hands stilled on the latches. Did he think I'd get in the way?

Otor's face was pale and twisted in agony as the two men brought him back to his post on the bridge, where his eyes looked fearfully about the cabin.

"Captain," Bolshakov shouted over the alarms. "What's happening?"

Luka answered grimly for his father. "The vrag."

Otor nodded, breathless, and then shook himself away from the others to rest his hands on the ship's interface. The ship lurched again, this time forward, and I was thrown back against the bulkhead as we sped away. "We cannot let them have the weapon!"

My crewmates had all left me behind. Copeland was crouched over a megobari pilot with a bloodied face. Jeong and

Shaw were helping two others put out one of the fires.

My heart raced but my body was frozen. Should I stay here out of the way? Could I actually help? Sunny's voice was absurdly calm in my head. *Cassie, an unknown ship has fired on this vessel. Evacuation suggested.*

I didn't stop to question how Sunny knew this. Maybe she was talking to the megobari ship somehow.

We can get away, I told myself, clutching frantically at the hope. The two megobari pilots still at their posts were sweating, staring into their consoles, hands clenched on the controls. Maybe we'd beat the vrag back to base.

But the megobari who were able to had all retrieved their helmets and put them back on. They knew better what was happening, and they were preparing for the worst.

I couldn't just *sit here*, but what could I do? I wasn't a member of this crew. I was barely a member of my own. I was a fool to think I was needed.

No, my role in this was the observer. The fail-safe. The go-between. The one who could communicate with Sunny.

That was it—my one useful skill at this moment. *Sunny, what do I do?*

But before she could answer, the ship lurched again with a sound like deep, groaning thunder. The lights flickered and dimmed. The bridge went dark, walls losing all color, and now only emergency lights outlined the floor. We were hit again, head-on this time. Screams of pain came from the dark.

I saw only shadows moving, heard only shouting. I could just barely see the outlines of Luka and his father, slumped over the controls.

Shaw was in front of me suddenly. "Cassie, are you okay?"

His face was a ghastly shadow in front of me, but he was intact. The whites of his eyes glinted in the floor lights.

"Yeah, I'm—"

But something sparked beside us, and shrapnel flew. Shaw dropped like a stone to the bulkhead.

I tugged in panic at my belt, but the latch was sticking. I screamed in frustration, the latch finally gave way, and I fell to my knees beside him.

The lights flickered back on at half strength, showing a scene of chaos and destruction. But I could only focus on Shaw, the sticky blood coating his suit, the hunk of metal embedded in his skin. "Copeland!" I screamed.

She was there in seconds, leaning over his other side to see the wound. Her eyes met mine over Shaw's body, and I saw in the grim set of her mouth that there was nothing she could do. Not now, not here.

I put my hands on his chest, felt the stuttering rise and fall, felt panic threaten to overtake me.

"What's happened?" Jeong was suddenly beside us. She caught sight of Shaw's wounds and groaned, her face going white.

I registered only a flash of confusion in her eyes before Luka skidded to his knees beside me.

He had something large and white in his hands. Bandages.

With Copeland's help, we pressed them against the bloodiest spots on Shaw's body with expert fingers. Shaw groaned and his eyes fluttered, and hope sparked in me.

Luka's eyes caught mine.

"Your father?"

"Okay. Shaw?"

"Not sure."

"Are you hurt?"

It was the first time I'd thought to consider it. I looked down at myself and found no visible wounds or tears in my suit. "I don't think so."

"They have done exactly as we feared," Luka said, his voice full of poison.

"Luka!" Otor shouted.

Luka held my gaze for a split second longer and then ran to the bridge. I looked down at Shaw, and Copeland spared a hand to push my shoulder. "Go. He's as stable as I can get him."

Jeong and I couldn't reach the bridge without stepping over bodies, so we took bandages to those who were still breathing. I glanced up to see Otor standing on the upper deck, cradling one of his arms awkwardly against his body. Luka's hand was touching his father's back, nodding as his father spoke quickly and quietly.

Just as I reached them, Otor shouted an order. "Eject the shuttles!"

Two megobari who had been helping mend wounds ran to consoles and touched hands to their control screens, lighting them up with violet and green.

I searched Luka's face, but his eyes were trained on his father. "He is dropping the weapon and the empty shuttles," he said tersely to me. "To confuse them."

His father watched a few more moments to ensure his order had been carried out to completion before responding. "The most important thing is to keep the weapon out of the hands of the vrag. Luka, they will not stop now that they have found us. They have no mercy, do you understand? We are not equipped to fight them here."

"We can't use the weapon?"

"I do not have time to explain now, but no—it cannot simply be aimed and fired."

Another hit, and a small explosion on the lower bridge. One of the megobari gunners fell to the floor.

Before Luka could reach it, Bolshakov had jumped ahead and took up the gun himself. Copeland ran to the aid of the fallen gunner.

Did that mean Shaw was okay, or that he was dead?

Otor suddenly seemed to notice me. He motioned me forward with his good arm and planted it on my shoulder. "I am sorry."

"What can we do?" I asked.

"Evade them," Luka said, just as another explosion knocked us into the support wall. The vrag must be right on us now. "Get back to base. We can't outfight them on this ship."

"No, my son. We cannot show them the entrance. They will

discover the last secrets we have left."

The screams of the wounded echoed the blaring alarms. Jeong and Copeland and one or two megobari were scrambling to keep up, but there weren't enough able-bodied crew to care for all of them, and the megobari that were standing needed to control the ship. I wanted to help them, not stand here *talking*. I started toward the chaos on the lower deck, and Otor grabbed my arm with his good hand to stop me.

"No," he said sharply. "We are lost."

Just then, an explosion that rocked the entire ship tossed all of us on the upper deck against the back wall. I slammed into the bulkhead and slid to the floor, dazed. It took a few seconds for my vision to come back, and then I mentally checked myself. Everything still there, still functional.

I struggled to right myself, but my brain had lost track of what was up and what was down. Patchy holes in the bulkhead, sparking and burning.

My eyes scanned frantically for the others and caught on Luka and Otor. I struggled on my hands and knees, the ship listing wildly, making it impossible to stand.

Otor was slumped, eyes struggling to stay open. I crawled on my elbows and knees, but Luka hadn't been hurt and beat me to his father.

But his father was pushing him away. "Go!" I heard him shout. "Luka, GO! Get the humans off this ship!"

What humans were left? Bolshakov was slumped over his station on the lower deck. Shaw might already be dead. Copeland was crawling along the floor one-handed, trying to give some kind of aid to an injured or dead megobari. Where was Jeong?

I used the half wall to pull myself up, and tried to find them in the chaos and death.

Luka's hand closed on my wrist. "We have to go."

I wrested it back from him as the ship shuddered, knocking us both to our knees. "Not without them!"

What I could see was terrible. Jeong lay beside a fallen megobari, lips blue, eyes blinking too slowly. There was a dime-sized hole in her helmet. My instincts roared to go get her, but what could I do?

I met eyes with Copeland, now on her feet, her suit splattered with red. She yelled to me, but I couldn't hear her. She was using her external comm, and sound didn't travel in a vacuum.

Another blast knocked us all to our backs, but Copeland was up and running and had her hands on me before I could get to my feet. "You get out of here!" she shouted, and suddenly my internal comm picked up her voice. She bodily pulled me up and shoved me into Luka, who was pulling me away. "Abandon ship! Gupta, you're our record keeper. Go! I'm the ranking officer now and that's a goddamn order!"

Suddenly Luka grabbed me around the waist, picking me up and dragging me backward from the bridge.

I struggled. Shouted. But he was like a machine, his arm immovable. "There's nothing for you to do here now."

Back on the bridge, I saw Otor still on the upper deck, struggling to stand on his own. There were not many left for him to command. He watched us go and I finally realized what was happening. Otor had ejected all the shuttles so they wouldn't know which one contained the weapon. There weren't enough for us all to escape.

Copeland, Otor . . . they were saving us because we were the youngest.

Luka pulled me down the hall at the far end of the bridge, past the alcove where I'd tried to hide from responsibility, and threw us both into a metal capsule with its door wide open.

The door slid closed as soon as we were inside. The capsule was crowded, not meant for two people. Chaos and death were on the other side of the glass now, and we were leaving them behind.

Luka wrapped his arms tight around me, tucked my head against his shoulder, and punched the release button with his elbow to free the capsule.

We shot away from the dying ship just as fire exploded out of the hatch, chasing us into the black as it consumed the bridge.

SEVEN

I SCREAMED ALL the way down.

Down and down and down, spinning like the inside of a washing machine on hyperdrive. My stomach flew against my heart and lodged in the back of my throat.

I was entangled in Luka's arms, crammed into a pod smaller than a broom closet, zooming like a rocket toward the jagged rocks of the moon below.

A terrible jerk knocked the wind out of me, and then our fall began to stabilize. For a few long, drawn-out seconds, I heard nothing but my own shattered breathing.

We slammed into the rocky surface of the moon. Though a little gentler than I expected, the impact jarred the two of us apart. I banged my elbows and my knees, and my helmet ricocheted off the interior of the pod, leaving me shell-shocked and dazed.

The capsule slid downhill through a shower of dirt, and then everything went quiet. At least, everything on the outside. My body still felt like it was spinning for several more minutes. I lay very still and struggled to keep from throwing up.

Still crushed into the small space beside me, Luka kicked at the door, grunting with the effort, until it gave way.

The surface of the moon was dark, almost pitch, but for the distinct twinkle of stars. A scattering of steady points of light might have been the other moons, or perhaps the inner planets of the system. Nothing but vast, airless desert in every direction.

Magnificent desolation, Buzz Aldrin had once said of the moon. We weren't meant to be here, in this lifeless astronomical graveyard.

Monstrous rocks that could've crushed an SUV broke up the landscape. We wouldn't get very far on foot.

Maybe the vrag couldn't see us in the dark. Our suits were black and insulated, concealing our heat signatures. Maybe it was the only reason we were still alive.

Luka worked himself up and out of the pod with some difficulty. It took him a few tries, even though the gravity was light. When he'd tumbled out and righted himself, he reached back in for me.

My muscles were jelly. My bones were bruised and battered, but Luka held me up like he was made of stone.

Luka was watching the sky, anxiously searching.

"Can you see them?" I asked. The sky was black with a scattering of silver glitter, beautiful even in its coldness. Sunrise was a threatening glint of white haze on the horizon.

And then I saw it. The megobari ship, racing low across the sky like a white comet, trailing debris and fire. It was far on the dark horizon, and speeding steadily away.

And then the other—a massive shadow in the night sky. Only visible for the way it blotted out the stars. It was a hundred times larger than the megobari ship, and *Exodus* hadn't been small.

The vrag ship was going to run them down.

My arms were draped across Luka, trying to keep myself up, hands gripping hard on to his hip and his shoulder. My wasted muscles had endured too much, and even standing was now too much to ask of them.

The white ship, though it looked disabled, slowly circled back. Limping toward its pursuer.

"No, no, no," Luka whispered. "You don't have weapons that can hurt them!"

The black vrag ship didn't change course, but it descended into the atmosphere to follow its quarry.

"They're headed straight for it. They're going to hit." I couldn't breathe. "Oh my God, Luka, they're doing it on purpose. They're trying to ram the ship."

There was someone still alive on that bridge.

I felt his body clench, like a spring tightening, as if he could reach out and physically stop the ship with his hands.

"No," Luka shouted into the sky. "Don't you dare. Don't you dare!"

The vrag ship opened fire.

Exodus broke apart. Explosions lit the night sky in red and orange and grayscale, but there was little left to destroy and no oxygen to fuel the flames. The pieces drifted slowly down, twinkling like falling glass.

The vrag ship hovered momentarily, as if making sure its quarry was truly dead. And then it disappeared into the darkness, my eyes unable to follow the shadow any longer.

A few seconds later, the shock wave rippled over us, blowing chunks of rock against my helmet and nearly knocking me down.

Luka stood with his back to me. His shaking hand reached up to his helmet, to his ear, and for a horrifying second I thought he was going to take it off.

But no. He was listening to the radio, over which I could hear nothing but static.

I waited, shaking, as burning debris fell away far over Luka's head like a halo of hell.

His eyes met mine. His lips parted, mouth fell open. He shook his head.

His arms hung loose by his sides, palms turned up, helpless. I fell into him and we held each other as the last of the false sunlight that had been his entire family fell across the fractured landscape and the last of the debris had fallen from the sky.

But we couldn't stay here forever. I slipped my arms from around him, numb and disbelieving, with only logic pushing me to act. "Luka, we have to go. We aren't going to last long out here. Luka. Look at me. Focus. Please. Tell me what we have to do."

He looked down at me as though he was startled to find me beside him. The lights in his helmet scattered deep shadows across the planes of his face. "The vrag will still be out there searching for survivors among the escape pods. We have to find the droneship that held the weapon. We must . . . get back to base."

I nodded through tears. "Okay. That's a start. Lead the way."

Luka had the location of the downed shuttle linked to his suit-board computer. We trudged in darkness over boulders and stones and dust that was never meant to be traversed by foot, two lone life-forms in a place we never should have been, that was never meant for us. I had to force my shaking legs to go beyond their endurance. The odds were so impossible I didn't dare think of them.

By rights, we should never have found what we were looking for. We never should have been able to cross the distance on foot to find the shuttle intact.

But we did. The shuttle drone, having landed itself with perfect control, was utterly undamaged and still functional.

Luka was able to open it with only a few deft touches, allowing us to crawl inside. The interior was possibly even more alien than the surface of the moon, but I was too tired to examine it. We were safe, for the moment.

There was only enough space for the two of us in our suits to sit facing each other with our legs crossed. Luka was able to turn on life support, giving us some warmth and light and air, but we kept our helmets on in case of accidental depressurization.

After a few false starts, Luka got the drone moving again, hovering only a handful of feet above the surface of the moon. He downloaded the location of the base into the shuttle, and it took off toward the light side of the moon.

Only once that task was done did Luka let himself sink to the floor, eyes glazing over and staring blankly at the wall.

I sat in front of him and tried to keep him going somehow. "Luka. Look at me. You just saved our lives." I touched his gloved hand with mine, but he didn't respond. "Luka, I would've died here without you. At least now we have a fighting chance. We'll take this weapon thing back to the base, and . . ." And what? Take it back to Earth, alone? Six months later?

But what the hell would two teenage kids be able to do against that *ship*? Against something that could destroy the megobari ship with such apparent ease? Without even a warning shot or a hail?

How could anything humans have compete? It'd be like flinging sticks at a tank.

No. Can't think like that. My rational brain shut down all extraneous thought. Survive this now. Save future problems for

Future Cassie to deal with. Current Cassie had plenty of problems of her own. Like the mysterious apparent mega-weapon we were now toting through utter darkness on a barren alien moon. Like the vrag ship that could still be hovering invisibly in the space above our heads. Like the fact that we were now the sole living things on this moon, and it was up to us to deal with these problems.

Breathe, breathe, breathe.

"We will handle this shit because we have to," I muttered to myself.

Luka's eyes flicked down to me. "What did you just say?"

"I said, we have to handle this shit because it's up to us now. Just the two of us. We have to survive. We have to get through this part, because we're not safe yet. Luka, do you know what this weapon does?"

Still blank-faced, he shook his head, helmet rocking against the bulkhead. His head tilted upward and he closed his eyes.

I felt a tingle of fear at realizing that Luka might be out of commission, and he was the only one now who knew the things that could get us home.

But maybe that wasn't entirely true.

Sunny? I ventured.

I'd closed the door on her while we fell, too focused externally to exchange information with her. I cautiously opened the door again and found her waiting.

Yes, Cassie.

Almost sighing in relief, I turned off my external comm and

spoke aloud so that Luka couldn't hear. "What resources do you have access to right now?"

I can store information and video recordings from your helmet cam. I can do calculations, process information, give production models and probabilities. I can monitor your health status. I can give limited data retrieval based on what I have stored in your suitboard memory. I require the tools on board Odysseus *for anything further.*

"Are you in communication with *Odysseus*? Can you tell how far away we are?"

The low-frequency radio signals on board are not strong enough to send or receive communications at this distance.

"Let me know when the signal gets any stronger or weaker." We could follow it like bread crumbs if necessary.

Yes, Cassie.

"Do you, uh . . . do you know what just happened?"

I have access to your memories, helmet cam footage, and vital signs.

Okay, creepy. "So you . . . you know that the other members of *Odysseus* are . . . gone. They were killed."

I have marked them as deceased in the mission log. Your suitboard record logs will be automatically uploaded to Odysseus *when we are within range.*

"Thanks, Sunny. Can you . . . can you sense where we are right now? Can you sense . . . the weapon we're carrying?"

There was a short pause. *I am reading unfamiliar energy signatures in the hold of this shuttle, but I do not have the capacity to decipher their meaning.*

Right. At the moment, Sunny was little more than my helmet, my suit, and my brain. While each of those three things had some pretty impressive capabilities, it didn't make her magical.

I settled back against the bulkhead across from Luka. Eyes still closed, he was in his own world.

"Sunny? Can you . . ." I didn't know what I was asking. I wanted . . . company. Consolation. The world outside was bleak and full of danger and we were small and alone and vulnerable. And I was so far from home. All I had was a computer hooked to my brain. How could she compensate? I felt dumb saying it out loud, so I posed my question in my head only: *Sunny, can you . . . make me feel better?*

In response, Sunny began playing Beethoven's Moonlight Sonata in my memory.

It was so sudden and unexpected and beautiful. An ode and a dirge.

I closed my eyes and, since no one else could see me, let the tears fall freely.

EIGHT

I DIDN'T ROUSE again until the shuttle came to a stop. Luka climbed silently to his feet, deftly moving his hands over the smooth control panel. He must have activated some remote entry system, as a panel beneath a boulder twice the size of the shuttle slid open, and the shuttle trundled inside. We descended into the cool dark far below, the shuttle's exterior lights illuminating our path.

"What are we going to do?" I asked. "What's our next step?"

He didn't speak to me for a few seconds. Just stared into space with his hand resting listless on the shuttle's control panel.

"Luka, what are we going to do?" I said again, louder.

I grabbed his arm and he blinked at me slowly, like he couldn't understand what I was doing. Someone had to take charge of keeping us alive, and I needed his knowledge. "Luka. We have to get back and warn Earth. No one knows those things are coming. Can we communicate from here? How do we get back? We need to plan."

"We have to . . ." Luka paused, looked around. His face was shell-shocked. He swallowed hard. "We have to find another ship. No message will reach Earth faster than we can ourselves. The vrag may already be on their way there. We need a mego-bari ship that can take us back to Earth quickly. Load it with food, supplies from *Odysseus*. And . . . and the weapon."

"Okay, good," I said, nodding to encourage him, holding back tears. Once I let the floodgates open, it would be hard to regain control.

Copeland, Jeong, Shaw, Bolshakov.

Gone.

Their last moments kept playing over in my mind, like a nightmare I couldn't escape, my brain trying to decipher where everything had gone wrong and what I could have done differently.

I had to keep thinking ahead or the horror would consume me.

The shuttle came to a stop. Luka opened the hatch and we climbed out. I tried catching a glimpse of the shuttle drone's cargo, but it was shrouded in darkness.

Luka led the way down the tunnel, and I hustled to catch up. "This weapon. Do you—nobody really told us what it *does*. Is it stable? Is it dangerous to us? To Earth, if we take it back?"

His eyes jerked to me when I said *if*, narrowing. "That is not something I know."

"If we need it, we need it. I just want to make sure we aren't going to kill ourselves trying to take it home. Is it secure in its container? Not, like . . . radioactive?"

He shook his head only slightly. "Not radioactive. It is inert, at the moment."

"Why didn't your people take it with them when they left, originally?"

"I was not born when it happened. Perhaps they tried, and failed in the attempt."

I swiveled away from him, wishing I hadn't gone there, hadn't poured more grief into his cup. "So we can't take *Odysseus* home?"

"Not unless you want to arrive six months after the vrag."

I cringed. "Right. So . . . where are the other ships?"

"The computer will know." He stopped in front of a bare stretch of wall, both hands pressing lightly against it.

"This is your computer?" I asked.

"*Everything* is the computer." His fingers flew over the flat surface like a speed painter, creating prisms in the dull canvas, interacting with strings of colors in ways that I couldn't understand. It certainly wasn't any kind of typing I'd ever seen—his fingertips swirled and swiped, never leaving the surface.

He let his hands fall, and the colors slowly faded back to white. "There is a hangar of spacecraft on a deeper level. We should go quickly."

"Wait. What else can you learn from the computer?" I asked. "I mean . . . does it show records of what happened here? This weapon, maybe—what it does? Maybe they even have more information on the vrag we could use."

He eyed me warily, but I could see that he hadn't thought of this before. "It is a massive computer, and very old. It stores more data than the sum total of your entire civilization. It may be useful, yes, but I don't know how to begin to sort through so much information."

Well, damn.

Cassie, I may be of assistance.

Sunny? Had she heard the entire conversation through my helmet's radio, or only my side of things? I wasn't used to computers interrupting my conversations.

She showed me, in intentions more than words, how she could sift through the information faster than either one of our slow, biological brains, find any information relevant to us, and store it in her own memory.

I tapped the side of my helmet. "I have a friend who says she can help."

Luka only raised his eyebrows. "I am not sure if your computer will be able to interface with this one, as it is not of our making."

"She seems to think she can. And anyway, don't all computers speak the same binary language?" I had no idea if that was actually true; his computer spoke in *colors*, after all. "Now . . . how do I plug her in?"

Cassie, you will have to remove your helmet. I will attempt to connect with the alien system wirelessly.

"If you say so." Luka watched curiously as I reached both my hands to undo the latches. I ripped it off and put the helmet on the console, taking a deep breath of alien air. There was a faint, unfamiliar scent to it that I couldn't place; something like heat and metal.

"Sunny's going to try to connect wirelessly to the computer." We waited. Lights on the wall before us stretched out like some kind of alien mural, not unlike the view screen on *Exodus*, flashing and dissipating like different colored water droplets falling and melting into snow. I kept trying to read some meaning into it, but I might as well have been trying to decipher messages in raindrops.

"Is it working?" I asked in a whisper. "Did Sunny connect?"

Luka watched the screen with attentive eyes. "Something is happening. I'm not exactly sure what. Can't you ask your computer?"

"No. I can ask, and I think she can hear me through the radio, but I can't hear her without the helmet on. We have to be directly connected."

We fell into uncomfortable silence. I had the urge to talk again, to say something, anything to break the silence. Grief and fear filled the empty moments. Had to keep acting like this was all normal, according to plan. Just keep following the plan.

Luka grabbed my arm. Something was happening on the screen. "I think it's working. There's a message here. It says Sunny will take approximately three hours to download the pertinent information."

"Then we have things to do."

We left Sunny to do her work. Luka and I traveled deeper into the bunker, taking alien versions of elevators and escalators down farther into the dark.

"How do you know where you're going?" I asked over the sound of our shoes hitting the oddly soft ground. "I thought you've never been here before?"

He touched his fingertips to the wall. It lit beneath his skin, revealing a network of illuminated, orderly lines, swirling in static circles like a tornado. How deep below the surface *were* we? "My people have achieved the ability to create maps."

Sarcasm, from Luka? I couldn't be quite sure.

He led me into a pitch-black cavern. Even in the darkness, it felt vast; the air was chilly and damp, and I had the feeling of being adrift in an inky ocean. The tang of moist dirt was in the air, and as lights began to dawn high over our heads, I realized why.

This was a massive natural cavern, entirely rough stone. No smart walls here. The ceiling glowed dull yellow. And as the light steadily grew more intense, I realized the entire cavern roof was actually *writhing*.

"Light worms. They feed on the rock," Luka said quietly. "Simple organisms, but quite useful. The only living thing to escape complete annihilation, besides ourselves."

Billions of individuals above our heads, a dome of golden light enough to fill up the entire football-stadium-sized cave. It was amazing. But what I saw beneath the lights completely took my mind off the ceiling.

A fleet of alien spacecraft lined up before us. Nearest to us was the smallest, four or five in a row that were about the size of a giant Humvee. A few, not unlike *Odysseus*. And on up from that, until the largest at the very end was another ship like *Exodus*, taking up an entire half of the cavern on its own.

"A small fleet," Luka said. "In storage."

"So . . . which one is our ride home?"

Luka headed down the row, and I followed at a distance behind. I couldn't help but marvel at each and every one. My heart was pumping. *No other human has ever gotten to see this.* And then I realized, Sunny wasn't here recording this. Nobody would ever believe me.

Then I pinched myself for being so selfish. At least I might still see home again.

Luka stopped in front of one that was roughly the height of three double-decker buses stacked on top of each other. It was rounded, like most of the megobarian technology I'd encountered, with a sharp sickle-edge disc at the front, not unlike a certain famous TV spaceship.

But beyond that, there was nothing remotely human about it. For one thing, it was a pale robin's-egg blue that shimmered unusual colors as the light shifted. I reached out and touched it, and the skin was ever so slightly flexible under my hand, like a turtle egg. I couldn't help but wonder where they got this, what it was made out of, how it worked. I owed it to everyone we'd lost to learn the answers.

"Not the biggest one?"

"The largest one requires at least six megobari to pilot it together. This is the fastest craft I can pilot alone."

Once he touched the side of the ship and ensured via some technological telepathy that it was functional, he sent me back upstairs to *Odysseus* by way of one of their weird elevators. Alone, underground on an alien world, I had a clenching in my chest at seeing *Odysseus* again. My last tangible link with Earth. The thing we'd built with such hope and expectation.

And we were leaving it behind in this alien mausoleum.

Swallowing hard, I pushed through my shifting feelings and went aboard. Turning my brain off, I worked fast unloading supplies, trying to outrun my emotions. Food was important. Food and water and medical supplies. Nothing else.

When I came back out, Luka was there. Behind him about a hundred feet, in the same place where his family had arrived the first time I saw them, was the blue ship.

"I won't even ask how you did that," I said, too weary to wonder anymore.

We moved supplies from *Odysseus* onto the megobari ship. There had been enough food inside *Odysseus* to last six people for a year. It would be more than enough for me and Luka, for what he assured me would not be a long journey home.

Inside, the blue ship was like *Exodus* in miniature: off-white and minimalist. I went alone to retrieve my helmet when Sunny's three hours were up. "You finished, Sunny?"

I transmitted backups of the data that seemed most promising, Cassie. They are saved on my hard drive aboard Odysseus.

Oh, no.

"Luka!" I shouted as I ran up the ramp into the megobari ship, still snapping my helmet on. He was kneeling over the last few packs, pulling straps tight. "Luka, we need to transfer Sunny's hard drive to this ship. Can we do that?"

He looked confused. "You have her on your suitboard."

I shook my head. "Just an auxiliary. She sends everything to the ship. All the records of the mission. The megobari data. All of it."

He hesitated. "Your hardware is not compatible with our hardware. It's not as though I could simply plug Sunny in." His arms stretched out, gesturing to the space around us.

My eyes followed, stomach sinking. He was right. There was no physical port anywhere. No circuit boards or wires. Only smooth surfaces. This ship was hundreds, maybe thousands of years evolved beyond the kind of computer Sunny was.

I growled in frustration, hands balling. "Without her memory stores there's hardly any point in going back to Earth with just the weapon and no idea how to activate it. And we have no proof of what happened here. No one on Earth will believe a word we say. Can you please at least look at it? See what we could do?"

Sighing, he let me lead him to the place where Sunny's central core was stored. He and I popped open the control panel together, and after a few minutes, I prodded, "Well?"

His face was inscrutable, eyebrows gathered as he stared into the network of chips and motherboards. But then he was shaking his head. "It would be like trying to play a record on your cell phone."

"Could we just take Sunny's memory chips with us, find something to plug them into when we get home?"

"This machine is so massive and complex, I do not even know where the memory storage units are, let alone the ones holding the data we need."

Sunny helpfully interjected from *Odysseus*'s speakers. "Cassie, my memory is fragmented, stored in numerous data banks and backup units throughout the ship. You would need to remove every single one to ensure you have a complete record."

We didn't have the time or ability to do that, even with Sunny helping us—the more of her brain we disconnected, the less helpful she'd be. We'd be taking her offline, and she was the only one who knew where her brain was even kept.

My suitboard would have to do. It was a much more limited memory, but maybe I could use the other crew members' extra suits as data accessories. I could retrofit and link them together into something workable.

The backups of their feeds had been sent to Sunny, too. Up until their last moments. I'd forgotten that. I had a first-person perspective of each of their deaths. Their last images of life.

A deep, gnawing pit opened in my chest, threatening to swallow me whole.

"There may be a way," Luka said, interrupting my spiral into dark thoughts. His expression was grim. "You are not going to like it."

NINE

LUKA LED ME wordlessly into one of the compartments off the bridge. There was strange equipment in this room, with three stations set up side by side that looked like examination tables. Some kind of empty research lab.

He gestured for me to follow him. While he got to work at one of the stations—a tall, glassy black cube that was either slightly translucent or just very reflective—I hoisted myself onto the table beside him to watch. The table lit a soft white light at my touch.

The machine began to whir softly, and Luka glanced up at me, his eyes catching the light from the glowing surface beneath me.

He held a delicate, shimmering black capsule, about the

size of a thimble, gingerly between his thumb and forefinger. I leaned toward him to get a better look. It glittered in the low light.

"I can download Sunny's program and her entire memory stores to this device. Alone, it is inert. Useless. It needs an entire system of support. A network of output, input, energy source, temperature control. For Sunny, all of that is built into *Odysseus*. She and the ship are nearly one and the same. Removing Sunny from *Odysseus* would diminish her capacity, making her nearly useless to us. There is only one other mobile platform that we know is compatible with the program that can provide all of the above."

"What?"

"You."

Understanding dawned slowly. "Luka. Tell me you don't mean . . ."

His silence was the answer.

"Wait, wait. This can't be our only option. Why can't we just—bring Sunny back with us on a memory chip or something?"

"Do you have a memory chip that can store this amount of data?"

"Well, no, but—when we get back—"

"Do you have ready access to a comparable machine on your planet? Sunny is already one of the most advanced systems your people have created. She is incredibly complex and delicate. She is as close to artificial intelligence as humans have yet achieved.

You can't simply plug her into any computer terminal on Earth."

He wasn't wrong. Sunny was so complex and unique that I hadn't even been able to practice interfacing with her in training, only a less-powerful prototype. There was only one of her, and she was integral to *Odysseus.*

SEE might have options, but the thought of approaching them for help made me wary. They weren't like NASA; they were a corporation looking for profit. And I'd never forget the cold look in Clayton Crane's eyes as he told the techs to keep Hanna locked in the HHM, even while she was pounding on the door in a panic.

I wasn't in a hurry to ask him for any favors.

I dropped my head into my palms. This was getting beyond even my ability to comprehend. I tried to trace all the possible threads to their apparent ends, but everything was becoming tangled.

"Your brain has already networked and interfaced with her programming," Luka said gently, taking a step closer. "I would do this for you, Cassie, except that your chances of success are so much better. Your brain waves were already demonstrated to be suitable, and you've had training. Not to mention that I . . . I already have one."

"So you've had this done?" I began to relax about an inch. It was alien medicine, but it was still medicine. Tried and refined and methodical. Not something we'd jury-rigged in a desperate hour.

He bowed his head forward, reaching up one hand to pull his

hair aside from one ear. I had to slide off the table and stand, our toes almost touching, to see what he wanted to show me: an inch-long white scar in the soft skin behind his earlobe, hidden in his hairline.

My soft exhale rustled his hair, and he straightened. "It is— or was—standard procedure. This is a research vessel equipped with medical robotic tools and what you would call 3-D printers. Each crew member would receive an implant, and we would then be linked to each other and to the ship. How do you think we are able to learn so many of your languages and communicate with the ship by touch, even after we changed our DNA?"

I shrugged. "Okay, that's . . . really cool."

A ghost of a smile passed over his face. "I can implant this safely using the tools we have on board. Your body would provide the electrical energy and temperature regulation necessary for Sunny's program to continue to run within you. Your nerve endings will interface with it like any other neuron." His voice went clinical; I could tell he was fighting to keep his face expressionless. "It would take some time to adjust, but you would be able to continue to communicate with Sunny, access her stored records, and make use of her considerable abilities. By the time we return to Earth, the connection may be permanent."

Luka wasn't a robot. The fact that he had removed emotion from his tone told me he was trying not to influence my decision.

He took a half step closer to me, offering the device in his palm for my inspection. His voice hitched lower, but was still absent of intonation. "Do you consent?"

I opened my mouth to respond but nothing came out. My first thought was yes, do it, whatever needs doing. But my self-preservation instinct was fast on the heels of that *yes*, yanking it right back into my mouth. "Pros and cons," I said hoarsely, then swallowed hard as I realized how dry my mouth was.

He didn't hesitate. He held up a hand and ticked off his reasons. "Pro. You gain a powerful computing accessory to your own mind, and with it, the information we may need to help save Earth. Con. The processing power in your head might be overwhelming. Your body may not be able to keep up with it. It's possible the heat output would not be well regulated by your hypothalamus and it could burn your skin. And this has never before been done on a human. The long-term effects are unknown."

My heartbeat sounded loud in my ears. "But I'll live? I won't be comatose or anything?"

"You have already been networked with Sunny with no ill effects. It will be little different from when you were networked via your helmet, except you will not be able to turn it off."

"What are the risks? Like, medically?"

"Minor risk of infection. Though there aren't many human pathogens here, and our machine will sterilize the injection site."

"What about rejection? Is my body going to attack the device?"

"It is inert. It's a foreign object, but not biological, so your immune system likely won't attack it. There might be some localized swelling or soreness."

I took a breath to steady myself. "Luka. Level with me here. What are you not telling me? Should I really do this?"

He exhaled, and he seemed smaller. Younger. When he turned his eyes on me, his gaze was the color of a cloudy sky. "My concern is the unknown. If this does not end well . . . it will be my fault."

I bit my bottom lip. He was still reeling from survivor's guilt.

"Cassie, I would not offer if I thought it was not worth the risk."

I steeled myself. "Then let's do it."

He was right in that the procedure was virtually painless. I sat very still while the robotic arm did its work, meditating on the image of Earth rotating alone in the void of space.

It was over in less than fifteen minutes. I wouldn't let myself think about the long-term consequences. What was done was done.

In the moments afterward, as fight-or-flight hormones circled my system, searching fruitlessly for an enemy to vanquish, Luka worked on the nearby console to ensure that Sunny was installed correctly in her new home.

Finally, he stepped away, eyes watching me with cautious curiosity. "Try it now."

"You all right in there, Sunny?" I asked, feeling odd and a little light-headed.

Sunny's cool voice sounded quietly in my mind, only this time without the barrier of an external medium between us. *Cassie, all my systems are functional. Thank you.*

Oh God, I had an artificial intelligence speaking directly to my brain.

Calm. Focus. "She's good. Is there anything else we need to do?" I asked, letting my hair fall back down, gingerly grazing the spot behind my ear that still tingled slightly as the anesthetic wore off. I could feel it there if I tried—the hard little cylinder, the cold spot touching my skull. I chose not to think about it.

"I would not try accessing the data at this point. Let yourself become acclimated first."

"How should I do that?"

"I can't answer that for you. How did you acclimate the first time?"

"By being semiconscious and in a dreamlike state while floating through space for about six months."

That didn't elicit the response I'd hoped for, but there was at least a twitch in the corner of his mouth that might've been mistaken for amusement. Then it was gone. He turned his back to me, resetting the machine and placing everything where it had been. "Give it time."

I took a shaky breath and slid off the table. The motion tilted the room violently to the side, and suddenly I couldn't feel the floor beneath me anymore.

Luka spun to catch me by the elbows, and I realized my legs

hadn't been ready to support me. "Take it easy," he murmured.

I forced strength back in my quadriceps and regained my footing. His hands drifted away, and I didn't waver again.

"I'll walk you back to the ship," he said, eyeing me warily up and down.

"I'm fine now."

He didn't say anything, but he walked with me down the hall anyway, keeping his distance but also a careful eye on me to make sure I was still steady.

And to be honest, I was grateful.

TEN

"WE ARE LOADED and ready for lift-off."

I'd already strapped in while waiting for Luka to make final preparations for launch. He stopped beside my chair, kneeling to meet my eyes. "How do you feel?"

"Just . . . a little light-headed. I think that's fair, all things considered."

His mouth twisted, but he nodded and moved to the seat slightly ahead and to my left, at what I'd already started to think of as the helm. He slid his helmet over his head and it sealed with a soft *shhh* of air.

"You read me?" came his voice, soft and close over the comm.

"I read you. You need any help?"

He glanced sideways at me, eyes tired and distracted. "The ship is designed to be piloted by one. But if we run into that vrag ship again, you can handle the guns."

My insides felt like lead. "I think I can do that."

Luka manipulated the control panel with deft touches. The door slid closed, and the ship started to hum.

G-forces pushed me back into my seat as the ship tilted and ascended. A hatch in the ceiling opened, letting us pass to the surface. Luka guided the ship expertly through the thin atmosphere and into the harsh, glaring radiation of Kepler-186.

Once we were reasonably sure the vrag were not waiting to ambush us, Luka navigated us away from the moon and we headed into the black.

My stomach pressed down into my intestines as the land grew farther away and smaller beneath us.

"Does this ship have a name?" I asked, speaking quietly so as not to be too much of a distraction.

"Why do you ask?"

"I would just feel better knowing its name."

"I don't think so. There's no designation in the computer."

"It's bad luck to fly a ship without a name, you know." I didn't know if that was true, but it sounded good.

There was a hint of humor in his reply. "Human superstition doesn't apply to megobarian technology."

"But there are humans on this ship," I said vaguely, wondering if he still counted himself among them.

"Then you should name it," he said, his eyes trained on the vast expanse of stars as we left solid ground far behind. The black of space wrapped around us, cold and merciless as the sea. "A human name. A lucky one."

It came to me suddenly, dredged out of the depths of some vague memories of school assignments. "Penelope."

He risked a quick glance at me. "Penelope?"

"The wife of Odysseus. She waited twenty years for him to return from war." *Lucky Penny*, I thought.

"Let's hope our Penelope is as faithful as the original." Luka drew in a few orders to the ship, and the walls around us subtly shimmered, the transparent display of the universe outside becoming clouded. "Not as good as an invisibility cloak, but this will at least minimize our heat signatures from the vrag."

"How long before we get back to Earth?" I asked.

"About a week."

"Are you serious?"

"An experienced pilot could get there in a few days. I'm not an experienced pilot."

He misread my incredulity. "It took *Odysseus six months* to get here!"

"I told you. We didn't give you our best." He looked over at me. "I'm about to turn on engines that utilize exotic matter to warp a gravity well in front of us, letting us perpetually fall into it in the direction of our choosing and move at superluminal speeds through the universe. Relatively, we won't be moving very fast, but I've never done this unsupervised before. You might want to brace yourself."

And then we opened up a bubble in space-time and twisted the universe around us.

ELEVEN

LUKA GOT THE ship to a point where it could fly itself, and leaned back into his seat.

The g-force had lessened. It didn't feel as though we were moving at all, but for the gentle vibrations of the ship.

"So we're moving through space-time right now," I breathed. "This . . . is amazing."

He twisted off his helmet and looked at me with lifted eyebrows. "You've done this before."

"Yeah, and I was in a steel tube, asleep. Can we see what it looks like? Outside?"

He tilted his head, as though the thought had never occurred to him. He touched his fingertips to the smooth interface again, and the bow of the ship went transparent.

I gasped out loud.

Putting my helmet on the floor, I unbuckled myself and approached the nearest wall. Directly in front of us was the darkness of space—no stars. Nothing at all, actually. A dark and limitless abyss. That must be the distortion of space-time, not allowing us to see light.

To our left and right, the light of distant stars seemed to stretch in stationary lines, like a long-exposure photo.

My heart sped up. Surreal didn't cut it. Right now, in this moment, we were outside of the regular course of time. Outside reality as we knew it. "And this is just normal to you?"

"No." His soft footfalls almost echoed behind me. The ship was so quiet now, everything so deceptively still. "None of this is normal."

We had kept ourselves busy on the surface, effectively keeping away the memory of seeing *Exodus* burn. But now that we had some downtime, the grief threatened to break over me like a dam.

But Luka . . . he'd seen his entire family die. In the moments of silence between us, I could see the horror of it dawning on him anew. His eyes had become distant.

I needed to keep him talking, focused on the task ahead. I needed him to be in the here and now with me.

"A wrinkle in space-time," I murmured, glancing back at him. "I'm standing here experiencing it and I still don't believe it."

He gave me a grimace. "I understand. There are things I

have seen that I do not want to believe." He left my side.

I caught up to him. Put my hand on his arm.

His eyes were full of tears, and he jerked his arm away.

"I'm so sorry, Luka," I said helplessly, emotion rising in my throat. "I'm sorry."

"Why would he have done that?" He choked on the words. The nightmare had caught up to him. "Why did he not evacuate everyone?"

No answer I gave would suffice. I tried anyway. "I . . . guess he didn't think he had a choice. Maybe he thought if he sacrificed himself, he could save you."

Luka shuddered and moved away from me, into the narrow passageway that led off the bridge.

I hesitated a few moments, wondering whether to leave him be. I thought about what I might want in that situation. Having someone to talk to might not help much, but being alone would feel far worse.

He had his back to me, hands braced along the rail. His head was bowed, shoulders tense. I approached him slowly and realized he was trembling.

"I should have stayed on board," he said through gritted teeth. "I should have died with them."

Cautiously, I placed my palm on the center of his back. "He wanted you to live."

"Living is . . . harder."

I took a step closer. Nodded against his shoulder, feeling the shaking tension in his muscles. "It is."

His breathing was ragged, eyes screwed shut.

My own tears hovered against my eyelashes, but I held them back. I slid my hand down his arm to rest over his clenched knuckles. "This is awful. I know it is." My voice cracked, betraying me. "But you're not alone."

He didn't respond, and I felt a choking in my throat. This was so far beyond my skill set. I didn't know how to do this—to comfort people. I didn't have a way to help. If Mitsuko had been here, or Emilio . . .

But Luka only had me, and I only had him. I swallowed and made my voice stronger than I felt. "I can't do this by myself, Luka. I cannot fly this ship. We're in this together, okay? And we're not out of the woods yet. I need you. We only have a few days before we get home, and those things are still out there. We need to be prepared. We need a plan."

After a long time, he gave a nod. His throat bobbed as he swallowed a few times, and he swiped at his eyes with the back of his hand. "Home."

I smiled. "Yeah. We're going home."

Hard to grieve with an audience. So after I thought Luka was more stable, I left him on the bridge while I explored the rest of the ship on my own.

Penelope wasn't very big. I'd already seen half of it just loading the supplies on board. There was a closet-sized infirmary and crew quarters for maybe six people, with bunks built into the bulkhead to save space, designed much like it had been on the moon base. I found a few small laboratories whose purpose I couldn't guess.

The only place left was the hangar deck—where Luka had loaded the droneship containing whatever secret weapon his family had died to protect.

He'd said it was inert, but I still felt a tingle of fear as I entered the compartment. Cabin lights came on automatically as I approached, revealing the stationary vehicle that towered over my head like a two-story tank, anchored now to the bulkhead. The droneship was obviously meant to handle all kinds of terrain, able to fly through space and traverse inhospitable land with massive rolling treads. There, at the front, was the space in which Luka and I had huddled in a pocket of air and grief. I headed around toward the other side.

And there it was. Clutched tightly in its rear cargo hold was a metal box, roughly the size of a compact car.

I couldn't reach it; it was mounted at least twelve feet high. There didn't seem to be anything special about it. I shivered anyway.

We knew nothing about what we were bringing home.

"Hey, Sunny?" I spoke quietly, feeling silly. "Do you know anything about this thing?"

I found I didn't need to be more specific. I could almost feel her reading me, a small and curious presence. Sunny had direct access to my occipital lobe now, and could read what my brain was interpreting from my eyes. She saw, heard, felt everything I did.

Creepy? Yes. Convenient? Also yes.

Cassie, I do not have access to my external sensors. I cannot tell you anything about this device that you don't already know.

Well, that was a limitation. I certainly didn't have as many data-collecting tools as she was used to. "You haven't been able to access any of the data you copied from the megobari computer yet?"

No, Cassie.

"Well, keep trying." Maybe she was trying to adjust to this new symbiosis as much as I was.

I continued around the other side of the droneship, and stopped short. There was something attached to the back of the crate—maybe a control panel or readout.

Impulsively, I climbed up the massive treads of the droneship, finding footholds and handholds as I went, until I was able to pull myself easily up to a grate where I could stand level with the weapon. There were symbols carved or stamped into the metal.

"Sunny, you'll let me know if this is a bad idea, right?"

Affirmative.

Not seeing any hinges or openings, I raised my hand gingerly to touch the small square I'd seen from the ground.

Even through my suit, I felt the static spark tingle my fingertips, but I didn't let go. *What are you?* I asked silently, and felt Sunny echo my curiosity in her calculating, machinelike way. My goals were her goals now.

Almost instantly, a small transparent window formed on the

side of the container nearest me. There must be some kind of computer intelligence monitoring whatever was inside that box, and it understood my command as easily as the ship obeyed Luka's.

Shaking now, I stepped closer to the transparent window. My breath caught in my throat.

I had no concept of what I expected the weapon to look like—okay, maybe I did expect it to look like a bomb, or at least some kind of projectile. Something that fit my very human mindset of ways my kind had historically killed each other.

But this . . . I didn't even understand what I was seeing.

A seething, warping, crackling prismatic mass of a color that was difficult to determine but that hurt my eyes to look at. A swirling energy kept barely at bay within a spherical framework of interconnected black lattice that hung suspended by some invisible force in the center of the chamber.

It was . . . almost alive. Churning and snapping like an electrical storm. The lattice must be what was keeping the energy contained, but what the hell *was* it? How did it work? How did you activate it? Luka's father had said this was something that could not be aimed. So was it more like a bomb? The energy— whatever was driving it—seemed ready to burst forth on command. What *was* its energy source?

Without really meaning to, I suddenly felt as though I had given Sunny a directive, and she had acknowledged it, without ever speaking a word. I felt her delve into her memory stores— somehow knowing, without really knowing, that she was trying to answer my questions as though I had posed them out loud to her.

I steered clear from the box and climbed down, leaping the last few to the floor. I looked up just in time to see the transparent window going opaque again.

Best to keep my distance from . . . all of that. There was no filter between me and Sunny anymore, no door to close to separate my internal thoughts from directives meant for her. I couldn't go around accidentally activating things on this ship before I knew what I was doing.

Especially not . . . whatever that was.

I set up camp back in the crew quarters, claiming a bunk and surrounding it with the things I'd grabbed on my detour through storage: freeze-dried food and drinks in the neat little NASA-brand packages; my Personal Preference Kit, or PPK, filled with a few sentimental items I'd been allowed to take on the flight; a few changes of clothes; and a blanket.

There was a small alcove near my chosen bunk. I carefully unpacked my PPK and laid out the photos of my family, and was struck for the first time that there were four more PPKs that I'd left on *Odysseus*.

Bolshakov. Copeland. Shaw. Jeong.

I repeated their names again. Four astronauts who'd never see Earth again. What had they brought with them? Photos of family who'd never see them again, who wouldn't even have bodies to bury? People they loved and didn't get to say good-bye to? Mementos of their lives back home?

The small knit bag in my hand slipped out of my fingers and onto the floor. In the rush to leave, I hadn't even thought to grab the others' personal items. What kind of person was I to think only of my own survival and not spare a thought for them? For their families?

Of all of them, of all their combined skill sets and abilities, I was the one who was still alive.

Why? It wasn't because I deserved to survive. I was the least experienced. The least trained.

I was alive because they sacrificed themselves. Like Luka's family had. I knew all the things I'd told him to try to ease his pain, and I'd meant them. There hadn't been anything else to do except escape. His family had chosen to stay behind to save him because they loved him.

But my crewmates? I barely knew them. They'd trained me and taught me, they'd treated me with respect, like an equal, but they hadn't loved me. And yet they died for me.

Because I was young. And because astronauts are inherently noble.

The real astronauts were dead and I wasn't. I was nobody. I hadn't changed the world—I hadn't even affected it. I was a lottery winner, that was all. I'd let them down. Let them die. And the world back home was in short supply of experienced astronauts in a time when we may have great need of them.

Was I worth the sacrifice they'd made?

And what the hell was I going to say when I got home?

TWELVE

CASSIE, LUKA REQUESTS your presence on the bridge.

I jolted upright. How had I fallen asleep? Groggy, I swung my legs off the bunk and inhaled, making sure there was oxygenated blood in my brain before I stood cautiously upright.

My body had been through a lot of stress in a short amount of time. The soreness and fatigue of my muscles had become a background static, something easily ignored, but if I kept pushing it, something was bound to break.

"Sunny? Did you wake me?"

Yes, Cassie. Luka has asked that you join him on the bridge.

"How do you know that?"

He sent a message over the ship's communication system, which I received.

Oh, freaky. Talk about the law of unintended consequences. I hadn't instructed Sunny to do that—but then, she'd been programmed to act with a certain level of autonomy, seeing as the crew would be unconscious. "Is it urgent?"

Nonemergency.

I changed into a fresh jumpsuit and boots, not bothering to do anything with my hair, and grabbed a few packets of food as I headed out the door.

Now that we were in flight, the megobari ship had come alive. The walls were no longer blank, but a gentle kaleidoscope of color. I felt as though I walked through an aquarium as I passed down the corridor, with colors floating by like sea creatures. A deep violet current led the way back to the bridge, with small yellow darts occasionally flitting past my head. I glimpsed red bubbles that seemed to fluctuate up and down the wall, blue splatters of paint, and clusters of rainbows along the way.

I had no idea what they were for or what they could possibly mean, but as I passed I tried to guess—instrument readouts, life-support status, telemetry, speed, trajectory.

I found Luka standing at the bridge, head down. He tilted his head slightly at my entrance.

"What is it?" I asked, joining him.

His face was drawn and tired, eyes a little vacant, but he seemed recovered from before. "I've been trying to discern what exactly it is that we have in our cargo hold. As I said, there is nothing in the ship's memory banks at all. And it seems completely shielded from our sensors."

"Which is probably a good thing. But . . . you found something, didn't you?"

"I wanted to make sure we were safe," he explained, rubbing at his eyes. "Whatever this is, it's locked in a containment field by one of the strongest materials my people knew to use."

"So it's not going to be tripped by accident?"

"Probably not. But it makes me think that whatever it contains . . . Cass, it's got to be more powerful than anything we know."

Concerned, I touched his shoulder lightly. "Nothing we can worry about now. Thank you for trying." I hesitated before adding, "I went to go see it."

"And?"

"I climbed up and I . . . touched it." His eyes widened, but he didn't interrupt. "I need to be more careful, I know. But I think I accidentally told it to show me what was inside. And Luka, it's . . . I don't even have words. It looks almost alive."

He swallowed hard. "Nothing else happened?"

"No. But I think it responds to touch commands the same as the rest of the ship."

He nodded, eyes going distant, thinking. "That would make sense. But it was locked down, a long time ago. It wouldn't . . . it *shouldn't* allow you to activate it from touch alone. There are levels of protections."

"Well, that makes me feel better. I guess we'll just have to hope that Sunny can help us figure out how to activate it when we need it. Any sign of the vrag?"

He shook his head, eyes sliding closed briefly. "No. Though it'd be difficult for us to discern them while we travel through space-time this way, it'd likewise be difficult for them to discern us."

"So we're safe for now."

"For now. As much as we can be, yes."

Biting my lip, I offered up the food pouches in my other hand. "Then we have a moment to breathe. You did good," I said gently, "making sure we were safe. Now you can rest for a bit. Eat something?"

He straightened, sighing, and I let my hand drop. He accepted the food I'd offered without looking at it. I'd assumed he would take it and leave. I was startled when his eyes met mine with open vulnerability and he asked: "Join me?"

I followed him back to the crew quarters, where he headed to the empty space in the middle of the room and conjured a table and two simple stools by touching a fingertip to a nearby console.

"I was born on Earth," Luka said after a moment. He tore open a package containing a granola bar and ate a bite before continuing. "It's always been my home. I didn't even realize we were different until I was older."

There was something about the way he'd said it that made me tread cautiously. The sadness had crept back into his eyes. "What made you realize you were . . . different?"

"At home, my family always spoke about everyone who

wasn't family not just as though they were strangers, but as though . . . they were something separate entirely. They were careful not to use phrases like 'the humans' around me, because they didn't want to give me phrases I'd repeat outside our house. But it was clear we kept to ourselves. No one had friends outside the family. Outsiders were rarely invited to our home unless necessary. I knew from television that we were odd in that way."

He seemed to want to talk, so I let him. We were both acting as though we were the same people who'd met on Earth, like nothing else had ever happened, which was a strange subspecies of relief.

He still looked like the guy I'd known back when I thought he was just a politician's son. But the old boy was gone, and this was someone different. I didn't have the space to process how I felt about that yet.

This was the true Luka—the full Luka, with no secrets. And it seemed like now that there was no need to hide anything, he wanted me to know everything.

He was someone I was going to have to get to know again. And as I listened to him talk—watched his mouth and hands—I wondered if we'd ever get back to the way we used to be.

But it wasn't something I could think about now. We only had a few days to ourselves on this ship. We needed to use them wisely. "Was it always your plan to . . . try to live with humans?"

"It was our hope, yes."

"It must have taken years. Learning the language . . . getting people into NASA . . ." I shook my head and offered him some trail mix, but he declined.

"It did. My family was on Earth many years before I was born. By then, my father had already secured a position in New York."

"So he really was a diplomat?" I asked cautiously, hoping not to trigger bad memories.

"Of course. He worked his way into the position quite on purpose."

"And you're really from Georgia?"

"I've only been there a couple of times, but yes, my family landed there and modeled themselves after the local population. When my family first landed on Earth, they wanted to do it somewhere isolated, of course. But their ultimate goal was America. New York City was a surprisingly easy place for aliens to blend in."

Startled that he'd made a joke, I laughed. He smiled wanly. "My aunts and uncles who spoke English best were working on getting jobs with NASA. The others stayed home and raised me. I could not go to school, of course. I couldn't be trusted not to give us away with some small mistake. Everyone else had spent years before I was born learning how to blend in. I needed to learn the major Earth languages as well as human body language. And humans rely so heavily on body language. That was difficult, to learn from those who were still students themselves."

Now it made sense. Why he'd always kept himself apart during selection and rarely spoke, even to answer questions in class. It'd been ingrained in him not to interact. "You did stand out at selection, though," I said quietly. "You were always in first place."

He grimaced. "I told my father that it would be suspicious. But he'd hinted heavily to Mr. Crane that his country might be interested in a multibillion-dollar business deal with SEE."

"And he'd happily negotiate favorable terms for the deal if his son was selected for the program?" I finished, seeing the puzzle finally complete. "And everyone would just assume it was nepotism or your father had bought your place."

Luka shook his head as he chewed the last of his granola bar and swallowed. "Yes. Which they did, of course. But my father was determined that I remain in the program until the last possible moment.

"It was the first time I had ever been around so many humans by myself. I was terrified of ruining everything my family had been orchestrating for so long. All the pieces, so painstakingly placed, so precariously stacked."

"Why did you have to be involved at all?"

"We could not get any of our people into the astronaut selection committee. We learned that NASA was planning to choose a fifth member from a pool of applicants specially chosen from around the world."

"Is that why you were at Marshall that day we met? Scouting out the competition?"

"Um . . . perhaps." He appeared suddenly sheepish. "My father was, in fact, going on a tour of the facility. It was coincidence that we met there, however."

"I thought this was all part of your plan. Who was chosen. Why the candidates all had to be under twenty-five."

"Our plan? No. Once I had learned more about you, I had . . . hoped the fifth would be you, but we did not influence that decision. You earned your place, Cassie."

He let that hang in the air a moment.

"Why did you want it to be me?" I asked quietly.

"I . . . was hopeful. That perhaps you might understand us." He glanced at me, and then away, as if he couldn't bear to hold my gaze. "I trusted you. I thought you were fair, and smart. You were one of the few who . . . gave me a chance."

My heart stuttered.

"Not that it matters now." He sat back, crumpling the empty food wrappers in his fist.

"Of course it does. What are you talking about?" I leaned forward, reaching across the table to touch the back of his hand. "Earth can still be a refuge for your people. I mean . . . there's the minor inconvenience of having to save it from aliens first, but . . ."

He shook his head dismissively and pushed away from the table, disposing of the garbage in a wall compartment. I followed him.

"I'm sorry," he said, not looking at me. "I just can't entertain the idea of . . . fulfilling my father's dream of an Earth refuge for my species. Not when he's gone, and Earth may not be a refuge long."

"Stop it," I said. "That's our home. We're not going to let them touch it. Understand me?"

119

His lips pressed together. "When you say it, I almost believe it."

I made him rest—threatening him with a tranquilizer gun if he didn't go to sleep voluntarily—and within minutes of his head hitting the bunk, he was snoring quietly.

As I was exiting the crew quarters, I had an idea—and cautiously touched the wall panel beside the door. I formed an intent and directed it. *Dim the lights.*

The lights dimmed, and I jumped.

Out in the hall, I whispered, "Sunny, are you responsible for me being able to communicate with the ship?"

Yes, Cassie. I can facilitate your communications with the ship's computer.

"Okay," I said in an unsteady voice. "You can understand *Penelope*? Can you translate what I'm seeing here?" I focused on a patch of wall that was pulsing orange.

Instantly, my mind was overflowing with numbers, equations, streams of numeric data that scrolled lightning-fast into my brain, overloading my senses like a room filled with a thousand songs all blasting at full volume. "Sunny, stop!"

The streams faded. "So," I breathed, pressing my palm against my forehead and trying to re-form my own thoughts. "You can talk with the alien computer because you're both speaking the universal language of numbers. But . . . you can't always translate that into something I understand or process. Is that right?"

That is accurate.

"I can work with that," I murmured. "So in order to translate, you'd need . . . what? Something external? A third party?" And as I said it, it made sense. Sunny wasn't designed to be in my brain, she was designed to be in *Odysseus*, with all its external hardware and multiple sources of software to feed data into her and help her understand its meaning.

Compared to that state-of-the-art ship, I was pretty dumb. I couldn't measure an accurate temperature or velocity, I couldn't see X-rays or infrared, couldn't determine what molecules made up a rock sample. She only had my five senses to work with—enhanced though they might be by human standards—a faulty memory bank, and no external hardware.

Well, that was a stumbling block, but it was more than I had before.

"Sunny, how are you doing with accessing that data you copied?"

I am still attempting to search for relevant information on subjects related to megobari plus weapon.

"How long do you think it will take you to search everything you copied?"

When she didn't reply right away, and I sensed that estimated time was ticking upward into *years*, I made her stop. And then rubbed at my incision, because it had started to itch.

I filed that problem away for later. "All right, then, Sunny. Luka said we need to get to know each other a little better. Back to basics. Let's try some meditation."

THIRTEEN

THE HATCH DOOR slid open, startling me out of my attempts to re-create the gentle sea where my consciousness had first spent time getting to know Sunny.

Luka's hair was a little mussed, eyes still blinking away sleep, but he looked marginally more alert. He proffered something toward me. "You . . . brought this with you?"

In his hand was a black piano key, half dipped in silver. Luka had given it to me, via Hanna, after he'd left the program. "Um, yeah. I did." I'd left it out on the alcove near my bed. "But I don't know what it's supposed to be."

Though he held it out, I let him keep hold of it. His hand trembled a little, letting the light dance off the gleaming surface. "You never opened it?"

"It opens?"

With a deft motion of his hand and slight pop, the black and silver halves of the rectangle opened on a hinge. Inside was a small electronic device built into the top half with a few tiny buttons. "It's a communication device. I wanted to . . . leave you a message. Before you launched. So you wouldn't be blindsided when you arrived." He shook his head, rueful. "I guess I should delete that."

I reached out to stop his hands. "No, don't. Please? I'd like to hear it."

His lips thinned, eyes downcast, but he nodded. "Just . . . not while I'm here. If you don't mind."

I had to bite back a smile. He was embarrassed. I'd never seen that emotion in him before.

He flipped it closed and handed it to me. I tried to spring the mechanism myself, finding with surprise how easy it actually was to open. "It should only open for you or for me. I have its pair. It allows us to maintain contact over great distance, on a secure line. Not quite the same way my people do—I had to modify it, so there is some time delay, depending on how far we are from each other."

He'd given this to me during the competition. After we'd kissed, after he'd left without telling me good-bye. I'd had it this entire time without knowing he'd left me a message to soften the blow. I let the meaning of that wash over me, feeling some of the resentment I'd held for him fade. "But you didn't leave me any instructions on how to use it."

"I trusted that you would learn it without too much difficulty."

This time I smiled for real. "Lot of good that did. And you trusted Hanna to deliver it to me?"

His head tilted slightly. "Why shouldn't I have?"

"I'm just . . . not sure that I would've."

"She is more trustworthy than you presume her to be."

I raised my eyebrows at that, but let it go. "It looks like a piano key."

His eyes pointedly remained downcast. "Yes."

"Why?"

Then his eyes met mine, holding my gaze for a moment longer than I'd expect. He'd meant something by it. "I had to disguise it as something."

My mind flew back to those times I'd tried helping Luka—before I knew who he was—learn to control his brain waves. Playing piano for him in the quiet little chapel on the astronaut training campus. And then I knew why he'd chosen this disguise.

"If you choose to send me a message, there are options for video, audio, and text-only. Text-only is fastest; video takes longer, of course. Depending on how far we are from each other. If you need to reach me instantly, text is the better option."

I reached for his hand. "This is . . . really nice. And will probably come in handy. Thank you."

He nodded and stepped away, but not before giving my hand a gentle squeeze.

I climbed to my feet also and called to him before he left the room. "Wait. You couldn't have known I would bring this with me, if I didn't figure out what it was. You didn't know we'd end up on the same side."

He stopped at the doorway, turned halfway, and shrugged. "I didn't. I just hoped."

FOURTEEN

LUKA SET THE ship's internal clock to Earth time, so we would experience the same twelve-hour day and night cycle our bodies were accustomed to.

The ship didn't require much supervision, but Luka did spend a few hours each day ensuring everything was running optimally. I had even fewer tasks available to me: eat, sleep, plan. I spent a lot of my time in my bunk, trying to let my body and mind recover, without succumbing to grief or homesickness. I used the time to slip into that gentle sea again. It wasn't quite the same without the drugs helping to maintain my mental state, but it was meditative and calming—and, I hoped, helping Sunny and me to continue to bond.

I needed to make my body stronger, too, in order to face

what was to come. I started each day with push-ups, lunges, squats, jumping jacks—only able to achieve a fraction of what had once been my standard. But bodies are remarkable at rising to challenges. Even if it cost me sweat and shaking muscles, I'd get back to where I used to be.

Luka and I drifted together and apart on an increasingly easy rhythm, meeting for meals, passing each other in the corridor or keeping each other company as we felt like it, falling into companionable silence when we ran out of ideas for how we were going to survive the future.

I spent more time in the presence of the weapon, sitting on the floor a respectful distance away, hoping to glean something about it through either Sunny's research or osmosis. Either one seemed a decent bet at this point.

Luka and I slept in the crew quarters. Separate bunks. We weren't ready to be as close as we had once been, but neither of us wanted to be alone.

On the sixth or seventh night, Luka's voice floated over to me in the dark, low and soothing, with the intonation of a wildlife documentary. "In most social species, it is typical for the individuals in a group to keep in constant communication. Birds, zebras, humans—if you notice, when they are together, they are always making noise. But the forest falls silent when a tiger approaches." The space between my ears filled up with mechanical humming before his voice returned, steady and reassuring. "That's why we are so discomfited by silence. Noise is the assurance that we are safe. Silence is a harbinger of danger."

"What are we going to do when we get back?" I asked, my voice hushed in the din. "What if the vrag beat us there?"

"We will have to be quick," he said. "And not give them the opportunity to shoot at us."

"Oh, that's a good plan. I hadn't thought of that."

"The vrag will not instigate an all-out war," Luka said. "Not at first. Their weakness is that they have only the one ship—they are alone. They'd rather use the planet as bait to lure the last remaining megobari to them."

"But why?" I asked. "Why, if they're vulnerable and alone, are they so intent on killing megobari instead of doing what your people are doing—trying to find a new home?"

"Revenge," he said simply. "They are too stupid to start again. They only know hate. They will kill us until their last breath."

"Humans will fight back," I assured him.

"But the vrag don't want to fight, they want to win. Even with their stolen ship, they are still one ship against an entire planet full of deadly weapons. They will try coercion first. Humans will be difficult for them to understand; they have not had the time to study you as we have. I'm not sure where they've been this whole time; maybe they've discovered other alien species and have learned a few things. They only know that we are interested in this planet, and that alone is enough to wish Earth harm." He paused. "If manipulation does not work, they will take advantage of the inevitable chaos of first contact and move in on their own."

"Move in?"

"They are using stolen megobarian technology. Very old technology, because they do not understand how to build their own. But even our outdated weapons are more advanced than anything on Earth. You saw how even *Exodus*, a research vessel, was unequipped to defend itself against the ship the vrag inhabit. I'm sure you don't need to imagine that power used against human technology."

I suppressed a chill, bringing the thermal blanket up around my chin. "So how do we fight them?"

"I'm still working on that."

"Luka . . . this weapon. I have a theory that maybe your people . . . chose not to use it. For a reason."

He gazed at the ceiling and I heard him suck in a weary breath. "That's not beyond the realm of possibility. But it's worth adding that they did not use it, and thus our world was destroyed."

It was a good point. "Sunny says there's more information than she can process at this time. It's taking all her processing power to search, and I don't even know that she'd be able to translate anything she found so that I can understand it." Which might be why I had not been hearing much from her lately. "I hope we can find out once we're back on Earth."

Luka turned his back to me and went quiet. But he wasn't asleep. "Cassie, we could be home by morning. And when we return . . ." He let the phrase dangle, a future and a fate yet uncertain.

"We'll do what we have to do."

"I should like to have a more concrete plan in place. We do not know what kind of situation we will be returning to. We must be prepared for all things . . . including the possibility that we may be parted."

I didn't like what he was implying. But he wasn't wrong.

We were flying alone through space and time, leaving our dead companions and the circumstances of their murder behind us. No one at home knew what had happened or what was coming for them. There was no way to know the state Earth would be in when we returned. Who knew what might have happened since we left?

There was no way to know. And I hated not knowing.

"My family set up safe houses back on Earth. I have one in particular in mind. It's isolated enough that I feel we can safely land *Penelope* nearby and keep it hidden. We can make the house our base of operations as we plan our next moves."

"What are we going to do about the weapon, though?"

He was quiet a moment. "Hide it. Study it. Keep it safe until we know how to use it."

"I hope we don't have to."

His silence lasted so long I fell asleep without knowing if he ever answered.

FIFTEEN

WHEN I WOKE up, something was different.

The humming. A specific variety of bone-jarring vibration that I'd become accustomed to over the past few days was just— gone.

Curious—and afraid—I touched the wall beside my bunk. *What is going on?*

Sunny responded immediately. *Cassie, the Alcubierre drive has deactivated. We have reached our destination.*

We'd made it?

Home!

I leaped out of my bunk, finding myself alone in the crew quarters. I ran down the corridor, tugging on my boots as I went, and found Luka where I expected him to be: standing at the bridge controls.

"I wanted to let you sleep," he said by way of explanation. "I thought you would need—"

"Is it . . . ," I asked, a grin splitting my face before I could even finish my sentence.

He slid his fingers across the interface, and black space enveloped us.

Through the transparent walls of the ship, a blue marble shimmered in the distance. A tiny silver pearl hovered in its orbit. Two jewels in an invisible crown.

A wave of relief washed over me, unscrewing muscles that had been wound tight for days.

"She's so beautiful," I murmured, unable to help myself. The back of my neck tingled.

There wasn't time to admire the view. *Penelope*'s scanners didn't pick up any suspicious readings, but Luka warned that the vrag had probably been here for days, and were more than capable of hiding their heat signatures.

"I sent a message to the other Megobari ships. In case they are within range to receive it, they will know what is going on here. If we fail, they may be our last chance to save Earth."

I nodded. Stick to the plan. First order of business: suit up. We dressed in our black spacesuits, taking turns to check that each was undamaged and ready to go.

Luka held my helmet between his palms. "Cassie. I'm wondering if it might be better for you to take the shuttle to Earth. Alone."

I bracketed my hands on my hips, feeling the tension ratchet up between my shoulder blades. "Why?"

"It would be easier to hide you and the droneship if we each went our separate ways. The vrag might already know we're here. We will light up like a beacon the moment we arrive."

I tried to steady my breathing. "I don't know how to use the shuttle."

"It's just an emergency escape pod, same as we used last time. The droneship isn't suited for passengers when it enters the atmosphere, but it will keep the weapon safe. You'll have some directional control but the shuttle moves like a brick, so just be careful. Once you land, don't forget to destroy the pod."

"Is this *Mission: Impossible*, or what?"

"I don't understand that reference. Cassie, this is important. I can set the shuttle to destruct on its own, but I can't know when you're at a safe distance. I trust you to do it. We can't have evidence of your landing for humans to find."

I looked at the view screen again, at the matching blue and silver crescents. "You don't think we could just . . . land *Penelope* on the White House lawn?"

He raised his eyebrows. "I *do* understand that reference. Sunny will help you," he said, putting my helmet into my hands. "Don't worry. This will be the easy part." Luka held my face and gazed down at me for a moment, eyes dark and somber. "I'll see you on the surface. Okay?"

I stiffened at the contact. We hadn't been so close in days. As he dropped his hands from me, I said, "You're going to be careful, right?"

Before he could answer, the bulkhead filled with flashes of red, a pulse of warning. Luka had only begun to respond when the entire ship tilted violently on its side, throwing me on a collision course with the opposite side of the bridge.

My back hit the wall with enough force to knock the wind out of me. Gravity was gone. I scrambled to grab hold of something, to right myself. Which way was up? The world was flashes of red, the ceiling now under my feet.

I might not have trained like a traditional astronaut, but I remembered what to do. I found a reference point and righted myself, finding my helmet floating nearby. I yanked it over my head and immediately felt Sunny's presence in surround sound. Her main brain may have been implanted in the back of my neck, but a remote copy of her program was still in my suit-board computer.

Cassie, this ship is being fired upon.

"Yeah, I figured!" I shouted over the alarms. I caught sight of Luka at the controls, anchoring himself to the floor. I pushed off the bulkhead with my feet and soared across empty space toward Luka, grabbing the console to keep from colliding into him.

He didn't need to tell me that the vrag had found us. The view screen was still up, showing Earth far ahead of us. Only now it seemed Earth was getting a little bigger. "What are you doing?"

He didn't look up. "I don't think they'll fire on us if we get close to Earth. I'm going to try to outrun them."

I stared at him. "Will that work?"

134

He shook his head and shrugged at the same time, his eyes a little wild. "No idea!"

The ship rattled again. "Are we hit?"

"Just a glance," Luka said. His hair was damp with sweat. "Why aren't they using their main weapons?"

"Maybe you're right—they don't want to have a firefight so close to Earth."

"The heat signatures are definitely going to attract some attention," he agreed, just before another glancing blow made *Penelope* shudder, and knocked me off my grip.

Luka reached out and grabbed my arm, swinging me back beside him. "Are you ready to go?"

"What do you mean?"

His eyes locked with mine. He turned, swiped some sort of color code into the interface, and a door slid open nearby. "Cassie?" He said it very slowly, despite the chaos going on around us. "It seems you are going to Earth alone after all."

"Luka? No, don't you dare—not *now*!" I saw Earth looming larger in the view screen. The swaths of red alarms drenched Luka's skin, flashed like lightning in his eyes. His face was shadows and angles and set in stone. I knew that look.

"I'll see you down there," he said. "I'm sending the droneship to the surface with the weapon. It'll hide itself somewhere near the safe house. You need to go with it and keep it from them. Sunny has the coordinates to the safe house and I'll meet you there when I can. Now GO!" His hand pushed against my back, urging me away.

I held on for one moment longer, trying to read his eyes. I

felt the logic of his plan pull at me and hated it.

I let go. Pushed off with my feet to the back of the bridge and into the open pod.

Seconds before the pod door closed, I had an image of Luka, standing on the bridge of a ship under fire. Like his father.

He wouldn't sacrifice himself for me the way his father had. He'd lost everyone else. He wouldn't do that to me. Would he?

Luka, don't you dare—

His eyes met mine and I heard his voice in my helmet. "Just like we planned, Cassie."

The door slammed shut, and then I was alone in the darkness of space.

Luka Kereselidze, you'd better not be lying.

SIXTEEN

I EXPECTED NOISE. But there was only a soft hiss of air as the pod released, and then nothing but silence.

A black void, pricked with stars, sped over me. But without a reference point, it was hard to tell I was moving at all. I didn't even catch a glimpse of *Penelope* burning silently behind.

The only sense I had of movement was how all my organs seemed to shift—my tongue was pushed back into my throat, my jaw against my skull, my internal organs into my spine. My arms and legs were welded into the pod. I had to force my diaphragm to open in order to inhale.

I was flying through empty space in an alien coffin.

Computer readouts danced in faint colors in the clear material in front of my face, but I couldn't understand them.

At this speed, all it would take would be a chunk of debris from *Penelope* or a micrometeoroid in the wrong place and I'd be dead.

I couldn't see Earth. I couldn't see *Penelope.*

I was hyperventilating but I couldn't calm down, couldn't think. My heartbeat was a long string of continuous beats, a drumroll. At this rate I'd use up all my oxygen long before reaching Earth.

Cassie, your remaining oxygen should be sufficient to reach Earth, based on your current velocity and trajectory.

Of course, Sunny could read the alien computer language. But I didn't miss her "should."

Earth. Where was Earth? What if Luka miscalculated the trajectory? Maybe I would shoot right past Earth and keep going through space forever until I shriveled up like a mummy, my carcass traversing the universe for millennia, eventually falling into a black hole a million light-years away from the place I was supposed to be.

Cassie, your trajectory is currently set to have you land at latitude 31.968599, longitude -99.901813—

"Sunny, I'm not a GPS satellite, I don't know what that means!"

—in the vicinity of Winters, Texas.

"Where the hell is Winters, Texas?!"

Sunny gave me the coordinates again, which I ignored, as I saw the ominous shadow looming in the distance.

The vrag ship. Black ship on black space, like a titan's

shadow, a nightmare rising out of the deepest corners of my dreams. Nothing but an absence of stars.

I didn't want to look at it, but I couldn't *not* see it. The transparent lid of the pod was half filled with its shadow, the other half with Earth—small and vulnerable in comparison, though I knew it was only a matter of perspective.

I must be thousands of miles away and it looked like a small planet, like a black hole that might pull me in. Maybe even big enough to have its own weak gravity.

Had the vrag ship spotted me? Maybe they were aiming their weapons at my helpless shuttle even now. I screwed my eyes shut, bracing to be blasted into vapor.

Cassie, the vrag ship is moving away from us.

My eyes flew open, scanning the darkness, finally seeing it—only visible from the faint glow of its engines.

Luka was leading the vrag away from Earth. Away from me.

"No!" I screamed. But the pod rotated again, pulling me away from the view.

Black gradually shifted to blue white as I fell into Earth's pull. My eyes watered with the effort of forcing my abs to keep my stomach in its rightful place, but I could see ice crystals form on the window and then melt and steam away as I fell and fell and fell.

Small rockets on all sides of the shuttle fired, repelling gravity, using air resistance to slow my fall and correct my descent. The shuttle rotated, tilted, and then I saw North America spread out like a map before me, clear as day and larger than life. It was both a still life and a living, breathing world. I saw the sunshine dancing on the water of the Gulf of Mexico. A sliver of shimmering ice somewhere in Canada. Strands of white clouds stretching like scarves across the Midwest. The Rocky Mountains, gray and snowcapped—the golden deserts—the emerald farmlands—the forested green hills of home.

Tears warmed my eyes. *Home.* Still here. Still green and blue and lovely.

The shuttle shook as I fell through the atmosphere, turbulence vibrating through my body. A small rumble as boosters deployed, fighting my descent, and the shuttle slowed—but what I guessed was the Texas panhandle was still rushing up to meet me at a terrifying rate, until I was so close I couldn't even tell where I was anymore.

The touchdown was incredibly gentle, like a feather falling on a cloud. The lower half skimmed the dirt and cactus until friction grabbed the rest of my coffin and gravity finally thudded me onto the hard dirt like a ton of cement.

I breathed. And breathed. And shook.

The door slid open, and I imagined rather than felt the hot summer air flooding into the shuttle.

I lay there, gazing into the impossibly blue sky, until my insides solidified again and my legs realized they were still attached to my body.

Home.

So gorgeous, that sky. So peaceful and safe.

Up there somewhere was Luka.

And up there, too, was an ugly vrag ship, waiting in the deep, like a shark, to devour my people. I lay there for a second hoping against hope I might see *Penelope* break through the clouds.

He'll find me. He said he would.

He couldn't let the vrag have the weapon.

I finally found the strength to stand up. Gravity hit me like a ton of bricks. My quadriceps screamed as I stumbled out of the shuttle and fell to my knees in the dirt. I felt a stab of pain, wondered if I'd broken a rib.

I hit the self-destruct command and crawled away. There was no explosion. The shuttle simply lit fire and melted into the dirt. In a matter of seconds, it was an unrecognizable black puddle.

Finally, when it was good and melted like a tar soup, I looked up at where I was, past rows and rows of immature corn.

And met eyes with four farmers standing in the field not fifty feet from me. One sat atop a tractor. All of them stared at me, slack-jawed.

Gingerly, I reached up and released my helmet, probably for the last time.

I pulled myself to my feet with some difficulty, helmet under one arm, waving hesitantly with the other. "Uh, hi, guys. I'm from . . . NASA. Could somebody call them for me, maybe?"

SEVENTEEN

TO BE HONEST, I don't know how often Texas farmers find crashed astronauts in their cornfields. Maybe it was a common occurrence. The farmers didn't seem nearly surprised enough to find a dirty, disheveled Indian teenager fall out of the sky. I was just thankful my suit had actual NASA logos on the shoulders, because those guys had shotguns in the back of their truck.

One of the farmers made a call while I sat in the kitchen, sipping from a sweating glass of lemonade while the others stared at me in gruff, disbelieving silence. I didn't think it was wise to engage them in small talk, but I did smile a lot and thank them for their hospitality.

Within an hour I saw a black SUV pull up the gravel driveway.

I approached the car cautiously from the passenger's side. The windows were tinted to an illegal opacity; I couldn't see the driver.

Suddenly the front passenger's-side door swung open, pushed from the inside.

Hanna was sitting in the driver's seat, big sunglasses shielding her eyes, short blond hair falling over one side of her face. "Are you gonna get in or what? It won't take Crane long to figure out I took his car, and I want to be far away when he does."

Stunned, I climbed onto the leather seat, set my helmet on the floorboard, and shut the door. Hanna didn't even wait for me to put on my seat belt before throwing the SUV in reverse.

"What is going on?" I demanded.

The SUV bounced over the gravel, rocking my abused bones and jostling my hand as I tried to latch my seat belt.

"You tell me," she retorted, eyes on the road. "Crane sent some people to come pick you up. Lucky for you, I intercepted the call. Now do you want to tell me why the hell you're calling Houston from some godforsaken cornfield in this backwoods hick town?"

"You don't know? Then why are you here?"

She shot me a glance over her sunglasses as she turned onto the main road. "I saw you go into space, Cassandra Gupta. And now you're back, alone, with no *Odysseus*, and a bounty on your head. Did you really meet aliens on Kepler-186f? Where is everyone else?"

"What the hell? Back up, back up." I turned in my seat to

face her, the seat belt cutting into my shoulder. "Did you just say a *bounty*?"

"Um, yes?" She shot me a look as though I was the unreasonable one. "They told us something was about to land on Earth, and it belonged to them, and whoever gave it back would be rewarded. And here you are."

"Who is *they*?"

She made an exasperated sound, as though I was the one making no sense. She jabbed her finger toward the sky. "Not a week after you launched, a ship larger than anything we'd ever seen suddenly appeared in orbit. It completely snuck up on everyone's sensors, and the world predictably freaked the fuck out. But it just *sat* there in the sky for days. A week later, it sent a message to Earth governments that it meant no harm, that it wanted to be friends with us, but that nothing should approach the ship or it would be shot down. We weren't sure why the aliens had come here after sending us that message to meet them at Kepler-186f, but thought maybe this was a small envoy? Is that right? We send some of our people there, they sent some of their people here?"

I realized belatedly that she was waiting for a response, but I was still trying to make sense of everything she'd just said. "No, I don't—what happened after the ship arrived? Have there been any attacks?"

Her eyebrows furrowed and she glanced at me. Her voice was skeptical, confused. "No. They've been good on their word so far—it's done nothing but quietly orbit for months, occasionally sending messages, even gifts to show their goodwill to certain countries. People calmed down pretty quick after that. Things almost went back to normal. But a month ago, the ship disappeared without a trace, and now suddenly it's back, and so are you. Your turn."

I sank back into my seat, feeling all strength leaving my limbs. The vrag had been here for *months*. Everyone in the world now knew about the existence of aliens. As soon as the megobari had gone, the vrag had swooped in and made themselves look friendly. Sickness hollowed my gut.

Hanna merged onto the interstate, turned on self-driving mode, and faced me directly. "Now are you going to tell me where the hell you've been, how you got back, and why I risked my career to help you?"

I closed my eyes, unable to take everything in. The vrag had put a bounty on me—did that mean Luka hadn't landed yet? Where *was* he?

Or maybe the vrag knew about the weapon? What was it that they'd seen fall to Earth?

Oh God, this was all wrong. Our plan was already falling apart.

She was waiting with dwindling patience, eyes lit with fanatical fire, for me to explain myself.

I had to tell her.

"Hanna. Those aliens in orbit now are called the vrag, and they're not the ones who invited us to Kepler-186f. They're the ones who destroyed it."

Aside from a slight narrowing of her eyes, Hanna didn't react. She was leaning forward on her knees, seat belt straining, hands clasped, one leg bouncing slightly in agitation.

So I told her everything—what happened when we landed, the megobari who'd sent us the message, and why.

Everything except the weapon we'd brought back.

She wasn't as surprised as I had been to learn of Luka's identity, but then Earth *had* already been rocked by the news that we weren't alone in the universe months ago, and there was an orbiting alien ship to prove it.

"Damn it" was all she said. "So all along? The whole competition? They were involved every step of the way?"

"Yes. Luka's one of the good guys. The megobari, not the vrag. The vrag attacked our ship without provocation—killed all our instructors from Project Adastra and the rest of Luka's family. Luka and I barely escaped. The vrag are not what they're pretending to be." I groaned, closing my eyes and leaning back. Everything had gone fubar in an instant.

"What happened to the ship?" she asked.

"We had to leave the ship behind—it was too slow to get us back here in time."

There was a grim set to her mouth. She didn't take it the way I'd expected. She just nodded once to herself and sat back in her seat. "If what you're saying is true—and, seeing as the rest of the crew didn't return with you, I guess it is—that might be the one thing that can convince Earth they're being tricked. The major players have been falling all over themselves to get the aliens—the vrag—on their side."

"But we don't have proof that the vrag are actually the bad guys." Not proof I could show anyone, at least. I mentally checked in with Sunny again, and she again responded in the negative. Still no breakthrough. "You said Crane was going to send someone to bring me back. Is that where we're going?"

She gripped the steering wheel a moment, as if forgetting that she didn't need to. "No. You don't want to go back there. The bounty, remember? Crane wasn't about to be chivalrous. He wants to turn you in. Or at least use you as a bargaining chip to get something from the vrag."

Of course. I was a fugitive now.

Her eyes bored into the steering wheel as it made minor adjustments on its own, the autopilot keeping us on course. Before I could ask her what she was thinking, she asked her own question. "What happened to Luka?"

Everything inside me went dark. "Last I saw him, he was leading the vrag away from my escape pod," I said quietly. "He swore to meet me back here. But I don't know. The vrag go after the megobari ships like rabid dogs. I don't—"

She cut me off with another question, then another, asking details about the megobari, what they'd looked like, what they wanted. I answered best I could, but my eyelids were growing heavy. I just wanted to shut my brain off.

"How did you get back?"

"We found another megobari ship, faster than *Odysseus*. But the vrag had beaten us back here and attacked us. I took an escape pod and landed in a field. And now you're all caught up to the present moment."

She didn't react, didn't emote at all. "So the aliens in orbit and the ones that sent us the message are different. You made contact with one, and we made contact with the other. They're hell-bent on killing each other and they brought their war here. And we don't know why the vrag are here now except maybe to spite the megobari. Does that about sum it up?"

"And more megobari are coming. We sent a distress signal to the few that remain."

Her face was solemn, eyebrows slightly raised. "And you came back here to . . . warn us?"

I nodded, wanting to sleep, wanting to just stop being conscious for a while and wake up to a world that made sense.

"Cassie. You don't understand. The aliens—the vrag—a few weeks ago, they sent a message saying that Earth was about to be invaded. That's why they had come here; our only chance was to ally with them. And they were offering their alliance to the highest bidder. I didn't understand at first. But now—Cass, they're going to make Earth governments compete against each other. The gifts the vrag have been giving are incredible—they've solved soil pollution in China, heat crises in Canada, malaria in Africa, and invasive species in Australia. Heads of state are tripping over themselves trying to do the vrag's bidding. They've been testing us, pitting us against each other. When the megobari get here . . ."

"Yeah. Earth will be more than willing to shoot them down."

I shook myself out of despair, trying to focus, to find forward momentum. I couldn't stop yet. Luka was still up there risking his life for me to be here, to find a solution. But the problems were so complex—they involved the entire world. How could I possibly fix this?

Maybe I couldn't. I wasn't anybody. I wasn't in charge. I had no platform.

But I had to try.

"Wait. You said you risked your career to come get me? Why would you do that?"

She shrugged, affecting nonchalance. "Look, whatever he was going to do to you—hand you over to the vrag, or keep you as a bargaining chip himself, or God knows what—I didn't want to work for a man like that anyway. And besides. You saved me from him once. I don't like owing favors."

I went quiet a minute. Hanna was always surprising me. "So I assume you have a plan? Where are we going?"

At this, she gave me a reckless grin. "It depends on who answers their phone."

She handed me her cell phone. "You can't go home, obviously. They'd grab you at the airport. I can't keep you at my place, because they're probably already there. So we're going to Houston. Call Mitsuko and tell her we'll be there in a few hours."

"Wait—no. I can't. I have to meet Luka. We have a plan."

She leveled her gaze at me, speaking slowly, as though she thought I wasn't capable of understanding. "We can't meet him in this car, Cass. I took out the GPS, but they'll track the plate. We have to get the feds off our trail first. Understand?"

Sliding down in my seat, I held the phone against my ear, listening to it ring on the other end. And ring. And ring. A tingle of nerves vibrating through me. Who would pick up a call from a random number in the middle of the day?

But the very last ring was interrupted by a voice so achingly familiar I wanted to sob.

"Hello?" Mitsuko's voice was unaffected by my anxiety, pleasant but tinged with the polite, cautious tone people use when they have no idea who's on the other line.

"Mitsuko." Her name rushed out of me in a sigh of relief. "It's me." And then I realized it'd been six months, and there was a very real possibility she would have no idea whose voice was speaking. "It's Cass—Cassandra. Gupta. From the ... from ..."

"Cass?" There was a stunned silence on the other end where I imagined her looking back at the caller ID on her phone in confusion. "Are you okay? Where are you? Are you back? Was the mission scrubbed? Why are you calling from a Dallas area code?"

A strangled laugh escaped me, relief and anxiety together. "Uh, it's a very long story. But here's the thing. I just got back. I'm on my way to Houston. I ... I need your help." Hanna nodded encouragingly, gesturing me to continue. I stammered, wondered how much detail to give away over the phone, how much detail she could handle. "Hanna's with me and we need a place to crash. Are you ... can we ... ?"

Silence on the other end. I held my breath. This was stupid. Who would agree to—

"Of course, Cass. And you're with Hanna? Oh Lord, I am dying to hear this story. Wait, Emilio will want to see you! Should I call him? Do you need food? Should I go shopping? Also, did you know there's a giant-ass spaceship orbiting Earth?"

I laughed in sheer exhaustion and relief. Told her yes to all of that, told her she was amazing, thanked her, promised to tell her everything when I saw her, and we hung up.

I looked down at the phone in my hand. At the date. June 30. I'd missed my high school graduation. Everybody in my class had gone on without me.

I wondered if I should call my parents.

Hanna reached out, palm up, waiting for her phone. I hesitated and she shot me a look. "No more calls," she said. "Crane will probably pull up my phone records—though it'll take some time—and we're already leaving quite a trail. You'll only put them on Crane's radar if you call right now. And don't plan on staying at Mitsuko's long—they'll come looking for you there next. Her husband's FBI, but I don't think it'll help us." I put the phone in her hand and she tucked it back into her pocket. "And now we need another plan, because this is as far as I got."

Thinking of the coordinates to the safe house and the weapon hiding itself somewhere nearby, I nodded. "I have one. I just hope it's good enough."

EIGHTEEN

"SO, OKAY, YOU'VE missed a lot." Hanna manipulated the car's console until videos and text filled the black windows.

She caught me up on what had been happening on Earth in my absence. All news channels were now dominated by round-the-clock coverage of said giant-ass alien spaceship orbiting Earth. The world had been holding its breath for six months, dangling on the precipice of war.

She talked over video clips. Scenes of riots, thousands of people marching on Capitol Hill and around the world. Talking-head newscasters with their disaster faces on. World leaders giving speeches in front of flags while camera flashes made them repeatedly wince. And then, of course, the alien groupies who were trying to storm Area 51 like it was the Bastille.

Constant surveillance of the vrag ship had apparently gleaned humanity very little. Radar bounced off its angles; heat sensors were blocked. The only reason we saw them now was because they *wanted* us to see them. Giant as it was, the ship had hidden itself easily from our detection methods on approach. No one had seen it coming.

Only now that it orbited Earth among our very own cloud of satellites was it able to be consistently observed. And yet we knew nothing.

Anything that had approached the ship—from unmanned spy drones to space trash—had been destroyed. But they had made no threats. Hanna had told me the truth. The vrag had foretold of a coming alien invasion, and now had every major world power vying for the rights to ally with them. They'd already started the smear campaign against the megobari, and their protection was being offered to any nation that promised allegiance. And, presumably, that help wasn't going to be offered for free.

It was just that easy. The vrag had pitted us against each other. Made us forget that our first allegiance was to the human race, not money or power.

The only way humanity had a chance was by presenting a united front. But we were too easily fractured. They'd found our weaknesses, the long-standing divisions and rivalries between peoples, and stepped in. The vrag were going to seep into those cracks like water and freeze, forcing us all farther apart.

The news mentioned that the vrag ship had, without warning,

disappeared for about a month, and had only reappeared within the past few days.

I closed my eyes as Hanna illuminated the details, and let the pieces organize themselves in my mind. The vrag must have been keeping a closer eye on the megobari than they knew since they arrived as soon as the megobari had gone. But why were they here? If they wanted to invade, they'd had ample time and opportunity while the megobari had been away. But they hadn't left their ship.

Were they baiting the megobari fleets to come to Earth to force an end to the war? Did they simply want to take another world from the megobari?

I wondered, not for the first time, why the vrag were like this. Maybe I couldn't hope to understand the motivation of an alien intelligence; maybe their reasons would make no sense to me. Maybe they really were, as Luka had said, mindless killing machines. Maybe.

But as far as anyone here knew, they hadn't harmed a soul on Earth—hadn't been threatening toward human lives at all except when we were on megobari ships. Perhaps they hadn't meant to kill my crew? They couldn't have known we were on board. Maybe we were just collateral damage.

My thoughts, as always, circled back to Luka. Was he still out there? Had he made it back to Earth? Was he safe? Was he waiting for me at our meeting place, wondering what had held me up?

Of all the scenarios we'd imagined returning to, this hadn't been one of them.

The not knowing was a bottomless pit. I could toss questions into it all day long and never get any answers. I had to shut off that part of my brain.

By the time the car was pulling off the interstate and heading onto residential roads, my eyes were blurring with fatigue, the sky was growing dark, and my stomach groaned in weak protest.

It felt surreal to pull into the parking lot of Mitsuko's apartment complex—seeing the details of her normal, everyday life for the first time. This girl I'd considered a close friend but had really only known for a few weeks in a very strange, isolated environment.

The forced intimacy of our selection had made us close quickly, but it had been a false kind of intimacy, a shallow one, based on a set of rules and circumstances that no longer existed. Was Mitsuko still the same person, here in real life? I braced myself to meet a stranger.

She was standing outside, leaning on her building's staircase as we exited the car, a lone figure in the cool blue light. The evening air was sticky and warm, the grass crunchy from drought. Birds flittered between the trees and the sun was melting into a warm puddle behind the apartment roofline.

I'd seen that sun with no filter, like the brightest searchlight in the dark.

For a moment I felt unsteady, until Hanna noticed me wavering and grabbed my elbow with a questioning furrow in her brow.

I took in a long breath, filled my lungs with the scent of life.

A scent I'd taken for granted, had almost forgotten. *Life. Earth.* The birdsong was so loud to my ears. The smell of the air, thick with scents of exhaust and tar and fast food and flowers.

The very fact of our existence was a miracle.

Mitsuko's eyes slid over to Hanna and then back to me as we approached. I was wearing the same space suit I'd worn for days, maybe weeks, and carrying my helmet. I was bizarrely out of place. "Wow, okay. So you weren't kidding." She examined my face, smoothing back my hair, like my mother would when she was trying to see if I had a fever, then handed me a mug of coffee. "Drink this. I have a feeling we're in for a long night."

Mitsuko pressed her thumbprint to the door lock and led us inside. It was a nice apartment, in a nice area. She must have found a good job. But then, of course she had. "Emilio will be over in, like, five minutes. He doesn't live far."

The apartment was clean and nicely decorated, warm and chic, but I barely registered details. Her husband, Michael, was in the kitchen laboring over something on the stove that smelled like peppers, and my stomach reminded me that it had been a long, long time since I'd eaten cooked food.

Mitsuko laughed, and the sound relaxed me despite the sense of urgency I still felt beneath the surface. "This is weird. Go sit. I'll find you some clothes to change into. I have to say, I did not expect you to show up in a literal space suit, Cass."

I sank into the comfort of a well-worn couch, let my eyes close, and thanked everything that was listening for good friends and soft landings.

But along with gratitude came the guilt. I'd brought the world's problems to her doorstep, and it wasn't her responsibility to deal with them. It was weird to intrude on her life like this. The amount of time I'd been gone was twice the length of time I'd known her.

I'd been a little jealous, on that last day before launch, that Emilio and Mitsuko would continue on with their normal lives while I risked mine for untold and unknown dangers. And now here I was, in the heart of her everyday life for the first time. It made me realize, too, the starkness of our age difference. She was an independent adult, and I hadn't even graduated high school.

I felt the couch cushions shift and opened my eyes to see Mitsuko beside me. Wordless, she gathered me into a tight, fragrant hug. She was a blur of glossy black hair and toned arms, until I blinked the tears away.

"I'm glad you're okay, Cass."

I smiled as best I could while my face was smashed into her hair. She held me longer than I'd expect a normal hug to last, releasing me only when Michael came in to announce dinner was ready.

I'd seen Michael only once, when I'd said good-bye to Mitsuko before the launch, and I'd been a little too distracted to notice much about him. His hair was short and military-precise, his face angular and handsome. I thought I remembered her saying something about him being in law enforcement. He was taller even than Mitsuko, with broad shoulders and a generally stoic expression. I hadn't heard him say more than a handful of words. I didn't have the energy to talk just yet, so I was grateful to mostly be left alone while the others spoke in undertones around me.

I changed into the spare clothes Mitsuko had brought me—everything was a bit too long, but after wearing the same skintight suit for days on end, it felt amazing just to be able to wear cotton that smelled like laundry detergent.

We sat down at the dinner table just as their front door opened. Emilio had let himself in with the fingerprint lock—Mitsuko must've programmed him into the system. He made a beeline for me. I'd barely gotten out of my chair when he grabbed me in the most enthusiastic hug I think I'd ever received.

When he pulled away, still keeping a grip on my shoulders, he was grinning. "It's really you, Cass! You fucking did it! Look at you, all grown up and back from space. And I won't even mention the fact that you called Mitsuko for help instead of me. Totally over it. Water under the bridge."

"Let the poor girl sit!" Mitsuko chided, whacking him in the arm with a cloth napkin. "She's starving. Oh my God, Emilio, can you chill?"

Still grinning, he settled into the open chair beside me. He'd let his hair grow back out, but the top where he'd once had a Mohawk was still longer than the rest. And other than being a little more tanned than when I'd first met him—we'd spent most of the competition indoors—he looked the same.

I dove into my plate, unable to restrain myself any longer. "This is the best meal I've had in my entire life," I said with my mouth full. "Just nobody tell my grandma I said that."

Mitsuko rolled her eyes.

"Hanna drove me here," I said by way of explanation, when Emilio spotted her across the table. "I was literally in a corn-field in the middle of nowhere. I wouldn't be here without her."

"No, you'd probably be in some SEE containment facility, being interrogated by Clayton Crane," Hanna said quietly.

Mitsuko lifted her eyebrows, giving Hanna her full attention for the first time. "Then we owe you."

Mitsuko must've told Michael that I was vegetarian, because the burritos on my plate were full of beans, rice, and peppers. I'd inhaled half of one before I realized everyone at the table was quietly sneaking glances at me as they chatted, but no one was talking about the elephant in the room. My attention was torn between Emilio and Mitsuko catching up about work— apparently they worked together at some NASA contractor—and the TV in the other room that was still showing a never-ending stream of Alien News. I couldn't tear my eyes from the footage, replayed every five minutes, of the vrag ship. A black, starless void, as seen from the camera of a passing surveillance satellite. Had it really been here for months? Waiting, watching?

And why?

It hadn't descended from low Earth orbit, hadn't breached the atmosphere. There had to be a reason.

I grew quietly restless, the easy conversations of my friends becoming an annoying background noise. I couldn't just *sit* here like a normal person. There were murderers circling overhead and here I was having dinner with friends. Luka was *waiting* for me. Alone, in danger. With that specter of a ship up there looking for him.

My leg started to bounce.

"Earth to Cass? You want me to take your plate?"

I snapped my grim attention back to Emilio. He'd been grinning at his dumb little joke, but the mood went somber as everyone else found what caught my attention.

"The world's gone topsy-turvy since you left, Cass," Mitsuko said quietly, putting down her plate. She put a hand on my knee to stop its anxious bouncing, her eyes full of worry—an expression I wasn't used to seeing from her. "I guess that's why you're here."

My eyes slid to Michael, an unasked question.

"We can trust him," Suko said, without her eyes leaving mine. "He knows everything that I do. Which isn't *much*," she prompted.

I caught them up on everything I'd told Hanna: waking up on the alien planet, meeting Luka and his family, and their deaths at the hands of the vrag.

Other than saying "Holy shit! Really?" when told about Luka's identity, Mitsuko and Emilio took it all in without comment.

"So now SEE, and a lot of other people, are probably looking for me. Which means I can't go home. And the vrag are *definitely* looking for me. I need to meet Luka at his family's safe house as soon as possible, so we can figure out our next move."

"Holy shit," Emilio said again, putting down his can of Coke. "I might need a stiffer drink."

"They'll be looking for me, too," Hanna added. "And probably everyone in this room."

There was a moment of tense silence.

I nodded once, decisive, dreading what I had to do. "So thank you for dinner, everyone. But I can't stay."

Mitsuko leveled her calm gaze at me. All trace of mirth had gone from her face. "What do you need us to do?"

I blinked. "You've done plenty. I can't ask you to do more. You've already put yourselves at risk just by letting me stay here."

"Cass. Where are you going to go? Where are you going to stay?" Mitsuko's voice was flat. "You don't have a car or money, or even any clothes that fit you."

"We're gonna help you regardless, so you might as well tell us what you need," Emilio said. "What else are friends for, if not helping you escape from a mad scientist's corporation, the US government, and a mother ship full of murderous aliens?"

"If your friends don't show up to help you save the world, you need to get new friends," Mitsuko agreed.

On the way here, I'd doubted they would even believe me, much less drop everything to help me. Would I have been as welcoming to someone I barely knew showing up without warning six months after we'd said good-bye, telling the kind of story I had?

"Wherever you're going, I'm going, too," Hanna said,

adamant. "I can't exactly go back now."

They were all staring at me expectantly. Waiting for me to tell them the plan.

I bit back a smile and forced my exhausted, overloaded brain to fire up a few more synapses. "First, I need to get to Luka. I have GPS coordinates for a safe house where we're supposed to meet. We'll plan our next move there. Second, I need to figure out how to convince the world that the vrag are not our new best friends and we need to get rid of them." I didn't tell them about the third thing: that Luka and I brought an alien weapon back with us, and I still hadn't figured out what it did or how to turn it on.

"You know that Crane has been working with the feds," Hanna told the others quietly. "SEE handles so many contracts for NASA, they basically *are* NASA now. The only functioning part, anyway. I heard that as soon as that vrag ship was spotted in orbit, Crane got a call directly from the president. Crane is her number-one man for dealing with the alien threat."

Emilio groaned. "Oh, boy. So Crane is a phone call away from mobilizing the feds to come find you guys."

Mitsuko stood up. "Well, then we need to leave, don't we?"

"What—right now?" Emilio looked perplexed.

"Didn't you hear her? Cass, how far away is this safe house?"

I told them the coordinates.

Michael pulled out his phone and began typing, but Mitsuko ripped the device out of his hands and threw it out of his reach. "What do you think you're doing? You can't type those numbers into Google." She rolled her eyes. "Were you not listening? SEE is working with the *feds.*"

"I'm a fed," he replied, a little insulted.

"Not like these guys," Hanna said darkly.

Mitsuko ignored them both. "The NSA is probably watching our phones right now. We need to get burners, stat." She started to wordlessly count out something on her fingers. "Okay. We need supplies and a rental car. Though it'd really help if we knew how far we had to drive."

I closed my eyes. Sunny didn't have access to *Odysseus's* sensors or GPS satellites anymore, and could only access her memory plus whatever I had stored in my brain. But maybe she had something in her memory that would help. I repeated the coordinates in my mind like a question and reached out, curious, searching for any hint of a foreign presence.

It didn't even take effort. The answer was simply in my mind, as though I had known it all along. "About eight hours. It's western Texas, somewhere outside Big Bend National Park."

Emilio whistled, impressed. He didn't ask how I knew. "Isolated. That's desert country out there."

With the dishes cleared, we moved the conversation to the living room couch. The softness of its cushions was calling my name, but I forced my eyes to remain open.

While Mitsuko busied herself making lists, Hanna excused herself to the restroom, and Emilio came to sit beside me, handing me a cold can of Coke. His energy was quiet and serious, so different from the kid I'd known him as. Now I saw that he'd aged considerably in the last few months. "Hey, bud. You okay? I mean, really. It sounds like you . . . you've been through a lot in the past few days."

"It's been rough," I said, barking a laugh to cover the break in my voice. "I'm really sorry about this, by the way."

His lips tightened and he studied me. "You know it's not an issue. Cass, come on. I told you that we'd gone through some serious shit together and I'd never forget that. You saved my life. That doesn't just . . . go away."

"It's just been so long that I . . . figured you guys would forget about me. Move on."

He raised his eyebrows at me expectantly. "I'm really glad to see you again. Even under these circumstances. And I'm glad you're okay."

I popped the can open. The sugar hit my tongue in an explosion that made my eyes water.

I'd been nervous that maybe the friendship we'd formed had been in my imagination, or would've faded with time and distance. But, again, I'd been wrong. I'd been wrong a lot.

I leaned my head back against the couch and just let myself be in the moment. Not since I woke from stasis had I been able to let my guard down even for an instant. But now I was safe, with friends, and had other people sharing my burden. It felt . . . nice.

I let my eyes slide closed.

Then the last few moments before I escaped in the pod flashed before my eyes, the moment lasting longer in my memory than in reality. The unmoored, stomach-dropping feeling of being shot out into space. And then that last view of Luka turning the ship away from Earth.

Please be okay.

I forced my eyes back open. Would I forever see the most traumatic moments of my life every time I closed my eyes?

Thankfully, Emilio and Michael were having some kind of discussion and didn't notice me startle out of my reverie.

"And this is better than you stealing parts from work . . . why?" Michael asked.

"Everyone uses the 3-D printer for personal stuff. I mean, you're not exactly *supposed* to, but they do. So it won't be out of the ordinary. As long as I space it out and maybe do it a few times when people aren't around. You never know when you might need an extra screwdriver."

"I didn't hear any of this," Michael said, going into the kitchen and returning with a can of beer for Emilio.

"You gotta stop buying this cheap shit, Mike."

"I buy it special for you. I know you secretly like it."

"Thanks for looking out. Asshole." But it was good-natured, friendly. Emilio grinned and popped the top of the can.

I watched the exchange with curiosity. This was like being inside a zoo exhibit full of animals I'd only ever seen from far away.

So this was what it was like to be an adult and have friends who lived in their own apartments, had their own jobs. It seemed nice. I'd never had much luck on the friend thing up until now. But maybe there was hope for my future.

Assuming we had a future.

Hanna returned, holding her phone aloft. "Whatever plans you all are making, you'd better hurry. The vrag are upping the ante. Cassie's name and picture just went up on the internet as a wanted person."

NINETEEN

MITSUKO GAVE A decisive nod and pushed to her feet. "Okay then. Target closes soon. I'm off to get supplies. Cass, you want anything special? Em?"

We both shook our heads, and Mitsuko swept out the door without asking Hanna if she wanted anything. Hanna didn't seem surprised, but I was—that Mitsuko could hold on to a grudge this long, under these circumstances.

Emilio turned to me. "Cass, are you okay? You look pale. Do you need to lie down?"

I couldn't absorb it all. The fact that my face was being broadcast across the state—maybe across the country—it wouldn't compute. Would my parents see? What would they think?

"No, I'm fine." I was still disturbed by my mini flashback,

and didn't know how I could sleep right now. "Hanna—are you sure you want to come?"

She looked at me for a long moment with an expression I couldn't read. "I can't exactly go back now. Crane is going to know what I did. And I don't want to be around him when he does." She grimaced.

Something struck my heart like a splinter. "So, you . . . what? You just gave up your job?" *For me?* I added silently. I couldn't believe she would just throw it away. Hanna, who'd always been out for herself.

She gave a barely discernable shrug.

"You can't do that," I protested.

"It's done," she said simply. "Yeah, it was a good job. But if we do things Crane's way, I don't know if there'd even be a job to go back to. He's . . . lost sight of things. All he cares about now, his sole mission, is to harness whatever power the vrag have dangled in front of him. He's obsessed with it."

I sighed, rubbing at the bridge of my nose. "I'd hoped maybe we could get him on board. I don't know how I'm going to convince the world otherwise."

"He'll never listen to the truth. The vrag have basically bribed people into thinking they're our fairy godmother. He wouldn't accept the alternative."

I had to hope that somebody would.

Mitsuko returned surprisingly fast, laden with plastic shopping bags.

Despite what I'd told Emilio, I did end up dozing on the couch. It had grown dark outside. I stretched and wiped my mouth with the back of my hand to make sure I hadn't been drooling before I joined the others.

There were at least a dozen full bags littering the table. What could she have possibly bought? At most I needed food, clothes, a phone, and transportation.

"This is too much," I said, confused.

Everyone stared at me blankly. Mitsuko spoke first. "We're coming with you. Obviously."

I hadn't been that far gone, had I? Was my memory still recovering? "I don't recall that being part of the plan. It's too dangerous for you guys."

"All of us are in danger now, Cass. We're collaborators. SEE is working with the government. They have free rein to do whatever they want and they wanted to lock you up, so who knows what they'll do to get you back. We want to come with you. Help you."

Was this really happening? Were we really about to go into hiding together? Become fugitives, like we'd committed some crime? This was crazy. Running from our own people—we should be working *together*. "NASA could help us," I countered.

"NASA doesn't have enough power now. And who knows who might turn you in, thinking they were doing the right thing?"

"Unless it was just one person. Somebody we trusted. My dad, or . . ."

"Pierce," Hanna and Emilio said together.

Colonel Pierce, retired NASA astronaut and first man on Mars, had been in charge of us during selection. When things had gone wrong during a simulation, Pierce had personally saved our lives.

Mitsuko took that into consideration. "Yeah, maybe he'd help us. But how?"

She had me there.

"They can't touch us. We're still American citizens with rights. Michael's a cop, or close enough," Emilio argued. "That should count, right?"

"FBI," Michael corrected him, but no one paid any attention.

"Michael might be fine or he might not be. But he can take care of himself. These are desperate times, Cass. And we can be useful." As if to demonstrate, Mitsuko gestured to the wealth of goods spilling from plastic Target bags.

Three prepaid burner phones with five hundred minutes each. A wad of hundred-dollar bills. Various road-trip-appropriate junk food items. Portable phone chargers. A small pantry's worth of shelf-stable food: trail mix, canned fruit, beans, energy bars, water bottles, Gatorade, instant coffee. Multiple sets of new clothes, a pair of tennis shoes, a huge set of toiletries, paper plates, toilet paper, laundry detergent, trash bags, a first-aid kit, batteries, walkie-talkies—on and on. Suko had bought us everything we might need to set up a household and stay there awhile.

"It was the max amount I could take out of the ATM,"

Mitsuko was saying. "But we can go again in the morning when we leave."

"It's too much." I put my hands on the back of my neck, suddenly realizing how sore my muscles were. "I can't take your money."

"You can and you will," Mitsuko said. "Because it's a loan, not a gift. And besides, it's a small price to pay to save the world."

The conversation went on without me, moving at the speed of light while I remained standing still. In a blur, I realized they were all making plans to come with me to the safe house, to rent a car, and were hammering out details.

And I didn't stop them. It felt so nice to have this burden lessened, if only a little. To have others help me shoulder it. To accept help. I didn't always have to do it alone, did I? They were right. Saving the world was a lot to handle by yourself.

I closed my eyes and felt myself waver slightly on my feet. I wasn't in any condition to outrun anybody right now.

My family, I thought again. What would happen to them? I should call them. But I said nothing. I felt like as long as they weren't spoken of, they were protected, far away in our brick two-story in our cookie-cutter suburb. Nothing to do with this.

"What about Cristiana?" Mitsuko asked.

At the mention of that name, Emilio went quiet. The stop in the conversation shook me awake. "Wait, who are we talking about?"

"His girlfriend," Mitsuko explained. "Who lives with him and will probably notice he's gone."

He grasped the top edge of the chair and frowned at it. "I don't want her involved," he said.

"So you're just going to leave her here without any explanation?" Mitsuko clearly didn't like that plan.

"I'll think of something," he said tightly. "But I can't ask her to—to go on the run. I don't know how to explain . . . all this."

"You have until tomorrow morning to figure it out," Mitsuko said.

"Why can't we leave now?" Night felt like a long eight hours to wait when we already had an eight-hour drive before I could make sure Luka was safe. Before *we* were safe.

"Oh, hon. You're exhausted. We'll all get some sleep and we can start fresh in the morning, okay?" There was a moment of quiet where I opened my eyes and Mitsuko squinted at me. "You need to sleep. Come on. I'll take care of you, Cass. Since, unlike some people, we have an actual guest room, and not a *video game room*, because we are actual, certified grown-ups." She gave Emilio a mock dirty look as we passed. He may have stuck his tongue out at her. Or maybe it was a finger. I didn't really look.

I was dead on my feet. All I could do was follow Suko obediently, which, I noticed, was what Michael did, too.

Mitsuko said good-bye to Emilio, Michael shook his hand, and then I hugged him good-bye. It was short but tight, heartfelt. "I'm really glad you're back," he said.

"Me too." He laughed as I pulled away, but I wasn't joking. "You're a lifesaver. You too, Suko. I didn't expect to just literally drop back into your lives and have you be one hundred percent in my corner right away. You don't know how much I needed this. I'm really grateful."

Emilio and Mitsuko wore twin smiles. "You dope," Suko said affectionately. "Of course we're in."

"Totally," Emilio agreed.

Michael said, "You don't get it, Cass. These two have been insanely jealous. They're just trying to live vicariously through you. You should've heard all the whining I've had to endure the past few months. 'Wonder where Cass is right now?' 'Wonder what Cass is doing right now?' 'Man, can you believe how lucky Cass is?'" He mimicked Emilio's and Mitsuko's inflections so accurately we all laughed.

"It wasn't all fun and amazing," I said quietly. "I'm afraid I brought death and destruction back with me."

"Oh, Cass." Mitsuko pulled me to her side, pressed my head into the crook of her neck.

After Emilio left for the night, Michael disappeared into a back bedroom and Hanna stayed on the living room couch as Mitsuko took my hand. "Come on. We only have a few hours till daybreak, and you're going to need them all."

"Suko," I said, following her down the hall. "Why are you being so nice to me?"

"I'm trying to build up my good karma. Oh, and you know me. I like being the center of attention. I'm just gonna try to stand close to you so I get to be near the action. It's selfish, really."

I huffed a laugh, thinking that was the end of the conversation. She opened a door to the left and I caught a glimpse of a queen bed with a plush navy comforter.

"I know you're exhausted, Cass. But listen. If you're right about all this, some major shit is about to go down, and nobody knows but us. We have a duty. We need to fight back. The regular people who are just going about their lives, minding their business, hoping someone else fixes this mess so they can go back to worrying about the dumb shit we all worry about? Nobody else is going to fight for them. So let us help you, Cass. This is too big a thing to do alone."

I couldn't muster the energy for the appropriate response. Just, "You're right. Thank you."

Her voice must have carried in the silence, because Michael returned, unexpectedly half-dressed, his shirt unbuttoned. I startled out of my fatigue and averted my eyes, blushing hard, but he marched right past me as though I weren't there. He walked straight to Mitsuko, grabbing her face in both his palms, and kissed her full on the mouth. "I knew I married you for a reason."

TWENTY

MITSUKO LEFT ME with an oversized T-shirt and pajama pants. "I'm just down the hall if you need anything." She smiled as she paused, hand on the door. "Good night, Cass. I'm so glad you're back safe."

Her words made me remember all those people who had not returned safe. Luka's family. My crew, my former instructors, all experienced astronauts: Bolshakov, Copeland, Shaw, Jeong.

Luka.

I changed, slipped under the blankets, and closed my eyes. But instead of sleep, I was back on the deck of the megobari ship as it exploded around me. The blood and fire and destruction. I fell deeper and deeper into the memory, never able to emerge, never able to escape.

○ ● ◐

I woke sweating, bolting upright in bed in the darkness of an unfamiliar room, clutching at my racing heart. A pale blue dawn glowed through the curtains, enough to illuminate the room.

As I willed my heart to slow, I tried to recall what was real and what was a dream.

Luka was not dead. I wouldn't accept it.

When I felt steady, I crept out of my room as quietly as I could and found the hall bathroom. I splashed water on my face and examined my reflection for the first time. It was like looking at someone you used to know. My hair was longer than it had ever been, my skin a pale shade of brown. My eyes looked shell-shocked and red. My frame was sickly, the muscles I'd earned after years of training wasted away.

I finished and edged out of the bathroom, careful not to make too much noise in the quiet apartment. But then I heard sounds of dishes clinking in the kitchen, and the smell of coffee wafted down the hall.

The kitchen was flooded with sunlight, windows open. I blinked in the light, surprised to see the collection of people seated together having breakfast. Everyone was here—even Hanna, who I'd forgotten about.

It was almost like we were back in the competition, all of us together again in the cafeteria.

I chose an open seat between Hanna and Emilio, and someone slid a plate of eggs and toast in front of me. Everyone else's plates were nearly empty, with only the remains of breakfast on them. "Guys, what time is it? You shouldn't have let me sleep so long."

"You needed it," Hanna said beside me.

"And it's not that late," Emilio said.

I took a long drink of the orange juice beside my plate—Mitsuko had actual place settings complete with napkin rings; it was super intimidating—and shot a look at Hanna. "Where did you sleep last night?"

She inclined her head toward the family room. "The couch."

I ate quickly while Mitsuko and Emilio looked up the best route on their phones.

"Wait, you guys are using your real phones?" I sputtered. "You know people are looking for us? Tell me you didn't type in the actual coordinates."

"Chill, Cass. We're professionals. Suko and I worked out a way to—"

His eyes flicked to Michael, who shook his head, covered his ears, and said, "I officially can't hear any of this."

Emilio flashed a grin and said in a confidential tone, "Anyway, we're anonymous. Just don't worry about how."

"What'd you tell your girlfriend?" Hanna asked Emilio.

"She's taking a vacation back to her parents' place in Michigan. I figured she'd be okay there. Luckily, she trusts me enough to just take my word that maybe she should get away for a while. And with this alien ship in the sky . . . well, let's just say that a lot of people have been acting strange."

I nodded. "I'm sorry, Emilio. Really."

He shook himself out, gave me a smile I didn't believe. "Hell, Cass. This is the next best thing to going into space. We get to save the world without ever having to leave the great state of Texas. Best of both worlds."

Michael cleared the plates away, started the dishwasher, and all of a sudden we were leaving, turning off lights and locking the door behind us.

I felt a sudden pang of guilt. They were leaving their homes and lives for me, and none of us knew when—or if—we'd be able to come back. This was too much sacrifice. And they didn't even know the worst part.

I stopped at the front door. I couldn't let them go into this not knowing the whole truth. "Guys. There's something you should know. Luka and I . . . The megobari had hidden a weapon they'd devised to use against the vrag. And we . . . we brought it back. We're not sure what it does or even how it works. And it's . . . big, you guys. But it might be our only chance to win this thing."

Hanna snorted. "Better and better."

Emilio's eyes went wide, and he made the sign of the cross.

Mitsuko gave him a bewildered look. "I've never seen you do that before."

"Yeah, well, no one ever told me that we're about to be caught in the middle of a war between two advanced alien species who both outgun us AND we have an alien nuke. I'm just hedging my bets."

"Where is it now?" Michael asked, concern etching his brow.

"It's hidden. Or should be. Somewhere near the safe house."

Mitsuko gave an exasperated sigh. "Then we'd better get going, kiddos, before somebody else finds it first."

The car Michael had rented was some kind of SUV, big and shiny and silver, with bags presumably full of the supplies Mitsuko had bought piled in the back. Mitsuko got behind the wheel and I sat in the back beside Hanna, while Emilio took shotgun.

Michael was leaning in the driver's-side window, murmuring good-byes to Mitsuko. They'd decided he would stay behind. He'd be more useful to us at home, with the resources from his job, if we needed help.

The air-conditioning was still blowing hot, new-car-scented air in my face; the leather was sticky against my thighs. The hours ahead of us weighed on me. I'd flipped open the communicator Luka had given me a dozen times, but nothing happened.

It was taking all my energy to not focus on why I couldn't get in touch with him.

Once we pulled onto the interstate, Mitsuko turned on self-driving mode and swiveled her chair toward me. "Have you called your parents yet?" Seeing the look on my face, her eyes narrowed into laserlike points. "Cassandra Gupta, you have an untraceable phone and eight solid hours in the car ahead of you. Call your family. Right. This. Instant."

I groaned, head hitting the back of the seat. And called up the communication module in the armrest.

It was a Tuesday. Midmorning. The sun was already bathing

the roads with shimmering waves of heat. So I wasn't surprised when Dadi's face appeared on the screen in front of me—except for the slight bit of surprise that she knew how to answer the video chat. Tears sprang to my eyes instantly. Dadi looked so much older, her gray hair frizzy in its loose bun, her eyes a bit confused and unfocused until she realized it was me.

She actually jumped away from the computer as though it had shot sparks, and then her face became so huge on the screen I was pretty sure she picked up the laptop and physically brought it to her face. A string of her surprised curse words was like music to my ears. "It can't be. Cassandra Gupta, what are you doing calling home? Your parents are worried sick. They called NASA, they called everyone looking for you! Where are you?"

"I'm safe, Dadi," I replied. "I'm back from . . . from space. I can't come home yet. Tell Mama and Papa I'm sorry. I miss you and love you guys. But I can't come home yet. I still have work to do."

She was already shaking her head. "No, no, no. Enough now. Your mother has endured enough. You come home now."

"Dadi, I can't. Please understand."

"Are you in trouble? Is someone keeping you locked in a room? Blink your eyes if yes! I will have your *chacha* trace this call and we will come and get you!"

Though I doubted my grandmother's faith in my uncle's ability to perform such a feat, I didn't doubt she'd sic the FBI or the Texas Rangers or whomever she could get to come after me in a heartbeat. "No! Nobody is keeping me locked in a room. I'm perfectly safe and with friends. Dadi, is Uncle Gauresh there? Can I see him?"

"He is out walking Saachi. You can see him when you come home! What's so important it would keep you from coming home? I'm getting old, you know. I might die soon!"

"Okay, Dadi." I hid my smile somewhere behind a heart aching with homesickness. "I hope I can come home soon, but there are things I have to do here first. I just wanted to call and let you know not to worry about me. I'm safe. Tell Mama and Papa for me, okay? Tell them I love them and will see them soon?"

"Bah! Tell them yourself when you get here!" And she disconnected the call.

I sat there a moment in shock, laughing a little to myself incredulously. *It could've been worse*, I thought. At least it wasn't Mama, crying and begging me to come home.

"Your grandma is amazing," Mitsuko said. "I want to be friends with her."

I smiled to cover up my grief. I hoped that wasn't the last time I spoke to her.

With Mitsuko and Emilio both engrossed in their own business on their terminals, the car went quiet again.

Having poured a little guilt out of my cup, I proceeded to devour the internet, speed-reading the news for the past six months, catching myself up with everything I had missed. Then I scanned pages and pages of new headlines, looking for anything that could lead to Luka. There was nothing.

I searched for anything and everything related to SEE, but their information was largely relegated to a corporate website with nothing but a list of the board of directors and CEO.

After a moment's hesitation, I also looked up the bios of the astronauts from my crew. I don't know what I was looking for. The names of family members, where they lived. Someone should tell their families what had happened to them. They needed to be put to rest, to be remembered.

But I didn't know how to go about finding their next of kin. Or if that news should even come from me at all. NASA would do a much better job at that than me.

NASA had worked with SEE on Project Adastra. How much did they know about Crane and his intentions? The entire project must've been covered up, erased from records. Did NASA know I was back?

Maybe with Sunny's records to back me up, *they* would believe me. But first, we had to make sure the records were still there, and see what was actually on them.

Outside, the interstate still spun past the windows, the car barreling us west on its predetermined course. For a nanosecond, I felt it all: The helplessness of our situation. The movement of us inside the car, crawling across the surface of a planet that was rotating a thousand miles an hour, and at the same time, speeding around the sun at eighteen miles per second, chasing it as the star shot through space, spinning its way around the center of the galaxy.

Running, running, always running, always chasing and

being chased. But we couldn't escape. We were small and power-less, ants trapped on our paradise of a planet, surrounded by the void, shooting endlessly through a vast and terrible universe. We had to protect our fragile home.

"T-minus six hours till we reach our destination," Emilio said, turning around in his seat toward me. "That's where you gotta be, chica."

He was right. Of all the places in the world, that was where Luka could find me. I held my grandma's elephant-head Ganesh necklace in my palm until it warmed from my heat, and prayed like I rarely had before.

All I could do now was wait, and hope that the world did not ignite before I could find a way to stop it.

I closed my eyes so I would stop looking at the clock.

We drove through San Antonio. We got fast food for lunch and filled the gas tank. Soon, there was nothing to look at out the windows but farm fences and cacti, and little to read but the status updates on the warrant out for my arrest. They'd added Hanna as a possible accomplice.

So Mitsuko bought us baseball caps, scissors, and hair dye, and at the next rest stop I chopped off my hair and Hanna gave herself a quick dye job in the sink.

Then we got back on the road—Hanna with fresh brown locks, still wet, and me with a sloppy bob that Mitsuko fussed over until it was even on both sides.

The whole world was looking for me. My parents might be

hearing about me on the news, worrying and wondering. My old classmates, what might they think? Even the other competitors from the selection. Seeing me and Hanna together six months after the competition ended; surely they'd find that suspicious.

And there was a leftover thread my brain kept tugging at, an unresolved worry—who had sabotaged our training mission inside the secure facility at Johnson and almost killed us all?

Sure, they'd said it had been an unfortunate error—a glitch. But no glitch on Earth could lock the hatch to our simulated space station environment, cut off our radio communications, and turn off our oxygen. Colonel Pierce hadn't believed it, and neither had I.

That mystery had never been solved, the perpetrators never caught. Could they be out here looking for me, too?

What other dangers were lurking, waiting for me? I didn't have the full picture yet. I had to be ready for anything.

When the others shook me out of my reverie, the sky had dimmed to a dusky orange, and we were the only car visible on the road.

Nothing, not even livestock or farms, was visible out the windows now, only sandy scrub and the jagged edges of red-rock mountains. We were truly in the middle of nowhere.

"Turn here," Emilio said.

"That's not what the GPS says," Mitsuko pointed out. I leaned forward to see the screen on the dashboard. And she was right. The map was telling her to go straight. There wasn't a road to turn onto for miles.

"No, it's wrong," Emilio said. "I plotted it out before we left."

"Well, there's no street there now," Mitsuko grumbled.

I was hyperalert, leaning forward in my seat, seat belt cutting a diagonal indent across my body.

The car made a sharp, sudden left, the steering wheel tearing itself out of Mitsuko's hands. Wheels grinding over gravel and dirt now, the vibrations shaking up all the way from my feet to my skull.

"What the hell? Autopilot just took over. GPS, what is my destination?" Mitsuko asked.

The computer-generated voice repeated our coordinates. The GPS display showed us veering off the single green line of the highway, heading off on our own into unmarked territory.

"What? I can't change it. I can't take over. What the hell's wrong with this rental?" Mitsuko punched buttons on the display in frustration until Emilio took over.

They kept trying to disengage the GPS. The manual override didn't respond. The steering wheel fought against Mitsuko's attempts to take over. I had a feeling she wasn't going to succeed. I didn't believe in coincidences, not anymore.

The car had a mind of its own, and unless we wanted to jump out of a moving vehicle, our only choice was to see where it led.

The lady voice of the GPS crooned, "You have arrived at your destination."

We all sat dumbfounded. There was nothing in front of us that was different in any way from the miles of empty scrubland we'd already been staring at for hours, except that the ground swelled slightly in front of us in a small hill, or dune.

A GPS couldn't malfunction like that. The doors unlocked themselves, and I reached over to unlatch mine, pulling off my seat belt with the other hand.

"Hey—" Emilio protested as the rush of dry heat replaced the air-conditioning.

I crawled out and my sneakers hit dirt, legs trembling a little as I approached the dune.

The closer I approached, the more the hill looked less like a quirk of nature and more like something purposeful. It was larger than it appeared from the car; it even cast a shadow on the surrounding sand.

I heard car doors slam shut behind me and the crunch of sneakers as my friends followed, but I didn't slow down.

As I approached the northern face of the hill, I stumbled to a stop, causing Mitsuko to collide into my back and then grab my elbow before I could fall.

Etched into the north face of the hill was a curve of glass and stone—windows, with a wooden door in the middle.

"What the hell? Is this some kind of . . . government . . . bunker?" Emilio sputtered beside me.

"It's an Earth-sheltered house," I said, my mouth already dry from the desert air, its heat pushing into me like a physical force. "Back in high school, I had a teacher who lived in one. He told us about it—it's eco-friendly, temperature controlled due to being half buried. He had goats that grazed on the roof." I had no doubt I was right. There was even a garden plot lined with wire fence not far from the entrance, clean and maintained. "This is the safe house."

"Out here in the heat—so far off the grid—it makes sense," Hanna said, but quietly.

We were all staring at it like it was an alien thing, even though it was obviously human in design and construction.

Isolated, undetectable, self-sustainable. It made sense, but suddenly I doubted. Who knew who could be living here? Maybe it was some survivalist nut. Maybe our GPS really had glitched and we were nowhere near where we were supposed to be. I'd read reports of that happening more since the vrag ship's appearance—satellites jamming, GPS sending people on wild-goose chases.

"Should we knock?" Emilio asked.

There was no need. A shadow moved behind one of the windows, and then the door began to open.

TWENTY-ONE

SUDDENLY, IMPOSSIBLY, LUKA was standing in front of us. He looked clean, uninjured, and only somewhat surprised to see all of us.

I approached him cautiously at first, as though he were a wild animal, not quite believing.

And then before I realized what I was doing, the distance between us was gone and I was hugging him, as though to reassure myself he was real and whole. "I thought you were dead."

He returned the embrace with gentle pressure, and when he pulled away, the light was back on in his eyes. "I saw your car approaching. I had hoped . . ." He gave a wry half smile. "I apologize for sabotaging your vehicle's navigation system."

"Are you okay? When I couldn't get you on the communicator . . ."

"I'm sorry I didn't answer. I couldn't know if you and the device had been taken. Perhaps I was too cautious, but I couldn't allow anyone to find this place."

"What happened? How did you even get here?"

His gaze shifted behind me, taking in the others I'd brought without comment. "First, we need to get out of the open. And get your car into the garage." His eyes darted to the empty space around us. Even knowing we were alone, I shared his paranoia. He stepped back inside and held open the door for me. "Please, come in."

"I'll take care of the car," Mitsuko said behind me, but I barely heard her.

I walked past Luka, my eyes adjusting slowly to the dark. As everyone else filed in behind me and Luka closed the door, I realized we were in an airlock of sorts. Another set of doors lay behind the first, and when Luka unlocked this one, it opened into a beautiful circular room with a high, rounded ceiling and rustic wood furnishings. Well-lit and cozy even while feeling open, the room was half kitchen, half living space. Everything seemed fairly new, the appliances modern.

"Welcome," Luka said, eyeing the group a bit uncomfortably.

I turned my eyes on Luka and absorbed every detail of him. It *was* him: alive and breathing, his skin and hair a little more bronzed, maybe from working that plot of land out front. It'd been a day since I'd seen him. His clothes were basic, nondescript, but clean and new.

Luka tilted his head meaningfully toward the kitchen and I followed him there, away from the others. I heard Emilio whistle and Hanna entered cautiously, settling on the couch, trying not to be obvious in her spying on Luka and me.

Luka spoke low and quickly. "Were you followed?"

"Not unless it was by an invisible car. We haven't seen another for miles."

Still tense, he asked, "Your friends—can we trust them?"

"You know them, too. They're not strangers."

The grim line of his mouth was telling. He didn't trust anyone.

"I wouldn't have brought them if I didn't trust them. I thought we could use all the help we can get. What happened after you shot me into space?"

He seemed to relax by a fraction, hand raking through his hair. "I could not lose the vrag ship; it is surprisingly fast. I launched all the escape pods and detonated them. I ran dark, auxiliary power only. In the field of debris near the asteroid belt, they lost my signature. I waited them out and then returned to Earth, landed nearby, hid the weapon and the ship in separate locations, and walked the rest of the way here." He said it all quickly, quietly, without emotion. But I knew enough of him to understand that when he seemed emotionless, he was simply disguising something he felt deeply.

"What is it?" I asked, when I could bear the silence no longer.

He exhaled slowly, troubled. His hands gripped into fists and he looked away, voice growing even quieter. "I could have ended it. I could have activated the weapon. I could have saved us and avenged my family, and I let cowardice stop me. And now we are here, and the vrag know it. When I arrived here and did not find you, I feared for your safety. I thought perhaps you had been detained."

"I almost was," I said, finding myself wanting to touch his shoulder, comfort him. So I did. His eyes alighted on me, cool and blue and concerned. "Hanna picked me up instead. It could have been . . . a lot worse."

His gaze flicked to her, sitting with her back to us, and then met my eyes again with a solemnity I didn't understand. "I'm glad."

"Anyway," I continued, clearing my throat. "The vrag have already been in touch with certain Earth governments. Apparently everyone, Crane included, thinks that the vrag and the aliens who sent us the *Odysseus* message are one and the same."

The quiet anger contorted his face slowly, like someone turning a crank: narrowing his eyes, furrowing his brow, setting his mouth in a bloodless line, tensing his jaw. A smaller crank churned in my chest as I wondered if I had said the wrong thing, equating his enemy and his people as interchangeable.

For a moment he didn't look at me. His gaze was far away. But then he snapped himself out of it. "I'm glad you made it here when you did."

"Why—what's happened?"

A muscle in his jaw jumped and he nodded to the others. "There is something everyone should know."

"How did you hack our car?" were the first words Hanna

spoke when we returned to the group. Mitsuko had returned with our bags. They had all settled into the brown leather couches arranged in a square, facing a fireplace and a flat-screen TV, which was tuned to a news network and muted.

Luka and I sat beside each other on the unoccupied couch, Luka sitting stiffly on the edge. Without blinking, he replied, "My people developed faster-than-light travel. I can manage accessing a simple satellite-powered global positioning system."

"And you knew ours was the correct car because . . . ?" Mitsuko asked.

"Because you keyed the GPS to the coordinates I gave you. It is highly improbable that anyone who is not you would have randomly inputted those numbers."

"Damn. I'm glad we're on the same side," Emilio said.

Mitsuko had been watching Luka's expression carefully. "What is it?" she asked, afraid. "What's going on?"

"So you have not heard?" he asked quietly.

"We didn't have Wi-Fi the last few miles," I said. "This area is a dead zone."

He nodded grimly. "The vrag have issued an ultimatum," he said. "They know that we landed, and roughly where. Your government must turn you and me over to the vrag by noon tomorrow, or the vrag ship will begin leveling American cities at a rate of one per day."

TWENTY-TWO

I'D NEVER HEARD so many profanities uttered by so many mouths at once.

"I'm afraid it gets worse," he said over the rising tide of outrage. "They have offered a reward to anyone who captures us alive. Our names and faces are being broadcast over the news nationwide." He nodded to the TV screen to illustrate his point.

A stab of fear went through me. And there we were—my smirking driver's license photograph and Luka's solemn passport photo, side by side.

"They're saying you're armed and dangerous? What a crock of bullshit," Mitsuko spat.

I felt sick. My *parents* were seeing this. That call I'd made earlier would only seem that much more suspicious now. The amount of pressure they must be under from police, from the government . . . what if they got arrested, too? I'd made them a target.

"Well, at least you picked a good place to hide out," Emilio muttered. "There's nobody around for miles."

Letting them blow up innocent people wasn't an option. We'd have to give ourselves up. We probably wouldn't live long after that. Someone else would have to figure out how to use the weapon. How much time did we have to get the truth out before that happened?

"Why now? Why would they instigate war with a very nuke-loving country over two people? That seems counterintuitive," Emilio said.

"They aren't afraid of us," Hanna said simply. "Or America's nuclear weapons. Don't you see?"

I searched Luka's gaze. His eyes were haunted. He'd come to the same conclusion I had. This was it. We couldn't run anymore.

I knew, just as deeply as I knew we'd have to turn ourselves in, that my friends wouldn't let me do it. They hadn't even let me come *here* alone. But I'd dragged them through enough.

Don't think about that last conversation with Dadi. Just don't.

"What's the plan, E.T.?" Emilio asked Luka cautiously.

I hadn't realized, but this was the first time they'd seen him after learning the truth. They were seeing him with new eyes, as I once had.

Luka glanced at me, eyebrows raised.

What *was* my plan? That I would go on local news with the

mission video footage and announce to the world that I had visited an alien planet, I had seen the vrag's violent nature first-hand, and that we had to fight back? That I had the answer right here, an alien superweapon that could destroy them all?

Yeah, that'd go over really well. Me and the billion other clowns out there could vie for airspace. Without the backing of SEE and the US government—which I'd never get now—I had no standing. Nobody listened to teenage girls, especially not brown ones.

I couldn't think of any way that I could get the truth out there without becoming just one more nonsensical voice in a sea of voices, all clamoring to be heard.

I had to find someone influential to boost my voice. Someone other people would believe.

Either that, or figure out what the weapon did, and how to use it.

It was up to me. Sunny—and any truth she might hold—was in *my* head. I'd need to find a way to access her. Tonight.

But that was the problem—I'd tried. Maybe it was too early—maybe the innervations that needed to happen hadn't had time to grow. The connections hadn't been formed.

"Cass," Emilio said suddenly, concerned. I'd drifted out of the conversation and startled to find my friends looking at me with matching expressions. "Are you okay?"

"There's something I haven't told you guys." I explained about Sunny, leaving out the part about the weapon. I needed to talk to Luka about that first to figure out what we were going to do. "I need to be able to get the information that's locked in my head out somehow."

Only Hanna looked unsurprised.

"We get the data off Sunny as fast as we can," I said. "And we get it to the people who can do something about it."

"Such as?" Hanna asked.

"People we trust. Pierce, maybe. I don't know if he has any real power at NASA now, but people respect the hell out of him. He has sway."

"Would Crane care if he knew the vrag were the bad guys? Wouldn't this threat override any hope of him being able to ally with them? Would *anybody* care?" Emilio asked.

"Not necessarily," Luka said. He glanced at the television. We all watched a moment, reading the scrolling news ticker and the closed captions of the president making a speech. "If America turns us in, the vrag will consider it an act of alliance. If they do not, it's an act of war."

"They want that alliance. So they won't care what we have to say," I said. "Even though it's the truth."

"Really, Cassie. Has anyone in power ever cared about the truth?" Hanna asked.

No. They hadn't. Not for a long time.

"Crane wants power," Hanna said. "That's all. He'll do whatever he has to do to get it."

We were all tired, energy sucked out and replaced with the anxiety of a ticking clock. Hanna disappeared into her room.

Mitsuko, Emilio, and I stayed glued to the TV for as long as we dared, hungry for news, waiting for some brilliant idea to strike.

Sometime that afternoon, after they'd issued the warning, the vrag underscored their threat by cratering a cornfield in north Texas. No deaths, but some farmers had been taken to the hospital. I didn't miss the fact that I had crash-landed in the vicinity.

The message was clear: next time, people would die.

A cold, swirling maelstrom of dread was churning inside me. Dread and *guilt*. I was frozen, watching TV and unable to make myself move away. If I didn't do something, tomorrow people were going to die.

But I couldn't tear my eyes off the screen. I sat there and let the waves of guilt roll over me. Felt the weight of the burner cell in my lap, with its now-full signal bars, and thought about calling my mom.

"Hey, I know I shouldn't be surprised, and in the scheme of things this is, like, the least important question, but—how do you get such a clear TV signal all the way out here?" Emilio's voice was somewhere near me, but I was barely registering it.

Luka gave him a pointed glance, eyebrows raised. "Faster-than-light travel," he said again, slowly.

"Okay, okay," Emilio said. "Just thought I'd ask."

Maybe taking that as an opening—maybe trying to change the subject or lessen the tension in the room—Luka briefed us quickly on the house. Sensing trouble and being ever-cautious,

Luka's family had been around the world for many decades installing fail-safes in many different countries. I suppose when you're a group of less than fifty aliens hiding in plain sight from your adopted planet's dominant species, it's in your best interests to set up a whole lot of places to hide. They even had secret caches of supplies, money, and identities stashed in a lockbox in the closet.

Luka's family trusted no humans; they'd no friends to rely on in times of trouble. Only each other.

I began to see the deep well of grief that Luka had kept a lid on during our journey back. He was more alone now than anyone could be.

He had no friends because he could not trust humans. Before SEE and the competition, I'd had no friends because I only wanted to win.

And now that I had friends, I'd dragged them here, into this.

Soon, everyone else claimed fatigue and went into their respective bedrooms. Luka and I were alone.

My eyes were burning, my limbs heavy, but I couldn't let myself sleep. I had only hours left to figure out what to do.

Luka was already unpacking the bags of kitchen goods. It didn't take long, but he was moving slowly, mechanically, like his mind was elsewhere and he was on autopilot. We'd eaten most of the trip food in the car, which was now hidden inside the garage attached to the house. I didn't know when—or if—Mitsuko planned to return it.

We stared at each other a moment. A draft washed over my

bare arms as the air-conditioning kicked on, making me shiver. Half buried in the earth, this place got cold quickly at night.

"What are we going to do?" I asked him. There was a touch of desperation in my voice that I hadn't meant to be there.

Luka turned his eyes to me slowly, like he was delaying the inevitable. "I'll go to the megobari," he said, determined. "Take the weapon to them. Then we can take out the vrag—hopefully before they ever know we are there."

My hands formed fists at my sides.

"It's the best chance we have," Luka said quietly.

"And how long will that take?" I asked, matching his tone. "We can't let the vrag hurt innocent people."

He said nothing.

"We don't even know what this weapon does. What if it—I don't know—opens up a black hole? It wouldn't even need to do that much. What if it poisons our air, or blasts Texas off the map? We don't know." My voice was edging into hysteria. "No, I'm going to figure out what it is. I'm gonna try to access whatever Sunny copied and figure out what the hell we brought back with us."

I whirled around, heart racing in anger, and there was Hanna, standing in the doorway. She'd been gone a while—I'd assumed she was asleep.

"How long have you been standing there?" I asked, breath coming fast for some reason.

"Long enough." She surveyed me appraisingly, arms crossed over her chest. "I think I have something that can help you."

We followed Hanna back to her room, a small, windowless space with a twin bunk bed pushed in the corner. She went to the nightstand, pulled out a drawer, and came back with a flat black device, like a tablet but thicker.

Sitting on the edge of the lower bunk, she swiped her index fingers across the surface and it shimmered to life. The tablet now seemed more liquid, somehow—like a bowl of water in a dark glass. Cool blue lights hovered over the surface, a holographic control panel.

"What the hell is that?" I whispered, hoping not to wake the others sleeping in the rooms next door.

"A little experimental device I took with me when I left SEE." She dipped her fingers back into the surface—literally, because now the surface wasn't solid, but some kind of permeable gel or . . . or something. I didn't have words to explain it. The hologram shifted slightly, but it was too small and backward for me to read. I sat beside her to get a closer look. "It's called Oracle."

She tilted her neck, the tendons straining, and used one finger to draw her hair up and away. A telltale scar marked the hollow space behind her ear. "You have a computer chip in your head," she said, matter-of-fact. "So do I. Mine is called Pinnacle."

At the look of shock on my face, she raised her eyebrows, her face becoming a little smug. "When you left, *I* became Crane's star pupil. Pinnacle is Sunny's smarter, faster big brother, and I've been working with it implanted in my brain for six months."

Luka eyed her suspiciously. "That is megobari technology. How did you—"

"Humans are intelligent, too," Hanna shot back. "At least, some of us are. It's not exactly a stretch. Humans have been perfecting human-computer interfaces for years. Your people aren't the only ones who can invent new technology. You all just gave us the push we needed when you sent that transmission."

Luka's mouth twisted angrily, but he didn't open it again.

"You did send us a bunch of schematics for building a ship like yours," I said. "Humans are quick learners."

Hanna shook her head, letting her hair fall back over her ear. "Oracle is an output node for Pinnacle that I interface with directly. They developed this along with Pinnacle, as a way for me to have an external processor of sorts. It should also allow you to have an output for whatever it is you're trying to get from Sunny, and share it with the rest of the world." A light beam trailed over her face, I assumed reading her biometrics, and then the hologram pulsed green. "It's ready."

"Ready for what?" I asked.

Hanna withdrew her hands from the touchscreen. "Just place your hand here and direct Sunny to show her what you want."

I took a steadying breath. "Will it work for me?"

"I see no reason why it wouldn't."

I reached a trembling hand to the screen, shivering as my fingertips made contact and *sank* into it, ever so slightly. The surface was slightly warm, making my fingertips tingle like I was touching raw electricity, like I was gathering static charge.

The microfilm coating the surface was something not quite aqueous, not quite solid, and a part of me couldn't help listing the possible materials—*aerogel? Semigel? Liquid crystal polymer? Carbon nanofoam?*—before I made myself concentrate on the task at hand.

"Sunny, play the visual records from *Odysseus*, starting at the beginning."

Sunny apparently understood me despite my lack of specificity, which most computers needed to get anything accomplished. But of course she didn't need it; she didn't even need my audible command. She read my *intent.* It was as effortless as deciding to brush a stray lock of hair out of my face and watching my hand obey.

The blue holographic display returned, became a ghostly sort of screen. The first few seconds of my helmet's shaky cam footage began to play on-screen, sans audio.

Sunny had started at the very beginning, when I'd first turned on my helmet cam. We were looking at the backs of space suits as, one by one, they jumped from *Odysseus* onto the surface of another world. It was one of the most, if not *the* most, important moments of my life, playing out on-screen like it was filmed on a Hollywood set. It was like literally taking a memory out of my head and putting it on display for everyone in the room to see. Creepy. And amazing.

Luka emanated stress and impatience, which was unusual for him. "We need to view the records from the megobari base. We need to know how to turn on the weapon."

The crew on-screen had spread out now, walking slowly and cautiously through a dark yellow cavern. I knew what was about to happen. Suddenly I realized I needed to cut off the feed.

"Sunny, turn it off, please." The video froze, and the display faded. I didn't want Luka to have to see his family on the screen. Without speaking aloud, I told Sunny: *Copy my helmet-cam recordings from up until the destruction of* Exodus *to Oracle and encrypt them.*

Luka had turned so I could see only his profile, and my eyes were afraid to linger too long on his face for fear of what I'd see there.

We didn't have time to dwell right now. "Sunny, please display the data you copied from the megobari moon base."

Megobari records are file-format incompatible with current processing system.

Dismayed, I pulled my hand away and the screen faded. "She says the file formats are incompatible. Maybe that's why I couldn't access them before? What should we do?"

"This computer is human built," Luka said. "It does not know how to interpret the information you are attempting to access. The megobari language is completely different from your own. I cannot change this."

"So, what do you mean . . . that's it?" I asked, incredulous. "After all this? Our systems just aren't compatible?"

Luka was stone-faced, his lips blanched. If this device from SEE couldn't do it, nothing could.

"I have an alternative," Hanna said. She touched her palm to

Oracle. "I think combining the processing power of both of our internal computers might be our shot at untangling the mess of megobari records. Sunny and Pinnacle could, possibly, convert the incompatible data into something we can understand—they both understand our brains, after all, and might be able to translate since Sunny did have access to the source language at one point in time. Hypothetically, we could use Oracle as a medium to interface directly with each other. Pinnacle's processing power added to Sunny's could be enough to translate those files. And we can save them to Oracle for playback or uploading."

"I don't understand how this will help," I said.

"When we both touch this interface node, it will allow direct communication between Sunny and Pinnacle. I will warn you that being connected to Pinnacle is . . ." A grimace flashed across her face. ". . . an overwhelming experience. I had months to work up to it, but you will not. You will have to fight it for control. There will be a lot of input for you to manage. Sunny and Pinnacle aren't designed to coexist in one machine, let alone a human brain. If you lose—there's not much I can do."

"Won't there be a similar risk to you?" The Hanna I knew wasn't in the habit of putting herself in harm's way unless there was some benefit to her.

"Sunny isn't designed the same way. She's more of a background presence, meant to monitor and observe, only coming to assist when called. Pinnacle is more . . . dominating." Hanna was not accustomed to giving much away, but the way her expression darkened at that made me wonder what she'd dealt with in my absence.

Luka was studying me intently. I could almost see the gears turning behind his eyes, weighing the options, the risks. "It is possible that could work. But, Cassie—your implant is so new. Your networking with Sunny has not even been fully established. It's risking a lot to stress your system."

I refused to accept that we were out of the game, just like that. "We have to try. We can't waste any more time."

A hard knot had formed at the base of my throat; I pressed a fist there to relieve the pressure. So much for hoping for the best. Did it really even matter if I fried my brain, if I was turning myself in to the vrag tomorrow?

Luka's worried eyes bored into me. I grasped for something positive to hang on to. "I've been linked to Sunny for a long time, when you think about it. Six months. I practiced with her. It . . . it should be fine. Don't give me that look."

"Oracle will monitor our vital signs," Hanna told him.

Luka nodded slowly, eyes never leaving mine. "If I think you're in danger, I'm pulling the plug."

"It'll be fine. Hardly the most dangerous thing I've ever done." I managed a smile.

As I reached out to touch the interface, Hanna's eyes caught mine. "You might be wrong about that."

TWENTY-THREE

I CLOSED MY eyes. Without drugs helping the process along, I needed a few minutes to find the place where my brain was quiet, where I used to go to find the door to let Sunny in. Only now Sunny was already here, silent and observant and invisible, and the one knocking on the door—*loudly* knocking—was a stranger.

I'd only just allowed the connection when that door burst open, with sensation and thought and data flooding in that was not my own. My own self was swept away by the crashing tide of information.

There was so much data, fragmented into a billion particles, that it made no sense at all; I was seeing the very atoms of things, trillions of individual bits of data that made no logical sense on their own. Pictures broken down into their pixels, life broken down into DNA. It was a universe of nonsense and static. I was helpless to slow down the flow or to hold on to a single bit of data.

Sunny had been quiet, gentle, sane, in comparison to this. This was the raw brain of a computer that could process information faster than my own and with no idea how to convert it so that I might understand. Pinnacle didn't know me; it was adapted to Hanna's electrical pathways, not mine. Pinnacle could have been trying to communicate with me or kill me; we didn't speak the same language.

I scrabbled, gasped, unable to feel my physical body or perceive where it was in space, drowning helplessly in the onslaught, my hand frozen to the interface node.

But then I felt something slower and more methodical emerge from the chaos, sorting it almost as fast as it came at me, and the information became a more manageable trickle.

"Sunny," I said, only I didn't say it, because I was nothing but my own thoughts in my head.

Sunny was orderly. She had spent so much time interfaced with my brain that she knew how it was organized. She set about putting the right bits of data in the right places, a super-powered secretary, collating and merging and formatting the bits into manageable chunks I could actually understand, if not hold on to.

Until, finally, I could think.

Sunny, I thought again.

Hello, Cassie. This felt right. Only now our connection was supremely intimate; she was glued to me, my conjoined twin, with our own secret language. Her voice was my voice; her thoughts were my thoughts. Though she had very few thoughts at the moment; most of her capacity was being taken up in processing the flow of information coming from Pinnacle.

And that's when I realized there wasn't just her presence in my mind. I began to feel it expand, more and more, a growing awareness of some curious predator circling me, observing, testing. A gnawing tide barely held back by Sunny's wall. Studying me, this creature it had never experienced before. Wanting to know me. *Learn* me.

Hanna was back there, somewhere, behind the onslaught of Pinnacle's overwhelming power. If she was directing it, I couldn't tell. This wasn't like when I had first been connected to Sunny-Lite and could sense Dr. Copeland's heartbeat during training. I felt nothing past Pinnacle's wall. Nothing except Pinnacle.

I began to understand how wrong this was. Pinnacle was searching for a place to land, to connect to me, but Sunny was already here. She had already learned my circuits.

To Pinnacle, I was a foreign language it was hungry to learn. It couldn't touch my circuits without touching Sunny's, and they were at odds. Sunny had merged with me so smoothly, so entirely, that I could not tell where she ended and I began. But Pinnacle was thousands of times more powerful. He would outlast her.

I was still hanging on by my fingertips to the rock of Sunny's borrowed sanity and couldn't spare much thought to do anything else. I held on to one directive.

Pinnacle needs to access the alien files, I thought, trying to direct its attention, not sure if it would even listen to me over Hanna. *Sunny, help Pinnacle access what you copied. Format it to be readable on our hardware.*

For a moment, my breath stopped—choked off, like someone had clamped a hand over my nose and mouth. Both computers grinding against their natures to work together, short-circuiting my own brain's attempt to keep me alive.

I felt my body rock backward, tilt, and then the pain in my throat as a ragged gasp brought air back into my body. Red blotted my vision and for a moment I was aware of my physical body again, before I was dragged back into the quiet place that was filled with data and light-speed calculations.

I couldn't even muster the energy now to send commands to Sunny. She—I—was running too hot, trying to outlast Pinnacle. She/I was approaching the limit of our abilities.

No thought. Only intent. *Sunny. Megobari. Records.*

I felt something open up just beyond my reach, like double-clicking a file folder and having its contents display on the wrong screen, one I couldn't see. It was there, but I couldn't get to it. Who was accessing it? Pinnacle? Hanna?

Sunny's hold began to slip. I felt white-hot fire where Pinnacle was beginning to network to my brain, overcoming Sunny and even my own thoughts, reaching deeper. All wrong, running backward, electricity being forced back along the wire, overloading the circuit.

I couldn't take it. Sunny was slipping away. Burning out. I was losing my shelter from the data storm. Pinnacle was sweeping me away, my nerves sending alarms of pain straight into the space behind my eyes—my lungs choking off—my own connection to my body being severed as Pinnacle took my place—

And then a light bulb burst inside my skull, leaving only darkness.

TWENTY-FOUR

IT WAS OVER for several seconds before I realized everything had stopped: the noise, the panic, the feeling I was slipping away. The pounding pain in my head was only echoes. I realized distantly that my body was convulsing, and that my limbs were being restrained, but it was like it was happening to someone else, a dream I'd had and could barely remember.

Were my eyes open? I couldn't process any input of visual data. I couldn't control my body, only feel its reactions through a mist like a drugged hallucination.

In a blind haze, the sensations of my body in space slowly filtered in, one at a time. The weight of my torso on the bed. The weight of shoes on my feet. The chill in one of my hands. The rustling of my hair against a pillow. The tears cooling on my cheeks. *Thud-thud-thud* in my chest.

I am real. I am a real person, I told myself. I was a person with a body that was still beating, still breathing.

I tried opening my eyes.

The edges of the world were painted with a thick brush, every line sharp. It was like seeing in high-definition. The picture was crisp, clear, and hurt my eyes.

I blinked rapidly and the sharp lines blurred, becoming a 3-D movie, lines upon lines upon . . .

I groaned and closed my eyes again.

"Cassie!" Hanna's voice was a sharp spike in my ear. I felt her small hand slapping my cheek, the pain sharp. It made me angry. "Wake up! Open your eyes!"

"Hurts," I managed to gasp.

"Do it anyway."

I groaned louder, dragging my eyes open through sheer force of will. The world had gone back to being crisp and altogether too real.

I am real. I am a real person. I didn't know why I kept repeating it to myself, but it seemed necessary.

"What the hell happened?" Hanna demanded. "I felt Pinnacle making contact. You were losing control. It was overcoming both of you."

She was moving too fast, eyes blinking rapidly, lips forming shapes. But at the same time I could see it in slow motion, like I was in another plane of existence. Seeing with two sets of eyes.

"Too much." I tried touching my head with my hand, but I had to concentrate on where my hand was in space. Couldn't feel it move, at first. Had to squint open my eyes to be sure.

There was a humming sound in my ears like computer fans running. A spot on the side of my neck was hot.

"I thought I was going to lose you," Hanna said, and for some reason she was angry.

"Me too," Luka said, his quiet voice on my other side the first reminder of his presence. "It looked like you were having a seizure."

"I'm not a doctor, but the EEG readouts seem to think so, too. Damn it!"

I forced my eyes to focus, roving around the room to find Luka beside me. The world seemed to shift again, to align properly this time. Not ultrasharp lines poking holes through my eyes, not blurry 3-D-without-the-glasses world.

Uncharacteristic fear etched his features. I looked down and realized he was holding my limp hand with a death grip.

I didn't notice the feel of it until I saw it. His hand was warm and solid and soft and real, and reminded me that I was real, too.

With that dose of reality—that lifeline—I sat up gingerly and tried sorting through my brain to assess the damage.

"You guys really use Pinnacle on human beings?" I groaned. "It almost fried my brain."

"I had months to work up to it," Hanna said, a note defensive. "And you didn't just have Pinnacle. You were connected to them both at once. That, we've never tried. You were the one who said you could handle it."

I shook my head, still in a daze, and touched my forehead delicately. "Remind me never to do it again."

"I won't have to," Luka said, his tone the audible version of putting one's foot down.

"Did it at least work?" Hanna asked anxiously.

"I'm not sure. Did you . . . see anything . . . on the screen?"

"Just interference. We can check the recording."

Everything was fading, like a dream. I couldn't tell if my eyes were open or if my mind was conjuring their worried faces out of thin air.

"You're okay now, I think," Hanna said, and there was a note of fear in her voice. She and Luka both hoisted me to my feet. "No one has ever done what she just did." She spoke the words over my head, to Luka. Even angry and coming down off adrenaline, there was a note of awe in Hanna's voice, of excitement.

Luka's grip tightened on my arm as they led me through darkened rooms, the tips of my sneakers dragging because I couldn't find the energy to lift my own feet. "And no one ever will again."

"Lay her down here." Hanna's voice filtered through the haze of my consciousness. "She might go into a postictal state. Does your head hurt?"

I groaned, covering my eyes with my hands. "Leave me alone."

"Hanna," Luka said, as I felt my body lifted onto a bed as though it were happening to someone else. "Can you tell me more about Pinnacle? Why was it made? Why did they implant it? What was their goal?"

My eyes were closed and my skull was pulsing with fiery pain, but the deep rumble of his voice brought me just to the edge of consciousness.

Hanna's reply was quiet, as though she was trying not to wake me. I felt her fingers taking the pulse on my wrist. "It was the successor to PROPHET—the program you call Sunny. They started working on it after Project Adastra was completed." I felt hands moving my limbs, adjusting me. I couldn't lift a finger to help. "After Adastra, I was moved on to another project, called Adonis. Its goal was to find more people with Cassie's ability to interface directly with superintelligent computer programs like Sunny. I was one of those people."

"To what end?" Now he was smoothing the hair out of my eyes, which was sweet. I'd have to remember to thank him when I was awake.

"Crane is obsessed with the idea that you can download your conscious brain into a computer and live forever. We accidentally discovered while trying to make the old man immortal that networking an advanced-enough computer to the right kind of human brain for the right amount of time can help a sufficiently advanced computer learn to be more . . . human."

That was interesting. I struggled to follow her words through the slog of quicksand that was my mind. "So . . . smart

215

human plus smart computer equals . . ."

"An even smarter computer. A true AI." She took in a long breath, paused. "That's what I was working on with SEE. And Cassie and Sunny might be our first real success."

Assuming I survive.

TWENTY-FIVE

I WOKE DAZED and alone, hearing muted voices outside the door. I blinked slowly at the ceiling several times before remembering where I was, before I could even sense the weight of my body pressing into the mattress.

Sunny, are you still there? Everything okay? After last night, I had to check.

Cassie, all my systems are functional.

Sunny had been a much quieter presence in my head as of late—only responding to me when addressed directly. Not like she'd ever been conversational, exactly. She didn't interrupt my own thoughts or conversations nearly as much.

I was beginning to wonder how much of her brain was becoming *my* brain—where I ended and she began. Perhaps she was using minimal resources to communicate with me while also still attempting to carry out my commands to search the megobari data, or she no longer needed to communicate with me except with the most simplistic words.

Maybe my body was beginning to use her functions without my conscious command. Maybe, eventually, she'd cease to feel separate from me at all. Even now she was there in my mind, listening, or feeling whatever I was feeling, and I sensed no response from her.

It'd be fascinating to study what was happening in my brain right now—if I wasn't the test subject.

Slowly, I made my way down the hall, rubbing the sleep from my eyes. I'd slept like the dead. No dreams. No nightmares.

Everyone was gathered in the main room, looking pale and anxious. As soon as I entered, everyone rose. Luka leaped to his feet and came straight to me. "How are you feeling?"

"A little out of it. But okay. What time is it?"

"Around nine," he said, tilting my chin up to examine my eyes, to see if my pupils reacted to the light.

"Sorry we didn't wake you," Mitsuko said. "Luka thought you needed sleep after what you guys did last night."

That made Emilio's eyebrows shoot up. "What . . . you guys did?"

"With Pinnacle. Get your mind out of the gutter." Mitsuko shot him a glare. "We're just discussing what to do next."

"We got the mission records. Mitsuko and Emilio are working on a way to securely upload them, unedited, to the internet."

"Did we get what we needed, though? About the weapon?" I moved to sit at the table and Luka was two steps ahead of me, pulling out my chair. I made a face at him. "Luka, I'm not sick."

His concerned expression didn't abate.

"We were waiting on you for that." Hanna was also laser-focused on me. Both of them were treating me like they expected an alien to burst from my chest at any moment. "I checked it last night after you passed out. I believe we were successful. There's only one thing—"

Mitsuko got up and brought me a cold Pop-Tart. "Give her a few minutes to ease into it, would you?" To me she said, "You need to eat something, at least."

I pushed the plate away, stomach roiling. "No, we can't wait. Tell me."

"Oracle appears to have a copy of whatever you asked it to save. But I can't access it. I think—since Sunny was the original one who copied and encoded it—Sunny has to be the one to play it back."

My head was spinning. For a moment this all felt ridiculous—the five of us, with stolen and experimental tech, playing with things we didn't understand, guessing and making it up as we went along. *We* were going to save the world?

Yes, I decided. We were. Nobody else seemed to be doing a better job of it.

I waved my hands impatiently, trying to hide my nerves. "Let me try."

Hanna placed Oracle in front of me.

Hesitantly—reminding myself that without Hanna touching it also, this was just an output node, nothing like last night—I laid my hand into its warm surface, my fingers sinking in a little, just as before.

"Whoa," Emilio murmured. "This is some space-age shit."

The holographic screen flickered to life. I felt Sunny's increased awareness, warming me like dawn.

Here goes nothing.

"Sunny, please access anything that you are able to show us from the megobari archives," I said, speaking aloud for the benefit of the others. I doubted this would work. I'd tried this exact query multiple times already. "Specifically related to mentions of a weapon they were developing to end the war."

I felt—or maybe imagined—her gearing up, focusing, her intention sending nerve pulses down my arm, through my palm, into Oracle. And then the waiting, as she searched.

Then the startle as Sunny addressed me. *Search results found. I have attempted to translate from source language. Some data may appear corrupted. Display?*

Wait—Luka could understand the megobari language. *Sunny, try displaying in original language first, if you can.*

I set eyes on Luka. "Sunny's going to try to display what she can. Can you translate?"

He nodded, gaze fixing on Oracle's holo-display, face going pale. "I think—"

Before he could finish, a spherical shape appeared in strands of light on the holographic display, a rich rainbow of shifting colors. Before I could even decipher exactly what I was seeing, the shape twisted into dozens of tiny shattering rainbows, fluttering down and out, and were replaced by drops of colored light that jumped from one side of the display to the other. The spheres of color hopped like staccato notes, like music if one could see sounds, a crackling energy that shifted and changed almost before you knew what you were seeing, so only the fading echoes on your retinas were left.

It was beautiful, if completely nonsensical. I stole my gaze away just long enough to gauge Luka's reaction, but he was completely absorbed in the light, his eyes darting from side to side as if reading. His face gave no indication of what, if anything, the display meant.

It lasted only a handful of seconds, and then the light faded, the whirring shards of color fading into nothing.

Everyone was waiting for him to speak, left breathless by the display that we could not begin to translate. How would Sunny have translated *color* and *shape* and *movement* into English sentences?

"Well, what was it?" Mitsuko finally pressed.

He had to swallow a few times before answering, his throat bobbing and voice unsteady. "This is a message from one of the last surviving outposts, near the end of the war. They had bunkered underground, racing against time to find a way to repel the invaders. And they . . . they knew they were doomed, regardless of the outcome of the war. The losses were too much. The outpost had stopped receiving supplies and communication with the home world. This message was recorded by one of the last living scientists—a message left in case another species stumbled across it one day. It said that my people discovered a way to beat back the vrag, but it would cost them. It would cost them everything to use it."

"And did they?"

"I don't know. This person didn't know. They . . . died before finding out, I think." He cleared his throat again.

"Is that it?" Mitsuko asked, leaning her palms on the table. "That's the message they left for us across all space and time? A warning? They don't even say what it is, what it does? An instruction manual would be helpful."

I shook my head. "It's a weapon of mass destruction. It's meant to kill a lot of things all at once. Something so terrible that it should only be used as a last resort. Or never."

Luka was staring into space. His voice was quiet, pleading. "Why *didn't* they use it?"

"Maybe they didn't get a chance," Hanna said darkly.

That made us all go quiet.

"Maybe it didn't work?" Emilio asked.

"Or they built more than one," I said. "We built more than one A-bomb, after all. Maybe this was their backup plan. Or . . . one of many?"

"That seems like something they would do," Luka agreed, but his brow was still furrowed in confusion. Instead of getting angry, he was closing himself off.

"So . . . are we any better off than we were before?" Emilio asked.

"Sunny, pull up anything you can find about what the weapon actually *does*," I said.

A singular held breath tied us all together as we waited for something to happen. And then a chaotic array of colors flittered across our retinas, incomprehensible to all but one.

I watched Luka—watched his eyes. They darted side to side, speed-reading what appeared to be an immense amount of information for how long the light show went on.

"What the hell does it say?" Mitsuko muttered.

Luka was too busy reading to respond.

"It's probably like a bee trying to describe the color of ultraviolet light to a human. You know, if bees could talk, I guess," Emilio said.

The light show blinked off suddenly and Luka pulled away from the group, turning his back to us.

I went to him and he pulled away from me, a hand riffling his hair. His other hand clenched, as though he were restraining himself from punching something. "My family died retrieving this. They wanted to bring it back here because they thought it was our only hope. But we would have been better off leaving it behind."

"It's not a weapon?" Mitsuko demanded.

"It doesn't work?" Hanna asked at the same time.

His shoulders tensed, his breathing erratic. "It is a weapon. It does work. And if we turn it on, it will kill every living thing on this planet."

TWENTY-SIX

"THEY MADE SKYFALL hoping to stop the war," Luka began. "To drop it on the vrag home world and detonate it remotely, rendering their planet sterilized and uninhabitable." He looked as though his spirit had left his body, eyes empty. "They never apparently got a chance to use it."

I squeezed his shoulder, but he might as well have been made of marble for how much it seemed to help.

"Our very own doomsday device," Mitsuko said.

Luka explained a little further. It worked the way all megobari tech worked: a direct neural link. Either via touch, or remote connection with the help of their implants, using some kind of password or code to overcome the firewall. That's what I got out of it, anyway. He didn't understand the exact mechanism;

the technology was beyond his experience. The megobari scientists who developed it had reached deep into theoretical physics, motivated by desperation. "The result is some kind of catastrophic destruction of the planet's atmosphere, something destabilizing enough that the entire biosphere collapses."

It was Emilio who gave it its name: Skyfall. Because it was about to bring all hell raining down on us.

I squeezed my eyes shut, hands ripping at my hair. "It's a planet-killer. And we brought it here."

We'd come back to save Earth. And we were the ones who'd destroy it.

"Unless it's detonated in space, yes. Then it may only affect a small area, depending on how far away from life-forms it is used," Luka said. He wasn't looking at any of us as he spoke, but focusing somewhere on the middle of the table. His fingertips traced the wood grain absently.

"So . . . we should destroy it. Or should we leave it in the desert and hope nobody finds it? Hide it? Bury it?" I asked. The flame of panic had been relit inside me. *We* had brought this threat back. *We* had put Earth in the crosshairs.

Luka was glaring into an untouched cup of herbal tea at the kitchen table, away and apart from the rest of us. "We can't destroy it without igniting it."

Emilio was leaning over, elbows on his knees, legs bouncing, brow furrowed. Mitsuko kept glancing at her phone, swiping it unlocked and then clicking it off again. Hanna was the only one who appeared to be listening to me.

But this was on us—on Luka and me. Not them. This solution was my responsibility. Luka was lost in the mire of his own guilt, so I had to deal with mine alone, assuming I had the luxury to work it out later.

Three hours left until the vrag blew up a city because I couldn't figure out what to do. Turn myself in, leave the weapon for the coming megobari to use? Turn myself in, leave my friends to clean up our mess by getting rid of the most dangerous weapon on Earth? Turn myself in, hope for the best?

Doomsday device.

I had to fix this. "So what do we do? Can we turn it against the vrag without hurting ourselves?"

"We cannot aim it—it is not a gun," Luka said. "It would explode like a dying star, throwing radiation in every direction." He met my eyes only for a moment. "However . . . it is possible we could still use it. If it's inside the vrag ship, and we could get it far enough away from Earth, it might be possible to detonate it remotely while leaving Earth intact."

"I vote for that option," Emilio broke in, leaning back and drumming his fingers on the empty chair beside him. "If anyone's asking."

"But the vrag ship's in orbit. Would low Earth orbit be far enough away?" I asked.

"No. Not if you wanted to ensure there would be no casualties. If it explodes in orbit, the vrag ship would rain debris down on the surface, likely in pieces too large to burn up on reentry."

"So . . . you are saying we'd have to basically trick the vrag into taking it, without them knowing we were just handing it over, and also make them get out of town, and yet still somehow detonate it. How do you expect that to happen?" Luka's eyes locked with mine, and I knew suddenly what he meant to do. "You . . . just want to give it to them."

"No!" Emilio almost laughed, thinking I was telling a joke, and then slowly realized I was not. "That's—dude, that's the exact opposite of what we've been trying to do."

"I will turn myself in," Luka said calmly, still not looking away from me. "I will fly the droneship into orbit, taking the weapon with me. They should not have reason to stay here once they have me. When I am inside the ship, I can detonate the weapon. If I am unable to do so . . . Cassie can do it for me from here."

"Um, no?" Mitsuko said, grabbing Luka's shoulder so that he was forced to turn toward her. "Even if we forget that either one of those successful outcomes leads to you being on the vrag ship when it explodes, what happens if neither of you are able to detonate it? Then you've given the vrag our only weapon and it's all over."

Luka didn't speak.

"No. Gotta be a better way." Emilio riffled his hand through his hair. "I just—give me a minute, I'll think of something."

Luka's family believed this weapon was the only thing that could save us.

But did we have another option? I tried to think of any human organization that I trusted to give this weapon to and came up empty. Human beings as a rule did not have a great track record with weapons of mass destruction. No one person should have the power to wipe out so much life at once.

"We can't take the risk of giving Skyfall to the vrag," I said decisively. "And we don't have the luxury of time right now to think of an alternative way to use it. Our main priority is to prevent the vrag from attacking us." I bit my lip; all my limbs were trembling with the knowledge of what I would have to do. "The only way we can do that is to give in to their demands."

"What?" Emilio and Mitsuko screeched at the same time, both jumping to their feet.

"Can you think of another way to prevent them from killing more innocent people?" They were silent. "Look, I don't intend on this being a suicide mission. We've survived two encounters with them before. We can do it again." That was stretching the truth, but they didn't have to know that.

"How are you going to get away, Cassie?" Mitsuko asked quietly. "Once they have you, then what?"

I smiled halfheartedly. "We don't know what they want us for. Maybe they just want to talk?" It was as brazen a lie as I'd ever told. I felt Hanna's laser stare, seeing right through me. "But we leave the weapon here. Okay? You guys are the only ones we can trust with Skyfall. If . . . something happens to us, Hanna can fly it into orbit and trigger it. Whether we are up there or not, understand me? She has Pinnacle; I think it works the same way." Hanna's eyes flashed, surprised.

"How will we know if you're okay?" Emilio asked.

I reached in my pocket for the communication device that Luka had given me, opened it, and tossed it to him. "Luka has the other. If we're able to communicate, we'll let you know what's happening. If you don't hear from us . . ."

Hanna nodded, her face solemn. "I'll do what is necessary."

"I can't believe we're having this conversation," Emilio muttered darkly.

"It's either this or we leave Skyfall in the desert."

Luka stood, his chair scraping loudly against the tile. "No."

Our eyes locked. Hurt swam beneath the surface of anger and cold determination on his face. I hadn't anticipated this reaction. "You can't tell me it'd be better to give it to Crane. Or the government. Your people wanted to use it against the vrag. Isn't this what they wanted?"

"That weapon doesn't belong to you." And what trickled cold down my chest wasn't the anger in his voice, it was the lack of emotion. He was drawing himself back. The way he'd been trained to do around humans.

I felt suddenly as though he and I were on opposite sides of a wide gulf, an insurmountable distance, even though we were only feet apart. "If we do not use the weapon, it must be given back to my people when they arrive. Megobari technology. Megobari only should decide what to do with it."

There was such force in his words that I felt my cheeks heat. "But it affects humans. It's on our planet. It could kill all of us. We should get a say in what happens to us, shouldn't we?"

"What makes you think you can trust these aliens more

than you can trust humans?" Hanna asked archly. She was still standing over the chair beside me, Oracle now deactivated on the table in front of her.

Mitsuko had been across from me, anxiously biting her thumbnail, but suddenly pushed her chair out and went to the kitchen to wash dishes.

Luka shot a look of venom over my head at Hanna. "My people are the only hope your people have of survival."

"From how I understand it, your people are the only reason my people are in danger to begin with."

He took the blow and gave it right back to her. "Humans have been killing this planet since they arrived at the top of the food chain. You pumped poison into the air and increased the temperature of Earth's atmosphere within a hundred years of your civilization discovering industry. Your leaders demonize and ignore scientific evidence so they can line their own pockets. People in your own country die from hunger and disease because your government blames them for being poor. You turn away innocent people escaping poverty, persecution, and war. I don't know why my father thought you might accept our people, but for the fact that we sought to help you in return. You can't even reproduce now without the intervention of science. Your species is dying out. How are your people equipped to deal with this decision of life and death better than mine?"

"My people didn't invent that weapon in the first place."

A loud metallic crash split the air, making everyone jump— Mitsuko, dropping a frying pan into the sink. "That's enough. You two—take a break. Go to your rooms and cool off."

"You have no authority over me," Luka said, his hands clenched over the back of the kitchen chair.

"What he said," Hanna retorted.

"We're all under a lot of pressure here, and you're not helping. Don't come back until you can learn to get along like the highly evolved life-forms you are."

With a final scrape of the kitchen chair as he jerked it out of his way, Luka left the room without another word.

Hanna picked up her things, calm and collected, and also left without so much as a parting word.

"So much for human-alien relations," Emilio muttered.

"If this is the best we can do, we won't even need an alien invasion. We'll tear each other apart before a single bomb is ever dropped." Mitsuko's voice was dripping disgust, and she was scrubbing the kitchen counters with a vengeance.

"Do you think Luka was right? Should we give the weapon to the megobari?" I felt suddenly like the ground I was standing on might crumble beneath my feet at any moment.

Mitsuko came in from the kitchen, still drying her hands with a dishcloth like she wanted to wring its neck. "It's too early to make decisions. This is bigger than all of us. Right now we have to focus on what we can do to stop the vrag from hurting anyone. The megobari aren't here yet; we can deal with them when, and if, they become an issue."

"You guys—you know I have to do this."

Emilio shook his head vehemently. "No, I don't know that," he said, voice breaking.

"I can't be a coward and risk innocent people," I said gently, feeling the deep well of regret and sorrow threatening to swallow me. "I have to go."

Emilio nodded and swiped at his eyes, his Adam's apple bobbing as he cleared his throat. "Yeah . . . so, who elected us to be in charge again, exactly? Because I'd like to abdicate."

"Me first," I whispered, swallowing back tears.

Luka was pulling away from me—and, I felt, from humanity as a whole.

But he'd just lost his family and he was alone. That would do a number on anyone.

I just didn't know what to do to help him. Maybe there was nothing I could do.

Except that wasn't a concept I could accept. And we didn't have much time left.

I opened the door to his room without knocking. He was standing in front of a bookshelf in the far corner, and startled at my entrance.

I closed the door behind me and stepped into the room.

"We have to turn ourselves in to the vrag," I said, adamant. "Soon. Now. Emilio's out there putting together the footage of the Adastra mission so that he can broadcast it worldwide. Mitsuko's going to figure out how to secure the transmission so that it's anonymous. Everyone will know what happened on that moon, and what the vrag are capable of. That should, hopefully, mobilize everyone against them. We just need to figure out what to do with that weapon when we leave, because I'm not so sure we'll be coming back."

He watched me steadily with that same expression he always wore, neutral but with engaged interest, like a concerned doctor listening to a patient. Then a slight furrow creased his brow.

We were dancing a strange, distant dance now. What we used to be, what we might have been a million years ago seemed to hover in the air like a ghost between us.

"Cassie, I am going to turn myself in. Not you." He crossed the room and caught my shoulders in his hands, and released me almost immediately, as if he regretted the action. "You have endangered yourself enough on my account. And Hanna is correct. My people were the ones who brought this danger to your doorstep. Let *me* try to fix it. You need to stay here. Find a way to use Skyfall."

I was the fail-safe. Again.

"Some part of me feels like you never came back," I whispered. "Like you're still back on that moon."

I knew they were the wrong words, as his face changed into something dark and troubled. "I'm sorry, I didn't mean—"

"A large part of me never left that moon, Cassie." His eyes were storm gray, clouded. "A large part of me died on that moon."

"I'm sorry. I keep thinking I could've . . ."

"Don't." He reached out, hand gripping my fingers as if to physically stop me.

"Part of all this is my fault."

"Why? I was the one who pushed you into the escape hatch."

"Exactly. If I hadn't been there, you could've stayed with your family—helped them to escape, instead of me."

His hand released mine, head tilting. "You think that? My father ordered us to abandon ship. Not because we were in the way, but because he wanted to save us. He would've remained on that ship regardless of what you or I would have done. There was nothing else we could've done except die with them. He didn't want that. Our ultimate mission was too important."

"You're remarkably composed about it."

"It's the only way I can make it right. Make it matter. We're alive right now to accomplish something."

"To save Earth?"

"And get revenge."

I knew Luka was conflicted. He viewed the vrag as monsters to be eradicated. I knew revenge motivated him—I wasn't exactly on their side, either, but if push came to shove, which would he choose? Avenging his family or saving Earth? What if there was a way to do one without the other?

Unlike Luka, I couldn't think of revenge.

He lingered before me, both of us caught in something, as the storm in my chest grew stronger, a ball of repressed emotion filling my lungs until I thought they might burst.

"Cassie." He said my name again, except this time it was gentle, softer, and the entire mood of the conversation shifted into unfamiliar territory. "You know that I care about you."

I sucked in a breath. Focused on the hollow of his throat, because I couldn't meet his eyes.

I wanted to say it back to him—if this was truth-telling time, it was my last chance. But would he feel deceived if I told him I cared about him, too, but didn't feel a pressing need to make out with him? Would we even have enough time together for it to matter?

Unable to find the right words, I reached for his hand and held it tight, hoping the gesture would say enough.

He squeezed my hand in response. "Please, Cassie. This all began with my people. I feel responsible to end it."

"They put a price on *both* our heads," I said quietly.

"They will be content with only mine. Trust me."

"I'm not going to let you do this by yourself. You know that."

He shook his head. Then, with a moment's hesitation, he closed the narrow space between us and pulled me into him. "You can't pilot *Penelope*."

I circled my arms around him and squeezed my eyes shut, reveling in the comfort of the embrace. But it felt like an ending, not a beginning. "Then I'll go with you."

His arms tensed over my shoulders. "Cassie, please. Let me go."

I clenched my fists and leaned away to look him in the eye. "But they'll kill you!"

"Perhaps not right away. I think it's more likely they'll use me as bait or a bargaining chip for the megobari that are coming."

Panic, fear, helplessness rose in my throat, choking me. I laid my head on his shoulder and tried to seal the feel of him in my memory forever. "I don't like this."

"I know."

"I'll find a way to get you back from them."

His voice was rueful. "I expected as much."

I craned my neck to see his face. "Luka . . . what should I do about the weapon?"

He sighed deeply. "Learn more about it. What it does. How to use it."

"I won't use it. Not while you're on board."

His eyes hardened. "If you have the chance, and you have no choice, then yes—you will. My life is a small price to pay for all of Earth. My father knew this truth, and so do I."

He held my face in his hands.

And then he told me where he'd hidden Skyfall.

TWENTY-SEVEN

I WENT BACK to the living room. I didn't tell Emilio or Mitsuko what had happened. Numb on the outside, panicked on the inside, I let them show me what they'd come up with for a secure uplink. Meanwhile, I was playing out strategies for how to maneuver this, how to win, and scrapping them, one after another. Not even Sunny could help me. We were both coming to the same conclusion.

All that was left was the one plan that I never wanted to consider.

They were both oblivious, luckily. "So we've rigged it all up—nobody will know where the upload originated from, but it will look like it came from NASA," Mitsuko said.

"How did you manage that?" I asked.

Emilio gave me a grin. "I hijacked Colonel Pierce's computer. It'll seem like it's coming from him directly."

"Will this get him into trouble?" I asked, concerned. We didn't need any fire coming down on him, too. "What if we just asked him to share it himself, and that way he can vouch for the veracity of the recordings?"

"Pierce is a *worldwide hero*. They can't do anything to him officially—he's the first man on Mars! People love him. Every word out of his mouth makes headline news. But asking him directly to vouch for us will take too much time, and what if he says no or starts asking questions?" Emilio typed frantically on the keyboard. "I've got it all queued up. As soon as I hit this button, the raw, unedited mission records—everyone's helmet cams all the way through to when we lost the footage—will hit the internet through Pierce's computer. I wrote up an intro and closed-captioned it all so people know what they're viewing, but otherwise, everything will be out there."

I let out a slow breath. *Everything.* People would doubt it, of course. Claim it was fake. But maybe enough of them would see. Enough scientists and government officials with backbones would come out in support, especially if they thought Pierce was behind releasing it. They would see the vrag for what they were.

What would happen next? Open war?

"That's awesome, guys. Well done. There's just . . . one more thing I need you to do." I took a shaky breath. Steeled myself. And I gave them the coordinates to find Skyfall.

Maybe they'd try to find another way. But we were out of time.

This time there'd be no plan B.

When I returned to Luka's room, I found him missing.

He'd slipped out of the house when no one was looking, through an exit only he must've known about.

I caught up to him a few hundred yards away. He was hard to miss—there wasn't anywhere to hide out here.

All he did when he heard my steps was shake his head ruefully and offer me a sip from his canteen. "I knew you had let me go too easy."

He hadn't brought anything else. He didn't think it necessary.

A heavy sickness in my gut grew denser the longer we walked, reality settling in over me. I didn't *want* to be doing this. I didn't *want* to leave my friends without saying good-bye, or leave my family wondering what had happened to me. But I also didn't want Luka facing his worst enemy alone. Or leave others to clean up a mess I had a hand in creating.

We'd left the house far behind, and the heat was dragging my steps even more than dread, when I asked him: "Are we going to make it in time?"

"I hijacked a satellite to send them a message. They know we're coming."

He was making a beeline for a massive rock, almost a hill in and of itself, half buried in the sand with scrub brush clinging to its bare edges. "Hey, uh . . ."

But I didn't get a chance to finish my question, because the rock suddenly shimmered and became . . . not a rock.

"Nice disguise," I said as I followed him to *Penelope*'s hatch. "You even had me fooled, and I was looking for it."

He touched its pale blue surface, and the ship let us in.

TWENTY-EIGHT

THE COMPUTER'S 3-D printer scanned our bodies and formed us new space suits, skintight black with veins of shifting iridescent blue, like an abalone shell, with helmets to match.

Hopefully we'd have time to get good use out of them.

Luka and I stood on the bridge in silence as he began the lift-off procedures. Not wanting to distract him but not wanting to be alone, I turned inward to Sunny. *What do you calculate our odds of survival to be, Sunny?*

Her response was cryptic and immediate. *Given the outcomes of your last two encounters with the vrag, and the damage done to the hull of* Penelope *at the last skirmish, it is statistically unlikely you will survive another encounter.*

Great. *How about you just play some upbeat music for me, Sunny?*

Sunny chose a piece out of my memory, a piece I'd once played for competition. And so, with Shostakovich's "Festive Overture" filling my senses, we lifted off from the ground in a spray of fine sand, upward through the thin veil of Earth, and into the deep black to meet our destiny.

The vrag ship appeared on our view screen just as the final triumphant notes of the overture were fading from my mind, banishing the last fleeting moments of joy from my heart.

Shaking, I placed my hand over Luka's. He turned over his palm and enveloped my hand in his.

Sunny, can you use my suit to interface with the ship and translate what's happening? I asked. I lightly rested my other hand on the console.

Yes, Cassie, came her response. *We are on a collision course with the vrag ship. T-minus seven minutes to impact.*

"Luka," I whispered. "Can you do that thing that your dad did once before? So we can see?"

He gave me the barest sideways glance; our helmets prevented much peripheral vision. Then he coded the order into the console and the entire bridge became transparent.

I turned my eyes to the endless universe spread out around us. The breath stopped in my body. It was a sea of death, yes; it would kill me in an instant and without a thought; it contained glittering wonders and gnawing horrors, unimaginable heat and deathly cold, things so large I could hardly even conceive of them. It cared nothing for me, for my beating heart or my dreams or what I loved. It contained everything in existence and yet it was defined by its vast emptiness. Humans could pick a direction and travel it for their entire race's existence and see nothing else but blackness ever again.

But out of the corner of my eye I could just see a sliver of brilliant, shining blue. The only color in the vast darkness. Our lush island marooned in this sea of death.

It was no wonder we now had interstellar refugees paddling up to our shores, ready to fight for a chance to cling to our lifeboat.

My jaw set, I turned from Earth and set my eyes forward.

Traveling a thousand miles an hour, with the behemoth of Earth spinning with deceptive slowness beneath us, the shadowed ship that was like a blot of ink came upon us much too quickly.

"Any change in the vrag ship, Sunny?" I said the words aloud, but softly.

Sunny didn't respond right away, which sent panic pushing against me like a tidal wave, trying to get in.

She was a computer. Anything that took longer than a nanosecond to calculate was a much bigger problem than I was going to be able to handle.

I held my breath until Sunny's ever-calm voice filtered through my mind. *Cassie, the vrag ship is powering up.*

My legs shook and I squeezed Luka's hand. A lizard-brain instinct, knowing I was doomed, still readied my body to fight.

But there was nothing to do. The vrag ship was a planet

and we were an asteroid. Our ship was a limping, injured bird compared to the beautiful, terrible monstrosity of a raptor looming ever larger. Its edges bled into the blackness of dark space behind it.

This was where I was going to die. "Powering up what?" I asked. Luka glanced at me.

Unknown.

"We should brace ourselves," Luka said quietly.

I closed my eyes and tried to bring up the picture of Earth as it was, glittering and calm behind me, unaffected by what would happen here. Only my heart seemed unable to accept reality; it was leaping and galloping like a stampeding stallion, driven by adrenaline and some base need to believe I could do something to survive this.

Nothing happened. *Nothing* stretched out in a long, long moment, for which I kept my eyes screwed tight, assuming time was simply expanding by some strange rule of relativity for my last seconds, giving me the illusion that I had more time than I did.

When it had been too long and I didn't feel dead yet, I opened my eyes. Death didn't appear to be on a collision course with me. In fact, we didn't seem to be on a collision course with anything. The vrag ship was still growing in the distance, but it didn't appear to be as fast.

"Sunny, why aren't we dead?" I whispered, not loud enough to tempt fate. I still wasn't sure death wasn't about to take my next breath.

Cassie, the vrag ship seems to be influencing our course.

"They're pulling us toward them," I murmured in amazement. "They're not firing." I had to suppress a hysterical laugh. I was living all my childhood science-fiction TV show dreams. A tractor beam. Of course.

Luka squeezed my hand. "Not yet."

I felt like a fish being reeled in on a line, pulled inevitably toward an uncertain fate.

All the times in my life where I had been bored, restless, annoyed, angry, dismissive—I regretted them. All the times I should have realized what I'd had, enjoying the fact that I lived in a paradise of blue sky and green grass and limitless air, and that I was loved.

I regretted all that lost time.

The closer we edged to the vrag ship, our path steady, the more I realized how truly vast it was. I was staring at a giant floating skyscraper. No, it was so much larger than that—so much larger, I didn't have words. It filled our view screen and went on and on. Luka was right—if this fell to Earth, even in pieces, it would cause massive destruction.

We were matching pace with the vrag ship, aligning orbits, a complex and delicate dance that was being masterfully controlled.

I wondered if even Bolshakov could have done as good a job.

And then I remembered that this ship had murdered Bolshakov.

As we approached, a pod door slid open, revealing a

pitch-blackness in which you could have lost my city. My heart-beat took over every movement in my body, trembling in time.

Even though she wasn't a real person, I was glad Sunny was with me. Sunny couldn't feel fear. Her logical, unemotional programming was almost like bravery, and it steadied me.

And then it was happening. Our ship passed from darkness into darkness, to a space within space.

The pod door closed and there was a jolt as something—I assumed—attached to our ship, locking our orbits, sealing us to the vrag mother ship.

Well, we weren't dead. That was a good start.

I took a few steadying breaths, and then a few more, not quite believing I'd survived this far.

The darkness beyond the window was inscrutable.

They welcomed us in. Are they stupid? Or am I the stupid one?

The second one felt truer.

"Should we . . . wait? Or should we go out there?" We'd run off the edge of the map, and I had no idea what path to take now.

"No air in this chamber," Luka murmured.

I took in a steadying breath. Each one that passed seemed worth marking, savoring. I had a sinking feeling that my remaining breaths were short in number.

No use sitting around in the dark wasting them.

We exited the hatch and eased down the gangplank, my legs shaking even more than I'd feared. Our helmets' exterior lights came to life in the dark chamber surrounding us, piercing the darkness in thin white beams, illuminating a whole lot of nothing. Our beams of light scattered before they hit any edges.

Cautiously, we moved beyond *Penelope*, sweeping our flashlights across the floor. "What should we do?" I whispered.

"Find a door?" he whispered back. "Let's—"

Whatever he was about to say turned into a shout as Luka was swept away from me, flipped upside down and pulled upward as if by some invisible hand from above.

"Luka!" I screamed, aiming my light upward frantically. The echo of his scream had already faded, and there was no trace of him. My light couldn't find the top of the chamber. It was so far above me, it might as well have been the sky.

My heart pounded a violent rhythm against my ribs as I ran in circles, calling his name, searching for him in the dark. Minutes buzzed by before I realized it was fruitless. They'd taken him, snatched him right from my side. I was powerless. Stupid. Small.

Alone.

Heart refusing to give up, I choked back sobs and edged my way carefully forward, picking a direction at random. Had they not wanted me at all? Would I be doomed to wander here until I ran out of oxygen, alone in the dark, waiting for invisible hands to grab me?

It was a long time before my heart started to slow. I didn't have a plan, I didn't have a direction, but I couldn't stop. Maybe Luka was dead already, or maybe not. But I had to go after him.

Sunny's robotic presence in my head was not so much a tangible thing as a suggestion of company, but it was a comfort nonetheless. She couldn't help me as much as she could when tethered to a ship loaded with sensors, but she could help. Alone, but not alone.

I ventured farther into the darkness, afraid I was doomed to tread water in an inky sea until I drowned.

I let loose a scream of horror and frustration and fear. "If you want me here, you have to give me some indication of where to go!"

And then without warning, lights blazed to life, blinding me like a supernova had exploded before my eyes. As I blinked back stars, the room began to take shape around me in fits and starts, sharp lines glowing in polarized colors.

WELCOME, HUMAN CASSANDRA GUPTA.

The voice was so loud, so everywhere-at-once, like a roar of solid bass, I clutched at my head and folded into myself, falling to my knees. It wasn't for a few seconds that I realized my ears weren't ringing because I hadn't *heard* the voice.

It had been inside my head.

It had taken over every space in my brain. So much louder than Sunny's voice, who had only ever spoken calmly and quietly like a friend in my ear. This voice had no intonation, no inflection, more robotic even than Sunny, who had been programmed to be lifelike.

I wasn't sure I had even differentiated the words correctly. But it was so unlike Sunny that I knew it must be something different, speaking *through* her and directly into me somehow. Taking over her programming.

Had the vrag mother ship just welcomed me by name? It had to be a mistake. Some automatic computer function that had read my biosignatures. Luka had said this used to be a megobari ship, after all.

"What was that, Sunny? Did something just—"

WE WILL BRING YOU TO US.

What the hell was going on?

My bewilderment was premature, because at that moment, gravity inverted, and the world flipped upside down.

And then I was flying.

TWENTY-NINE

FLYING, OR FALLING? Really, one needed gravity to differentiate between the two, and I didn't have that luxury at the moment.

I was also screaming too loud for any logical thought to make itself known.

My stomach was ricocheting around my abdominal cavity, my muscles clenching reflexively against the pressure. Gray metal flew by me and I had the impression I was falling down hundreds of stories' worth of empty skyscraper.

Vaguely, in the back of my mind, some logic tried to tell me I couldn't be falling because we were in orbit—in space where there was no gravity—and whatever this was, was in opposition to the gravitylike force of earlier—but it was a little too hard, and pointless, to piece it together when I was speeding along the length of an alien mother ship like a girl-shaped bullet train.

I had the vague sense of passing through something pale blue and insubstantial, a barrier like the thin skin of a bubble, and wondered if my brain was just shutting down.

The flying/falling lasted only long enough for me to worry what might happen if I actually did puke, which way would it go—and then the strange jolt as gravity—or my body, or the environment—flipped on its head again.

My feet found purchase, but I fell hard to my knees, unable to keep my body upright with quivering muscles and a stomach that was dangerously close to reversing gravity itself.

Cassie, your perspiration and heart rate indicate stress. Attempt to slow your breathing.

Sunny, in my head. Her calm and unaffected voice was so unlike the turned-to-eleven boom of the Other. I hadn't had the presence of mind to ask for her help before.

I found I couldn't exactly form words, but she read my intentions. *Your suit is equipped with first-aid modules. Should I administer antiemetic neurotransmitters?*

"Do it."

Within seconds, the knots in my stomach eased, and I felt a steadiness seep into my quads, replacing the instability of my muscles. I climbed to my feet, unsteady as a newborn deer. "Thanks, Sunny. How did you—"

I stopped. Had to. Words left my brain.

I was surrounded by dozens—hundreds—of floating . . . things. Creatures, or plants, or something in between—some as small as fireflies, some as large as pickup trucks, clinging to pillars of pale stone that rose like redwoods all around me.

All of them glowing, pulsing, in impossibly bright fluorescent colors.

They filled the acres of space above my head, moving past me in undulating waves, unaffected by my presence, each going its own way. As I watched, the creatures would occasionally leap from one stone-tree to another, appearing to fly like nothing on Earth could fly, in pulsating waves of their bodies. They landed effortlessly, using long talons on the ends of their long arms to pierce the skin of the stone-trees and cling and crawl like rock climbers.

My attention was diverted as small orbs of orange and green lights blinked lazily by my face. I peered at the closest one. It could've fit in the palm of my hand.

It was *alive*. Cilialike protrusions fluttered as it moved through the air, like microscopic amoebas or pond scum, but macro instead of micro. A baby version of the massive creatures above?

I was standing on the floor of some bizarre alien ocean. Instead of salt water, space. Aliens like deep-sea creatures, creatures like jellyfish and octopuses and sea slugs that didn't have names in any human language.

A large one passed near my head, floating or flying or swimming by, as black as night but shot through with electric-blue streaks that pulsed violet in time with some mysterious beat. It was trailing translucent arms full of wicked-looking spines.

I ducked unconsciously. But the creature moved past, seeming unaware or unconcerned by the odd creature in a space suit.

How did these things move? They almost appeared to be swimming. Was this still a vacuum, or had I passed without notice into a chamber with some sort of atmosphere?

I looked up. And up, and up, and up, at the acres of space over my head.

About two or three stories high, silver arches that seemed ancient, with the aged patina of old metal, crisscrossed in the stone treetops. The arches seemed original to the ship, but the trees . . .

Dozens of tall, narrow spires reaching so high I couldn't see where they ended—like pine trees with branches that all reached upward instead of outward. Trees with no leaves, but whose topmost branches seemed covered with lichenlike growths of brilliant, tiny flowers.

The spires seemed out of place in the architecture, more organic and colorful than the otherwise black and metallic space. The creatures were living on the spires, smaller ones swinging among the weird upside-down branches and larger ones seeming to float between the trunks at the higher elevations.

Somewhere far above, blue light hummed and pulsed like something living, and open corridors branched off the arches into dark places I couldn't fathom.

I turned around to see an entire section of exterior wall was clear, a window the size of a skyscraper. And through the window, beneath an unimpeded and breathtaking view of the Milky Way, was a narrow slice of the bright and impossibly blue Earth below us, swathed in perfect white clouds.

I sucked in a breath, dizzy at such a view of the universe. But were these creatures even aware of it? They didn't appear to have faces, let alone eyes.

Was that why none of them were trying to kill me? Did they not sense me? Or was I not considered a threat?

It was almost as if an alien god had heard Earth sea creatures described to it and had re-created them in its own image. A drug-trip version of the sea.

As I studied them, I realized there were three different types of the weird sea creatures. There were the small buglike ones that moved slowly and clumped together in softly glowing masses in the branches and hovered in sparser numbers around me like dust motes.

There were the ones the size of my arm, sluglike and beautiful, crawling up the trunks of the tree pillars, glowing and flashing lazily in bright, colorful patterns.

And finally there were the ones the size of cars and trucks, formless shapes that seemed to be a central body and many yards of arms of varying sizes, some thin as hair, some thick like wire cables, some ending in sharp spines that were mainly kept tucked into the body.

These had bodies that glowed and changed, too, undulating as though they had no bones, but in the snatches of light their skin glittered and shone like something metallic, making me think they were covered in some layer of bony plating like inter-locking fish scales.

Which ones were the vrag? All of the above? None?

Sunny, talk to me, I thought, awe taking my voice away. *What am I looking at?*

Sunny stayed silent. I'd only ever known her to do that while struggling to calculate, and thought maybe this question was beyond her.

I changed tack. *Is there atmosphere in this chamber?*

There are nonearthlike atmospheric conditions at this level, Cassie.

They had themselves a little mini biodome here. Well, bio-cylinder, anyway.

One of the smaller octopuslike creatures, this one glowing rosy red tinged with pink edges, bumped gently into my arm. It instantly turned the bright emerald green of summer grass, as if in surprise, and then weaved its way past me, unconcerned.

I watched, mesmerized, as it defied whatever gravity was holding me to the floor. But it came close enough for me to see pulsing tubes among its tentacles. I searched my memory's cataloged index of sea creatures and thought I remembered that octopuses—or was it squid?—used jets of water to propel them-selves through the ocean. But if this was the aliens' method of floating, what did they use? Some form of compressed gas? I could feel nothing so delicate as air passing across my insulated suit, but anything more substantial would have given me some form of sensory feedback.

A thin, wirelike tentacle brushed my helmet as it passed, jolting me in surprise. Burning. Almost like a . . .

A static charge. These things were electric.

Shit shit shit.

"Sunny, you still there?" I asked out loud. "Did that mess with you at all?"

No, Cassie. Only a temporary power surge. I am still here.

I took a steadying breath and then an unsteady step toward one of the thick treelike trunks. I touched it gingerly with my gloved fingertips. It was solid. A few feet above my head, one of the sluglike creatures inched along the skin of the pillar, gliding slowly over small spots of color like tight, spiral fractals of flowers that glowed softly in the darkness.

Just then, a large octopuslike creature a shade of soft lavender pulsing with blue spots latched on to the pillar over my head with its long spike-ended arm.

Pebbles like metal shavings fell audibly onto my helmet. I brushed them away without taking my eyes off the creatures. My neck began to ache, but I couldn't look away.

None of these things seemed to notice me at all. Not that I would be able to tell what they noticed or didn't notice.

Something had brought me here. Something wanted me to see this.

Where do I go? I thought. *What am I supposed to be seeing here?*

As I watched, the lavender octopuslike creature above me speared into the stone again and again with its razor talons. Finally, one long talon drew out something glowing and wriggling, pierced onto its sharp blade. Swiftly, the creature brought the worm into the center of its body, to a circular mouth ringed with tiny razorlike teeth, and closed over it.

Shuddering, I backed quickly away. They hadn't been violent to me, but they were obviously dangerous. Those talons could cut cleanly through my space suit.

Where was Luka? Where had they taken him? And why?

I had to find him.

As I watched, I realized there was a pattern to their movements. The large ones moved slow and leisurely, but they were all coming to and from the same place: a large opening to the far right of the chamber.

I pointed my feet in that direction, toward an arch that looked as though it had been forcibly chipped away at, perhaps to make it larger.

The closer I came to the arch, the more a current thrummed up my body, warm and vibrating. It felt like the ship was encouraging me, saying *yes, yes, this way.*

This was not what I was expecting. But I didn't feel fear. No one had threatened me; I had been kept safe and welcomed in. I was suspicious, yes, and scared for Luka, but not yet afraid for myself.

Until I crossed under the arch, I was not afraid.

In the massive chamber, a grayish-white mass filled the entire space, suspended or hanging from some ceiling that was so high above I could not even see it, stretched out from wall to curving wall.

It was like some monster out of a child's nightmare. A horror with no face. Both a fat spider and its web, nearly the height of *Odysseus*, with thousands of legs the size of trees, each of them pulsing, reaching, circling, undulating. The overall color was pearlescent white, but with colors that danced under the skin of its many appendages.

It reminded me of auroras and lightning storms on Earth. Flashes of blue like crackling electricity traveling up one arm, fading into lazy green tendrils of color that dissipated as they neared the body's center.

A thousand scrabbling, reaching claws. I couldn't make sense of it beyond this. Too much movement, too much color; it was like an optical illusion in constant motion. A few thin, wirelike tendrils floated in the air, miles long. The glowing octopus creatures were beautiful mermaids compared to this—this monstrosity of a Lovecraftian horror. I couldn't decide if I was disgusted and repulsed or fascinated and enchanted. I was all things at once.

The horror of it dawning slowly, I was frozen to the spot, gaping.

But then one of the tendrils began snaking its way toward me and I fell backward in my gut instinct to get away, scrambling on my hands and feet like a crab, still unable to tear my eyes from it, sick chills breaking out over my skin as though I could feel the touch of these spidery legs crawling across my body like a hundred tarantulas with grasping claws—

The arm shot toward me, whiplike, wrapping multiple times

around my torso and stopping my retreat cold.

I gasped against the binding of my rib cage, trying to scratch or pull at the arm. But there was no response. I might as well have been trying to cut steel cables with my fingernails.

Cassie, she says to be calm. Sunny's ridiculously unperturbed voice came to me. *She wishes only to talk.*

I wasn't sure what to do until I realized that it held me firmly, not painfully. Waiting me out. I felt watched by the impossibly huge tarantula being despite it not having any visible eyes.

Gradually, I forced myself to see it as less horrible. Its arms never stopped waving and undulating, calm, gentle, patient. Now it was like seagrass in a tidepool. I had the bizarre thought that it was trying to calm me down.

Wait.

"Sunny—how *the hell* do you know what it wants?"

I realized with a sinking sensation that Sunny might not be Sunny anymore.

God-Mother communicates with electrical energy as I communicate with you, Sunny told me. *She is using considerable amounts of her energy to relay messages through radio bands.*

A creeping sensation filtered over my scalp as I realized what was happening. "Stop Wi-Fi-ing into my brain!" I shouted.

She wants you to be calm. She will give you reason to trust.

And with that, one of the larger, thicker arms moved closer. Held still, I could do nothing but watch as the arm—wider across than my own body twice over—unfurled some distance away from me and retreated, revealing Luka.

The arm holding me loosened, allowing me to cross the short distance and catch Luka's limp body as it fell. He looked just as he had when I'd last seen him, no worse for wear, helmet still intact. Whole and alive, condensation on the inside of his mask telling me he still breathed.

His eyes fluttered open as I knelt over him anxiously. He peered up at me with a grimace. "Cassie?"

Relief exhaled out of me in a rush. I bent over him, tightening my arms around his shoulders even as he struggled to sit up. I pulled away to let us both get to our feet but did not let go of his hands. "Are you okay?"

He seemed dazed. "I am . . . unhurt. What are we doing here?"

"I have no idea." Why had it taken him and not me? Why did it give him back? How could I even guess at the motivations of something I didn't understand at all?

Sunny's voice in my head stopped me. *God-Mother's wish is to communicate with you directly, Cassie, as you are now doing with me.*

"What, you mean like . . . letting that thing connect to my brain? No way!"

Luka, party only to my side of the exchange, looked alarmed, and then his eyes darkened with suspicion.

It is the only way she can explain why you are here, Sunny told me. *The vrag do not have verbal language. You will not be at risk, Cassie. I will protect your brain from undue influence.*

"You mean she has the capacity to control me?"

I do not know, but it is probable she has many skills beyond my capacity to understand.

"Mine, too," I agreed softly, looking up into the wide expanse of alien intelligence looming over us.

"You are communicating with your AI?" he asked.

"The thing, the alien . . . it and Sunny are . . . communicating through electromagnetic waves or something. Sunny calls it God-Mother, and God-Mother wants to communicate directly with my neurons like Sunny does."

"Cassie, *no*," he said, alarm sparking his eyes as he grabbed my hands. "This thing—*it lies*. I know only a little, but—I think this is the hive mind of these vrag. It's like a biological computer, pure nerve endings. You won't be able to go against its will."

A chill of fear went through me. And yet, I felt an odd surety that this was something I needed to do. Maybe it was Sunny's reassurance that she could protect me, or the fact that the vrag had had ample opportunity to hurt me and hadn't. "It brought me here, to you. It didn't hurt you, and it could have. It just wants to talk. If we can find a way to work this out peacefully, it's best for everyone, isn't it?"

"Cassie." His voice was flat with anger now, something I'd rarely heard from him. "Vrag *killed my family*. Don't let it in your mind. It's trying to trick you. It's given you no reason to trust."

"Did it try this with you?" I asked.

He pulled his hands from mine and put them to his face, turning away in frustration. "It . . . tried. I believe. I can't understand it in any form of words. It's . . . it's like being near a power plant, all raw electricity. I . . . felt . . . that it wanted to." He

261

turned back to me. "I did *not* let it."

"It didn't force you, then. You were its prisoner and you're still you—it hasn't tried to coerce you." I took his hands again. "Something's going on here. This isn't how I expected this to go. But we're trapped here on this ship unless we can communicate. I think it brought us here to tell us something. Don't you think we need to understand why?"

"Please don't do it, Cassie." He was shaking his head, pleading now. "Do not do this."

I couldn't believe I was considering it, but I was. Maybe it *was* God-Mother's weird electrical energy trying to coerce me. But more so it was my own curiosity. An alien species that was *so very alien.* Wanting to impart some secret knowledge to me. The chance of me coming all this way and then not seeing it through was pretty close to zero.

Did I trust a computer program to have the capacity to protect me like this? Did I trust that this computer program was not capable of lying or being manipulated? Should I trust Luka, or my instinct?

"Will you do it with me?" I asked. "Please. Think of Earth. If we can somehow avoid war and save Earth, this is worth doing. Isn't it?"

He shook his head, more pained than I'd ever seen him. "My family, Cassie."

I came closer, pulling his helmet against my own. "Don't you want to know why? To understand? To end the killing?"

His shoulders shook with repressed emotions. He was

shaking his head as he said, "I do not want to do this. But you're right. I see no other choice."

"Together, then."

He nodded, his eyes screwed shut.

Take off your helmet, Sunny said.

I took a breath. "It's safe? I can breathe?"

You can breathe, Sunny said. *God-Mother has altered the gas ratios of this chamber to make them nearer to Earth levels. But she cannot stay in this state for long.*

With trembling hands, and a sense of logic that was screaming at me that I was going to get both Luka and myself killed, I reached up and unlatched my helmet.

THIRTY

ONE OF THE wiry appendages floated gently toward me. I flinched. It wavered in front of me, waiting, patient.

Alarm bells were jangling in my head and my heart. But I was so intensely curious. I'd already lent my brain to Sunny and to Pinnacle. This would be an entirely new plane of existence, of communication.

I'd always wanted to go where mankind had never gone before. I only felt guilt that I was dragging Luka along, half unwilling. But whatever we might discover, I wanted us both to know it.

I nodded, more to myself than the creature—which couldn't see me anyway. "Okay," I whispered.

The hovering arm wavered. Waiting for express permission? How could it tell?

Cautiously, I lowered my head in offering. Luka did not move, head pressed into my shoulder, as if unwilling to see what was about to happen.

The tentacle advanced, making contact with the top of my scalp and threading itself, almost gently, through my coiled hair. The end split into even finer ends, and I felt a dozen tiny tingles like static pulling upward at my hair follicles. I shuddered involuntarily.

And then, all at once, like the flip of a light switch, I was no longer inside my body. I was joined with the immensity of a being older than me, who had traveled far and seen much, yet had no words to communicate to me.

At the same time, I felt distantly connected to Luka's body. I was aware of him, of his breathing, of his anxiety—the tone of his thoughts, if not the thoughts themselves. Whatever was happening directly to me was happening indirectly to him through our touch.

And then all at once I felt swept away from my consciousness and Luka's, both of us taken away from ourselves into the consciousness of another. Of something greater, larger.

Instead of words, I felt its intentions, as wholesome and pure and true as if they were my own. Her intent was to help and be helped. She was tired of endless war, of waging it alone and gaining nothing. Tired of hating and being hated.

Her emotions came across to me in a strange, floating sea, slowly at first: Fear. Curiosity. Anger directed outward, not at me. Distrust of Luka and confusion over his intentions. Hope, and despair. I knew without words that she was revealing herself to me on purpose, and that she read similar emotions in me.

God-Mother was tired. God-Mother was dying. Too many budding cycles, too far from her home star. She was afraid for her people. Her children, in fact. All the vrag that were left, all the creatures I had seen, had all budded from her considerable body as the tiny firefly polyps had grown into the indescribably bizarre and beautiful creatures that flew through stone trees. I felt and somehow saw without seeing, like my mind flashing on a dozen security screens at once, multiple caverns like the one I had left: room after room of this ship, repurposed, filled to the brim with stone trees and thousands of vrag floating among them. I felt God-Mother's knowledge and awareness of each one, how she knew the status and location of all her children within range.

They each were a separate, individual entity, and yet also all part of one whole, and that whole was God-Mother.

She had carried them, the last of them, across the oceans of stars. But they did not live as long as she. Generations had lived and died in this ship, cycles upon cycles, until even the memory of their home trees and stars had faded, and she was the last one alive who remembered.

I saw how she stopped telling her children the truth, because it was too sad to teach the young ones again and again what they had lost, what they would never understand and would never achieve again. Her children didn't live as long as she did. Cycles lived and died, lived and died, and she let history be forgotten.

She let them live shadowy lives aboard their stolen space-craft, happy in ignorance, stealing a half life that she alone knew was a sad replica of what had once been and that she knew could not last indefinitely.

God-Mother's intentions turned dark, sad; black and gray like smoke. In my mind, memories that were not my own unfolded like opening flowers. A sense of peace came over me, butter yellow tinged with brown. She showed me the planet on which she was born: the home trees that from her small view seemed to pierce the hazy stars, which to her eyes were twinkling stones always out of reach.

There was light, and wind, and food to be found in plenty in the trunks of the stone trees that the polyps built over their many generations. These trees were bright and colorful, swatches painted like abstract masterpieces, the evidence of many years of the contributions of the pupae.

God-Mother's children inhabited the trees around her, living in peace, spending their days searching out the grubs that grew in the thick bark.

The young polyps, her newly budded children, ate the fungi and deposited layers of energy-laden substrate onto the trees as they grew, strengthening them as the grubs ate them from within. The polyps fed the trees, the grubs ate the trees, the juveniles and adults ate the grubs. It was a circle of life-giving that was in balance, and God-Mother was well and innocent and content with her new family and their place in their world.

I felt God-Mother's own body as though I had lived in it, the world awash in the joyful and carefree colors of her budded-off children growing and flying around her, in eyes that could see little but swatches of color. Like a watercolor painting, animated in slow motion. She had no desires but a continual existence. She had no ambitions of conquest. Her children knew only what she told them, and she told them *the sun is bright, the trees are full of grubs, be at peace.*

The vrag clung to the trees using their talon-tipped arms, glided from branch to branch with their air valves and long, strong arms. Even though God-Mother was too big and slow and remained suspended in her branches, high in the shelter of the treetops, she—and I—felt the lightness of them all, the low gravity giving little resistance.

The vrag communicated with each other through light and color on their skin, occasionally connecting specific messages through direct neural links with the trailing ends of neurons that floated like cat's whiskers, well past their bodies. And when necessary, God-Mother could call them all together, warn them of danger, or pass along commands with her special ability to send shortwave radio signals. She was the transmitter; they were the receivers. When needed, God-Mother could call to the other leaders like herself, such as during breeding cycles. But she never got the chance.

Each memory was like a snapshot; an image contained with feeling and emotion and understanding. The next came without warning, blending seamlessly and jumping ahead in time.

God-Mother was showing me what she wanted me to know.

The vrag did not have eyes like humans. I saw through her visual memory only smears of the bright colors of her home and her people. So when the Others arrived, I knew them only as she had known them: as upright columns of black, moving over the land in jerky, solid movements, lacking grace. The Others were strange in their lack of color. To God-Mother, who survived by her sense of color, they had no faces and no voices. Emotionless, inscrutable. Terrifying.

God-Mother tried communicating with them, but their colors did not change. She tried reaching out with her neural tails, but her tails bounced off their rubbery skin and smooth heads.

In the part of my mind that was still just my own, I had a sinking feeling as I realized what had happened. I had an even darker feeling about what I was about to see.

The next memories were not images; her world was now ink black. She was in the dark for a very long time. But because she was God-Mother, and all her children had once been a part of her body, she could still sense their energy while they were nearby. She had the many neural sensor cells in her body directed outward, searching, hoping, listening so hard. Some of her children were nearby. She was lost in the dark, and so were they, and they were full of confusion and pain and hurt and hopelessness, and they cried out to her. She tried sending messages of comfort, but received no response.

God-Mother knew it was the fault of the Others. The Others had done this. They had trapped her and enough of her family that she could feel them around her. She sensed the ones who had escaped capture like missing limbs and mourned for them. They would soon die without her, cut off like severed fingers, unable to function alone.

The Others kept her cut off, too, lost and blind in the dark. For her, it was complete sensory deprivation. They did not touch her much after the beginning, perhaps sensing her ability to manipulate energy. All she could do for a very long time was listen to the wailing cries of her children, unable to help them.

Until the cries stopped.

The silence, she realized, was worse.

Now she was even more alone.

Was she the only one left?

Her body was trying to replace the lost ones. But she repressed the reflex. There should be no young born into this place of death and darkness.

Until They came back. They gave her light. They gave her food.

She did not want either, but her body craved both.

They made her give them more of her children.

In my mind, in her memories, God-Mother railed and moaned without voice, bright red and fiery purple like lightning, her sorrow and helpless fury so palpable and heartrending that I heard myself cry out. Giving voice to her pain where she could not. Letting her use my mouth. Sharing her pain.

This memory lasted long. God-Mother did not know how

long she was held captive. How many children were taken from her. She stopped hearing their cries; they were taken too far away, out of range. She didn't know what happened to them.

Not until much later.

She was not the only God-Mother of her people. No, of course, there were many. She had come from one herself. But the Mothers rarely ever met. Each family had its own territory. That was best, or else there were fights over the best trees and the most space. There had been wars, occasionally, but she had been young then and her family small.

God-Mother languished alone, in a place lacking all color. She was desperate for some response from her children.

She waited and hoped to die.

All at once, her darkness was split with blinding light. There was chaos—rumblings so loud she could feel them vibrating from one arm, all the way through to the next. Suddenly, color! An explosion of color so loud God-Mother was stunned by it. She almost did not remember how to reflect her own colors. Her body had been sickly beige and lifeless for so long.

She was freed by children not her own. A fellow God-Mother, one whom she had never met, had not even sensed, had broken her people free. For the first time in so long, God-Mother felt the touch of another of her people, her neurons crackling with the electricity of community, blazing to life again, sharing the story of their liberation.

For the first time in their communal memory, the Mothers

joined forces. They directed their children to fight back.

God-Mother shared only the vaguest notions of these memories. The fighting. The killing. The endless and growing war. How she had more children—many more—born into death, sent to fight as soon as they grew large enough. She birthed legions.

They were not a warlike species. Their talons were for gripping, their poison for hunting, their scaly hides tough and specially designed to protect from the intense radiation of their star and thin atmosphere.

They were, accidentally, the perfect soldiers. They could survive nuclear bombs. Their boneless bodies could fit into spaces no megobari would expect, their skin changing colors to conceal them. The Mothers could bud thousands of children in weeks, their fast life cycles allowing juveniles to mature quickly. They could communicate instantly and silently with their children, their language in radio waves, directing them with machinelike perfection.

War was against their nature, but God-Mother's nature had been forever changed. Now she knew hate. Now she wanted revenge.

Their poison, she quickly learned, killed many megobari. Their bladed arms cut them down with ease. The vrag were ideally suited killing machines, each family a self-regenerating guerrilla unit, acting independently of each other, unpredictable and destructive.

Sensing the depth of my understanding, God-Mother brought

her story to a close. How the megobari home world—where the vrag had been taken en masse for experimentation and harvesting of the parts of their bodies considered valuable—was destroyed in one moment.

God-Mother had sensed something terrible was going to happen. Both sides had escalated to monstrosity, the megobari striking back hard and fast, her people doing the same, learning quickly, out of necessity, how to turn the megobari's weapons against them. She got off-world with her kin on a stolen warship, with the aim to escape back to her own world.

But her own world was no more. And soon, neither was the megobari's.

An eye for an eye. A planet for a planet.

This God-Mother was clever. She knew when to stop fighting and when to run. The other Mothers had tasted blood and wanted more; they could not see beyond their vengeance. They died when the megobari world fell.

She hid out the aftermath of the war in the shadow of the ruined world of her birth. When she found it safe to venture out, somehow, this God-Mother found herself the last surviving Mother. The scattered vrag that existed in space or on other worlds would wither and die without close and constant contact with their Mother.

Only her family was left intact, as whole as it would ever be again.

They were as orphaned as the megobari, refugees. Their stolen starship, all black inside, might as well have been a tomb. It did not speak to them. God-Mother found a way to connect her neural tails to the computer and direct it with her mind.

God-Mother felt and watched me gasp with curiosity. Yes, she seemed to say with her intentions. Just as you speak with your computer. It is the same.

This was technology that the megobari had been studying. Stolen from the vrag, forcefully, at the expense of their bodies and lives. They found a way to use it, twist it, for their own aims. But it belonged first to the vrag.

She found that the megobari had harvested and used their food grub for cheap sources of light, and directed her ship to the outposts of the megobari bases to find food for her people. They farmed the grubs and grew their trees anew in their stolen ship, and it became their entire world.

God-Mother was releasing me slowly from her memories, easing me back into awareness of my own body, which was now hunched over on the ground. I opened my eyes with some difficulty, taking in the reality of the massive God-Mother hanging in the rafters above and in front of me.

Luka, as soon as he came back to himself, forcefully pulled away from me and fell to his knees. Head in his hands, fingers scrubbing against his scalp, as though to physically remove all traces of God-Mother from his mind.

I reached out to touch him and stopped short.

"You mean us no harm?" I knew she couldn't hear me. But my voice, my thought, traveled to her through our connection.

I felt her lack of desire to hurt me. Luka, she was prepared to defend herself against, if necessary. Somehow she knew the reality of who he was.

As though to refute her intent, I shared a memory of my own: the image of the vrag ship *Exodus* burning in an alien sky. Luka and I holding each other in grief, helpless and stranded.

I felt the rise of smug victory in God-Mother before she tamped it down. *Yes*, I felt her rumble with emphasis. *Yes, I did this and it was right.*

I felt her knowledge of Luka, her initial hatred of him, her wanting to kill him, another of the oppressors. She didn't have eyes to see him, but she knew what he was, recognized the way his electricity echoed like static from his body. But after chasing us across space, she sensed our youth, our fear, and my humanity.

She was curious about me. She found me particularly suscep-tible to her external neural sensors. She was able to read me like a book despite the vast distances between our ships. She had never felt the mental presence of another sentient creature who was not one of her children.

She had wished for this moment, our physical connection, ever since. Just as I had wanted answers, so had she. She longed for answers. Why were the oppressors here at this planet? Why had they communicated with humans, and why did they return to the scene of their crime? And most important: Where were the rest of them?

Once here, she had found our internet—and thus her answers. All of our cultures, our languages, ready and cataloged for the taking. She'd consumed our cultures in a few short weeks. By now she had been linked to the computer for so long that they were basically symbiotic; her neural network was enmeshed in the computer and she had the ability to learn and retain vast amounts of knowledge near instantly.

After I'd returned to Earth, God-Mother was easily able to track my movements. I had been traveling along the path she had made for me. All along, it was supposed to lead here, to this, by her design.

"You've brought your war to us," I told her, voice pleading. "This has nothing to do with my planet. We don't have the ability to fight back. Please leave us alone."

At this, Luka's head jerked back up. I reached out to him, cautiously. With God-Mother still touching me, I was not sure he wanted my touch.

But he glanced at my hand, swallowed hard, and took it.

Her people had been brought into a war not of their making, she told me.

Luka jerked softly. "Can you understand her?" I asked.

The light of understanding, of fear, flickered in his expression and then went dark and slack as he began the same sensory overload. Filtered through me, maybe it wasn't such an onslaught of memory and intention.

Her answer came in solemn tones: they had not wanted war, either. But war came, and they had to fight back or be destroyed.

"Please," I told her again. "Please. Humans have no other colonies. No other planets in this system are habitable. My people have no ability to survive what you did to the megobari home

world. I want to help you end your war against the megobari.
Please, let me help you. Have mercy, and spare us."

Her response was surprise. *What* we *did?* Her emotions were
deep navy and violet, like the murky depths of the ocean. *No,
Human-Cassandra, we did not kill the megobari world. The megobari burned their own world.*

THIRTY-ONE

NO, I THOUGHT. *That's not true.*

We had turned the tide of the war, God-Mother continued, unabated. *Until we overran them on their own planet. Thus, their leaders declared it a lost cause, and instead of deploying their weapon on our world, unleashed it instead upon their own—the only way they saw to kill us all at once.*

I rocked backward at the same time Luka jerked his hand out of mine.

No. She was lying. What kind of species would do that? Cutting off their nose to spite their face? Destroying an entire planet's worth of life? Not the reasonable, patient people I'd seen in Luka's family. So cautious. So diligent.

Like dawn breaking over a bloody battlefield, I saw the horror of it all clearly.

"Luka," I rasped, my voice shredded. "Skyfall. Your people used it on their own planet."

I wanted to be wrong. Why would the megobari have done this, knowing they were killing themselves? Who would do that willingly? Burn down their own house just to get rid of their enemy? It was beyond scorched earth, beyond a last resort. It was stupidity.

It was evil.

"They must have been truly desperate," he murmured, still in shock. "Perhaps they didn't know the extent of the damage they would do."

He had a point. Humans had first used the atom bomb in order to end what they thought would be a terrible and bloody war, albeit against civilians. We had been lucky, as a species, to survive the Cold War. Perhaps they had walked a similar path, and their luck edged the other way.

"I think they knew. I think some of them—maybe just a small sect—knowingly sacrificed your world to win the war. You said the only ones who survived were off-world at the time? And that included who, exactly?"

He looked bewildered; it took a long time for him to respond. "Some small scientific and research colonists, like my family."

"The government? The military?"

"I—I don't know. Yes? They might have gone off-world once the war turned against us, for protection. . . ."

Cassie, God-Mother has sensed the weapon on Earth. She believes it is a smaller version of the one deployed against her people.

"That's one consolation," I said bitterly. At Luka's questioning

279

glance, I relayed that information to him.

"Perhaps my father did not know the truth. Or perhaps he thought it was worth the risk," he said quietly.

"Or his hatred of the vrag mattered more than anything else." Drenched with residual emotions from God-Mother, I staggered upright, breathing heavy and trying to push back the tide of emotion that threatened to drown me.

Luka had not gotten that far yet. He was still on his knees, bent double, forehead nearly touching the ground but for his hands. His fingers clutched at his hair.

"Luka? Did you see everything I saw?"

He groaned and punched the floor. "Yes."

"We have to stop this," I said. "No matter what happened in the past, it needs to end *now*."

God-Mother couldn't hear me, but she could read my intentions.

I am dying, she said, plainly and without emotion. She was tired of being alone and carrying the pain of her people. She wanted to stop running and stop killing. And the only way she could see to do that was to make peace with the megobari.

She showed me her idea: they would kill her if she came close, if she attempted to contact them. She had never been able to connect her neural network to one of theirs—either they were incompatible or they had never shown exposed skin to her. She was sure that if she could just connect with one of them, share with one of them what she shared with me, they could stop their terrible war.

I wasn't so optimistic.

She asked for my help. With the echoes of her children's cries still in my head, I agreed before I had even formed the intent.

God-Mother's memory was long. She did not forget. But soon she would be gone, and her race would be finished.

It wasn't right.

And now I realized that humanity was not threatened by the vrag. God-Mother did not wish to invade; her species couldn't survive in our gravity.

No, she knew that the megobari were coming. Earth was too enticing to them to leave alone. God-Mother's promise to the governments of Earth to help protect them against the coming invasion of megobari had been genuine. And as the last surviving witness to what the megobari had done to her, she knew what no one else could show us: the truth.

I thought of the weapon, and what scared people might do if they thought they had no other choice.

No, the real threat was within.

We needed to get back to Earth.

THIRTY-TWO

GOD-MOTHER SAW AND understood every electrical impulse that traveled down my neurons before they even formed a conscious thought in my head. She knew what I needed.

For a creature without depth perception, much less an understanding of numbers or letters, she had a surprisingly good grasp on physics. I supposed it helped that she was plugged into a giant computer connected to a ship filled with sophisticated sensors, all of which were receiving feedback from humanity's network of GPS satellites.

The sum total of human knowledge of space travel couldn't have filled a thimble compared to what God-Mother could do. A free-living, self-aware neuron. The things she could accomplish. Had *already* accomplished with the gifts she'd given

Earth. I wished we might've had more time, but we had to get that weapon off Earth and hidden before it was discovered.

She offered to send us back in a pod of her own, so as to avoid detection and suspicion. Not wanting to test my luck again with suspicious farmhands, I agreed.

She opened a door in her chamber and directed us down a darkened corridor that narrowed considerably as we went. I wanted to ask Luka what he was thinking, how he was dealing, or even what he thought of this nonsensical layout of a ship. But we might as well have been two planets in synchronous orbit. Distant, moving in the same direction, and never able to meet.

God-Mother showed us to a small spherical craft, something a step up from an escape pod. Luka and I strapped into seats twice our size, back to back, as the ship revved itself to life.

Luka was sullen and silent as God-Mother cast us out of her ship with the precise timing and trajectory for us to fall back to Earth exactly where we needed to be. I could place my hand on the soft interior of the sphere and make minute corrections to its trajectory if necessary.

We landed in a moonlit field a few miles from the safe house, sky dark enough to glimpse the stars we'd left behind in the gauzy curtain of atmosphere.

Head still spinning from the dizzying fall, I stumbled out of the pod and yanked Luka out by the arm when he proved too slow. As soon as he'd exited, the pod began to dissolve into a steaming black mass of oozing liquid, like bubbling lava cooling quickly into a swath of pavement.

I was desperate to reach my friends. We'd survived what I'd expected to be certain death, a suicide mission, and everything we thought we'd known was wrong. I needed to fix it.

But this had grown beyond me. Beyond me and Luka. The two of us had gotten into this mess that maybe we weren't qualified to fix. At the very least, we could undo our mistakes and let the truth come out.

A different truth than the one we'd uploaded yesterday. A fuller truth.

The half-buried house was dark, all shadows and soft moonlight coming in from the window. It was deathly quiet.

I flipped on the lights and scrambled backward into Luka, a scream dying in my throat.

There was a man standing in the living room.

THIRTY-THREE

LUKA SNAPPED OUT of his fugue. His arm came up to shield me, putting himself between me and the strange man.

With all we'd faced, he'd never tried to physically protect me until now.

My hands clenched into fists, and I scanned the room for something I could grab for a weapon. Only two candidates nearby: a hardback book on the coffee table and a lamp that might be made of glass.

"What are you doing here?" Luka's words were clipped. Low. Dangerous.

Not *Who are you?* Not *How did you get in here?*

The man didn't move. The corners of his mouth tugged sideways, more of a grimace than a smile. He was maybe late twenties. Clean-cut brown hair. His face was vaguely familiar.

His eyes were bright with fanatical energy, trained on Luka with single-minded intent. "Hello, Lukas. You've made quite a mess of things, haven't you?" He pronounced *Luka* with a strange lilt on the second syllable, an almost imperceptible *s* at the end.

He was broad-shouldered, thick. Hands like a gorilla. He could probably take a swing and break Luka's face without exerting any effort.

When Luka didn't answer, he circled his muscled arm wide and pivoted his upper body as if to show off the room. "I thought that this place was to be a refuge for our people in times of need. No matter the time. No matter the need."

I don't know what I expected. But the man's voice was not as thick as his body was; it was thin and young and strong. He was even *mocking*. Mocking Luka's speech patterns.

"What could you possibly need?" Luka's voice was so spiteful and dangerous I took a half step back, as though he might start snarling at me next.

The man took a handful of steps toward Luka. *"The weapon."*

"What weapon?" The man cocked an eyebrow at him and Luka bristled. "It's not here."

"You don't know how right you are." The man stalked across the room, pacing before us.

"Where are my friends?" I demanded.

"I locked them in their rooms. Do you know what you've done? Of course not." He leaned against the back of the couch.

The man turned his oil-slick eyes to me for the first time, his chin jerking up. "Who is this?"

Luka seemed more angry than afraid, and I had no intention of appearing fragile. I gently pushed Luka's arm aside and moved closer. I kept my fingers encircling his wrist, as much a reassurance as a restraint. His pulse trilled like a hummingbird's heart under my fingers. "I'm Cassie."

"My name is Tamaz. As these strange human mouthpieces cannot form the sounds of my true name, it'll have to do."

An electric tickle ran down the back of my neck.

His eyes slid to Luka, whose arm still tensed like he meant to shield me. "Where is your father?" Tamaz's voice was hard, but not mocking now. Did he really not know?

It was two heartbeats before Luka replied. "Dead. All of them are dead."

Tamaz tucked his chin into his chest, anger flaring his nostrils. "The vrag?" he asked quietly, with an undercurrent of rage.

Luka gave a slow nod. "They were there, as you feared. Always a step ahead." Then, cautiously: "You and I are the only two left on this planet."

There was a muted flash of surprise over Tamaz's features— he drew his head back as if the news had physically hit him. But then it was gone, and he spoke again as if nothing had been said. "Not anymore."

"Would someone like to clue me in?" I asked.

"This doesn't concern you—"

"Spit any more of your vile words at her and I will stop your human mouth from forming any sounds at all." Luka was holding steady in his staring contest with Tamaz. "You're a liar and a traitor." To me, in an aside: "Until he renounced our family and left us, Tamaz was my father's brother. My uncle. He . . . disagreed with the course of action my father had decided to take." A pause, where Luka's eyes and voice went hard. "And I believe he was the one who tried to suffocate us inside SLH."

"I didn't *plan* to kill you, Lukas. I was simply trying to scrub the mission. Your father left me little choice."

And it hit me, all at once, why his face was so familiar. Tamaz had been one of the blue-jumpsuited men who had worked as our Mission Control during our SLH simulation. He had gone by the name Tom. I remembered his name badge, how he'd had a beard and glasses then. I'd heard his voice over the radio night after night, giving instruction.

I hadn't heard him on the night we had been locked in the simulation and starved of oxygen.

"You knew he was there all along?" I asked Luka accusingly.

"He was meant to be there. At the time. To be another set of eyes and ears. Before he abandoned his family. That was when I first suspected you, Tamaz." Luka's lip curled in disgust. "I didn't want to believe it was you. That you could put me—put all of them, innocent humans—in such danger."

"I only wanted your father to give up his reckless idea."

"You almost *killed* us," I growled. Luka was now holding on to my wrist, but I didn't need to be held back.

Tamaz didn't even look at me. He just shrugged. "But you survived. And it didn't work, did it? It only spurred them on. The humans really can be as foolhardy and power-hungry as my brother had once been."

"Do not speak of him." Luka's voice was shaking with hatred. Under my hands, his muscles had gone to steel as his fingernails dug into his palm. "In fact, do not speak at all unless it is to tell us *why you are here.*"

"Your father is gone, Luka. And you being the dutiful son, you succeeded in carrying out his mission to bring back the weapon, didn't you? Did he ever tell you its true purpose?" He paused for confirmation, but Luka didn't give him one. "I suppose not. You have no idea what you have done, do you?"

"Yes, we do," I said, stepping forward.

"You have no idea, little girl," the man repeated, eyes barely grazing me before addressing Luka again. "Lukas, I knew what your father was planning, and I tried to stop it. And now, soon, there will not be anyone left to remember that any of us existed at all."

"The weapon is hidden," Luka said through gritted teeth. "Safe."

"Is it? Have you *seen* it? Because a few hours ago, one of your new friends just delivered it to Clayton Crane."

"What?" Luka and I demanded at once.

"Your friend, the blond one, who worked for Crane? She never stopped working for him. She called him earlier this evening. Didn't you notice that your vehicle was missing?"

No, I hadn't noticed.

"He's a liar, Cassie," Luka murmured, though he sounded unsure. "I wouldn't believe him."

The hall to the bedrooms was on the other side of the room. I'd have to leave Luka's side and walk past Tamaz to see if Hanna was still there.

He watched me consider the option, a look of grave amusement on his face. "Believe me or don't," Tamaz said offhandedly. "You'll see soon enough. All bets are off now that the vrag have made threats. Your government doesn't like feeling powerless. As soon as Crane figures out how to operate it, this planet's time is up."

Luka and I shared a second's worth of a glance. "We can stop this," I said. "We're going to fix it."

But Tamaz was right. Luka and I had brought Skyfall back in ignorance, maybe—with good intentions. But I knew it was dangerous, and I'd been careless, too trusting. Too willing to believe that Hanna was my friend first. But she only ever looked out for herself.

Hanna must've overheard me telling Mitsuko and Emilio about the weapon's coordinates. That would've been a grand way to get back in Crane's good graces—if she had been telling me the truth at all. Maybe she *had* worked for him all along. Had it been Crane's idea to send Hanna to me, knowing I'd trust her, my former roommate, over him?

Or had it been Hanna, whispering in his ear? *Let me go get her. She'll trust me.*

My one saving grace was the fact that they wouldn't be able to use the megobari technology. It required direct touch, control . . .

But—oh God.

Pinnacle.

Hanna had Pinnacle inside her head. As soon as Crane put two and two together—or Hanna put it together for him—all it would take would be one little provocation before the government pressured Crane to use the only weapon they had.

If they even waited for provocation at all.

"This is why I came, Lukas," Tamaz began again, his voice gentling somewhat as he watched us put the pieces together. "We're all that's left. And the humans—the greedy, self-destructive, shortsighted people who have been ruining this planet since long before we arrived—have a weapon that will end it once and for all. We have only one chance."

Luka's voice wavered, throat bobbing as he swallowed. "What is it?"

"Escape. A forward team of megobari commandos has arrived ahead of the fleet to investigate your report of vrag presence. They have a small, fast ship, quiet enough to slip through the atmosphere before anyone's the wiser. They can take us back with them. We can return to searching for a new home with the fleet."

Luka shook his head in disbelief. "The fleet? No, *this* is my home. We may still have a chance to make this a home for our people. What is the investigative squad going to do? Have you had contact with them?"

"Only cursory, over the radio, like a *caveman*. Standard protocol to let me know they were en route. But commandos don't exactly share their plans with the likes of *me*. After all, I'm more or less human to them now."

Luka turned his profile toward me, speaking low. "This . . . does not bode well."

"They won't help us? I thought your people wanted to save Earth. To colonize it."

He winced. "My family, yes. My *people*? I have no idea. We are not all of the same mind. They have . . . conflicting priorities."

"More important than finding a new home?"

"They were willing to destroy their own to eliminate the vrag. They will not hesitate to sacrifice yours." This came not from Luka but from Tamaz.

"How do you know this?" Luka asked.

Tamaz shook his head slowly, as if mourning Luka's ignorance. "Why do you think I parted ways with the family?"

Luka's brow furrowed, and his lips parted, but he could not speak.

"If you want, we might be able to convince the powers that be to allow your friend to come, too. But we're getting off this rock sooner rather than later—and believe me, when they turn that thing on, all that's left *will* be rock."

"I thought you cared about this place," Luka protested. "You obviously have found some enjoyment in life on Earth."

"One does what one must," Tamaz muttered. "It's not that

Earth is a cesspool. It has its perks. But it's no Eden, Lukas. These people don't even *know* what they have in this planet. They don't value it. They throw garbage into the very water they drink and dig the ground out from under them for a fuel source that pollutes the air they breathe. They let their own neighbors die of sickness and starvation, and your father thought they would take *us* in?" He barked a humorless laugh. "They don't even want to deal with refugees of their own kind. This place is an overcrowded slum. A tinderbox. In another hundred years, Earth wouldn't have been habitable anyway, even *with* your father's virus. We will find an unpolluted world to make our own."

"Wait—virus?" I cut in.

Luka looked as blank as I felt. He shook his head, confused.

"Oh, you didn't know that, did you? Of course not. Why would he tell you?" Tamar grimaced, the bearer of unpleasant tidings. "Your father—patron saint of uplifting primitive species, the planet-saving do-gooder—he infected the human race with a genetic virus. Just a small segment of DNA replaced by one your father invented, and passed from generation to generation. He released it almost as soon as we found this planet. Long before you were born, Lukas, before he'd even designed the virus that could disguise us as the native fauna. He ran the numbers—the projections of human population over the next couple of centuries—and extrapolated the data. Assuming the birth rate continued on an upward slide, and human life expectancy continued to rise, exceeding the carrying capacity of

Earth was nearly assured, even within our long lifetime. So he introduced a virus into the population that would . . . *curtail* that rate. Just a little, just enough to make sure there was room for us in humanity's future. It was genius, I thought. It might actually help them, he reasoned—there was already so much fighting over their resources, and so much strain on the planet to keep you all alive. The slower the population grew, the less competition, the better for us all. It might've been his best work. All he had to do was drop it in a few major population areas and it infected over one-third of the Earth's population within decades. The more babies they had, the more the virus spread, and the fewer babies *those* babies would grow up to conceive."

I stepped away from both of them, breaking my hold on Luka's hand.

Luka, lips parted, eyes wide, just stared at Tamaz in horror.

Tamaz almost seemed to be enjoying this, reminiscing over the unsung genius of his brother's work. "Your people eventually advanced enough to figure out how to combat the problem, of course, but you never did figure out the cause. Back when we'd first infected you, DNA was an unknown concept to you. When it was discovered, you all just assumed that little segment of virus was a naturally occurring mutation. You would've thought it harmless, useless, inert. Not that it would've mattered; there's nothing you can do about it now. Funny—in a sad way—how much you people could overlook the most dangerous concerns you face as a species to squabble over such petty things that you, as a culture, give such weight to."

A flash of hot anger, followed by a cold sweat of dread, washed over me in waves. I was speechless.

"That's why we wanted to *work* with them," Luka said through gritted teeth. "To help them scale back the damage and show them a better way. To make their lifestyles sustainable and save one of the few garden planets that can support species like ourselves. As though we knew better," he added bitterly. "As though we are blameless."

"It was a nice idea, I'll give your dad credit. But the humans are greedy and stupid, and the megobari are greedy and superior. And neither are above violence to achieve their goals. There was no peaceful cooperation in your future. One would have exterminated the other from the face of the Earth before you two even had a chance to pick out wedding rings."

Tamaz approached Luka, face congenial, and placed a reassuring hand on Luka's shoulder. "We'll find somewhere else, Lukas. And until then, the fleet will be our home."

"I was born *here*," Luka snapped, shrugging out from under the other man's hand. "And I will not run away." His breathing was ragged. "You're the last of my family, Tamaz. I know you hate that I call you that name—but it is the only name I've ever known. This is the only *home* I've ever known. Please. In all your years on Earth, did you not see anything worth saving?"

Tamaz regarded him a long time. Then one eyebrow quirked up. "Do you even have a plan? The weapon is in the hands of powerful and foolhardy humans. There are still warrants out for the two of you."

"Still?" I asked.

Tamaz shrugged, uncaring. "Presumably the American government wishes to understand why two teenagers are so highly desired by a hostile enemy."

"That's why we need your help, Tamaz," Luka said.

Tamaz raised his eyebrows into his hairline. "Now you need my help? You start this conversation by demanding what I'm doing here, refuse the help I offer, and ask for *more?*"

"Nothing could be clearer to me at this moment than the fact that I do not know everything," Luka said carefully. "The fact that I have been ignorant—have been *kept* ignorant—of the truth, and I have allowed myself to believe without question that we were in the right. I don't know what to think anymore, Tamaz. I don't trust that I know the best path. Please, Tamaz. Help us save these people."

Tamaz tilted his head curiously and leaned back against the kitchen table, arms crossing over his chest. "Where . . . precisely . . . have you been?"

"Stay, and I will tell you."

I wasn't sure what Luka was doing—if Tamaz *could* help us, even if he wanted to. But he was right in that we didn't know what we were doing. And being on a Most Wanted list was certainly going to hamper any plans we might come up with.

Tamaz considered the proposal. His face lost the pretenses of arrogance and disdain, and for a moment I fooled myself into thinking that I saw someone worthwhile. Then he spoke. "I know you mean well, Lukas. But you do not owe these people your life. This mess is older than all of us. You cannot fix it—none of us can. We can only save ourselves."

Luka's eyes went wide in a flash, and then he looked wounded. Betrayed. "So be it." He blew past me and threw open the front door. Dawn light showed on his haggard face, illuminating the fury barely contained in his eyes. "If you're not going to help us, you can get out."

Tamaz closed his eyes and nodded, as though he expected this unfortunate outcome. He obeyed, pausing in front of Luka briefly. "I do care about you, nephew. And I do not want you to throw your life away in a hopeless war when I can still save you. If you change your mind, you know where to reach me."

Luka glared at him as he left, and locked the door after him. Then he stormed into the kitchen and braced his hands on the countertop, his face flushed.

I approached him cautiously, my own heart still pounding. There was still the knowledge bouncing around in my head that the megobari had poisoned humanity's gene pool to limit our size—a gross manipulation whose ramifications I had only begun to wrap my head around. *My parents couldn't conceive because of what his parents did and that's why I'm here—*

Luka seemed to gather himself somewhat. Then he slid one hand from the counter to open and slam shut a drawer.

I jumped, surprised at his anger. But I should have known better.

Responding to some cue of Luka's doing, the smooth face of the plaster wall to our left slid open to reveal a screen of black-and-white security camera footage. We watched together in silence as the camera's eye followed Tamaz down the path and into his car, and then he drove away.

"How much time do we have?" Luka asked dully.

It took me a moment to realize what he meant. "I don't know. Maybe days? Hours? Maybe he won't turn it on at all unless there's provocation." Crane may have been ruthless, but he wasn't stupid. He wouldn't destroy the vrag while he could still stand to gain something from them. He probably still thought he could ally with them. Or strong-arm the vrag into giving him whatever it was he wanted. Crane's greed might be our saving grace.

Or he might take that power he'd been given and doom us all with it.

THIRTY-FOUR

ONLY ONCE THE dust from Tamaz's car had disappeared into the horizon did Luka relax even one iota.

"I'm sorry." Luka's shoulders slumped, the fight gone out of him. Head hanging. Sweat darkening his hairline. He still hadn't looked at me.

"For?" I crossed the room toward him, one step at a time.

"For . . . everything. For what just happened. For what might happen very soon. For what my family did to your DNA before you were born. Before either of us were born, I'd already betrayed you. At every turn, it seems, I have acted against your best interests."

I came closer. His back was a network of taut muscles, each so tense as to be almost individually distinguishable beneath his shirt. Gingerly, hoping touch could convey what words couldn't, I laid my hand between his shoulder blades, and felt the slightest exhalation deflate his rib cage. A muscle beneath my hand loosened, only just.

"I wouldn't say that." There was a storm brewing inside me, but on the outside I felt oddly calm. Too much had happened, and my mind was no longer able to take it in. It felt like being left in the wake of a tornado—utter destruction and silence. Nothing to do but pick up what pieces you could scavenge and focus on your most pressing needs: food, water, shelter. "You're still with me."

"You don't . . ." His voice was small. "Blame me?"

"I haven't . . . sorted out how I feel about that yet. But like you said—you weren't born and neither was I. You obviously didn't know enough to lie about it. I *do* think you could have told me there was another member of your family still living here."

"I didn't know where he was. I assumed he'd still be back in Georgia." He cleared his throat and kept going, as if he needed to explain. "We had been close, before. He had been like a father to me, while my own father was busy. He was the one who made me read classic literature to perfect my English. He read me *The Count of Monte Cristo*. Both of us loved that book—though now I think for different reasons. He was . . . a different person then. Or perhaps I saw a different version of him."

I dropped my hand from his back and stood by his side. "He will work against us now," Luka continued bitterly. "He will tell

300

the others that the humans have Skyfall. Whatever that investigative squad can do to finally rid the universe of their mistake, they will do. They will incite the vrag to violence against Earth, if that's what it will take for Crane to activate the device."

My hand fell from him. "They care so much about killing an innocent species that they will kill two of them?"

He finally turned toward me, leaning the small of his back into the wall. His shoulders were hunched. "I'm sorry I did not see it before. I think . . . I think the reason Tamaz wanted me to read that Dumas book was to see that vengeance against a wrongdoing was right, and good, and empowering. But I only ever saw it as empty and destructive. And now that I know what truly happened . . ."

"You believe God-Mother?"

He avoided my eyes. "I did not want to. I wanted to believe it was a trick. But Tamaz more or less confirmed it. He knew what we were bringing back. How else could he? He was one of the few who escaped that day. And now perhaps I know why my entire family escaped, when so few did. Why they knew where to find that weapon undisturbed after so many years." He looked like he might be sick. "My father helped design it."

"You are *not* them," I said firmly. "You are a *good person*. And I trust you." Finding my words limp and inadequate, I wrapped my arms around him instead and held him tight. "We'll find a way to fix this. We will."

When his arms pulled me against him, I felt stronger somehow.

Maybe I don't like kissing, but I do like this.

"We have to stop Crane," I whispered into his shoulder. "That's first. We can figure out everything else—the vrag and your people and my people—after. We have to get Skyfall out of play."

"We cannot simply walk in and take it from him." He pulled back from me a little to study my face. "Skyfall operates like all the megobari tech. He needs someone able to operate it. We should be safe until then."

I shook my head. *"Hanna."*

His brow furrowed, and then the light dawned in his eyes. He cursed. "Do you think she would really do that? Just to find favor with Crane?"

I'd asked myself the same question. Was her ambition so great as to cast a shadow over all her sense and morals? "We have to get to SEE. We can figure out the specifics on the way."

"Great. What do you want us to do?" Mitsuko came into the kitchen, rubbing at the back of her head. Emilio followed, limping slightly and blinking.

Luka and I flew apart—a bit too fast to escape suspicion— but Mitsuko just grinned.

I rushed to Emilio. "What happened to you guys?"

He waved me off. "I'm fine. Your boy wanted us out of the way for this conversation, E.T.—tossed us into this room at the end of the hall that locked from the outside. But we were listening at the door. Luckily you guys were loud."

"My lock-picking skills came in handy, *finally*," Mitsuko said, brandishing a handful of bobby pins.

Emilio sobered quickly. "You're not planning to head straight into the belly of the beast, right, Cass?"

I shot a surreptitious look at Luka, who drew himself up to his full height and said nothing.

"Because you know that Crane will just take you prisoner. Make you disappear. He'll make you operate the doomsday device yourself."

"He can't do that," Mitsuko said. "Luka was crap at the EEG." Then, at my pointed look, the light bulb went off in her head. "Oh. Duh. You were faking."

"I was faking," Luka confirmed. "What can we do, then?"

Mitsuko interjected. "I'll take Cass back. They can't hurt me, not really, since Michael's out of their reach and my parents are in Japan. Emilio, you and Luka . . . well . . . maybe see about those megobari commandos the big guy mentioned? I'd like to not run into the best of your best in a dark alley."

Luka and I met eyes. His jaw worked. "I do not wish to part from Cassie. Not now."

"Me neither," I said, but quietly.

Mitsuko rolled her eyes. "Fine, ride back to Houston with us and we'll figure that shit out on the way. Wait, you *do* have another car, right? Because that bitch stole my rental."

"You saw her take off? Hanna?" I asked.

"Yeah. Heard the car start up before sunrise, woke me up. Got outside just in time to see her taillights." She rubbed at her forehead, looking like she'd sucked on a lemon. "I'm telling you,

Cass, she was in on this the whole time."

"Good news, though!" Emilio said, brightening. He dove for the remote control and flipped on the television. "Our message made it out."

There was Colonel Pierce, looking pissed to be up so early, mouth moving silently as the closed captioning filled the screen below him, a few seconds behind. And in the cutaway screen, playing beside his face, was my helmet-cam footage of the death of *Exodus*.

THIRTY-FIVE

AS LUKA'S FAMILY had planned for every eventuality, he did happen to have an SUV in the garage, though it was dusty and needed fresh gas.

We piled silently into the car, our meager belongings in the trunk. Luka driving, me sitting beside him, Emilio and Mitsuko in the back.

Hanna's absence was a glaring, angry wound among us.

We continued playing the news footage in the car. Emilio and Mitsuko's transmission had been successful; the world now had access to the fatal end of Project Adastra. And they all believed it had been leaked by retired astronaut, first man on Mars, Colonel Pierce.

Our gamble had worked. Pierce didn't lie about the true

source of the transmission—he couldn't, since he didn't know—but he was on live TV proclaiming that as far as he was concerned, everything we were seeing was true and accurate. And that without further evidence from eyewitnesses, it seemed that the vrag were only posing as our friendly neighborhood aliens.

As validating as it was to see the truth being spread, and Pierce backing it up, his assertions that only Luka and I could tell the full story were not going to help.

Not long after the sun had grown to full strength, we pulled off the interstate to a truck stop.

Emilio and Mitsuko hopped out—Mitsuko to put gas in the car and Emilio to head inside to pay—leaving Luka and me alone in the car, trying to keep our heads down and remain inconspicuous.

Luka hadn't spoken much since we'd left. Either determined to ignore me, or too lost in thought to acknowledge me. So I slid down in my seat and pretended like he wasn't there.

Until he seemed to snap out of it. His hand snaked across the leather seat to hold mine, gingerly, loosely, leaving me room to pull away. "I don't know how to apologize to you for everything that's happened."

"Then don't. I don't need an apology."

His brow crinkled. "You don't?"

"Bad things happen. These circumstances . . . you didn't put them into motion. And you're helping us to fix them. So . . . we're good."

One by one, the crinkles smoothed. He offered a pale

imitation of a smile, but it was more pained than happy. "This could still end very badly."

I looked down at our joined hands. Squeezed. "I know."

All we could do was hold hands. I studied his knuckles a moment, wondering. I enjoyed this amount of contact. I liked his hands, his smile. Would this ever be anything more? Did I want it to be?

I closed my eyes and wondered if I'd live long enough to find out. If I'd ever have a chance to get bored of this feeling, where everything inside me felt warm and at peace and exactly where it should be.

And then the car door opened and Mitsuko was sliding inside. She met my eye. I expected a joke, expected to be laughed at or teased. But there was nothing. Only an acknowledgment. That we were coming down to the final hours of whatever this may be—a new beginning for humanity, or its end. Then she looked away, affording us what little privacy there was to be had.

Emilio returned with an armful of chips, trail mix, and candy, and Luka started the car.

After we'd eaten our truck stop brunch, Emilio called his girlfriend to check on her. He spoke quietly, words muffled beneath the noise of the interstate and the near-constant pop-ups of ads animating the dash as we passed their corresponding billboards. Mitsuko was on her burner phone with Michael. Luka and I had a shared bubble of privacy in the front seat.

I couldn't think of anything to say that I hadn't already. I

was drained. Sunny might be quietly helping me sort and cata-
log the information overload of the past few days—I assumed
she was working hard at that, since I rarely noticed her presence now—but the constant fear and sleep deprivation were
swirling reality into a dreamlike state. Beneath it all, a pulsing
anger at Hanna's betrayal colored everything else. All I wanted
to do was sleep. But even when I closed my eyes, I saw red.

*Sunny, can you maybe just—turn off my brain and let me sleep
awhile?*

Suddenly the background noise of my brain was muted and
all I heard was the hum of the road, lulling me into a dreamless
sleep.

"We'll be there soon," Luka said.

I opened my eyes to see the Houston skyline on the horizon,
doused with evening sun. Luka's hand was on my arm, gently
waking me.

The car was still driving itself. Luka pulled his hand back
and crossed his arms over his chest. Mitsuko was dozing behind
me, and Emilio was gazing out the window.

My stomach felt hollow. I'd eaten nothing but cheese crack-
ers and mixed nuts all day. My legs ached with disuse. The
danger we were headed into didn't feel real.

Luka was still facing the road, as though he didn't trust the
car to keep us safe, but he snuck a cautious glance at me. "I
would be lying if I did not tell you I considered leaving this
place and taking you with me."

That made me sit up straighter. "I wouldn't go. I wouldn't leave my family, or them," I said, jerking my head to the back seat. "I couldn't."

He didn't seem surprised, only a little sad. "I know. I've been wondering . . . if we're successful . . . if I should be allowed to stay here. Much less with you."

Now I regarded him with more gentleness. "Of course you should stay," I whispered, mindful that our bubble of privacy was both transient and permeable. "This is where you belong."

"I can't help but wonder what kind of life we may have . . . together. Should we succeed. And survive."

The fact that he noted those two things separately was disconcerting. "Me too," I admitted. "Though I think we can save that conversation for later. We'll figure it out, okay? Cross that bridge when we come to it." I emphasized the *when* a little too much. "Wait, but—you're not seriously considering leaving with the megobari?"

"The megobari need to leave Earth alone. We've meddled enough." His voice dropped. "*You* deserve to be left alone, if you choose."

I reached over for his hand. "I can't speak for the rest of Earth, but that's not what I choose."

He squeezed my hand and relaxed a little more in his seat, beginning to smile. "Thank you. I—"

Mitsuko screamed.

Luka reacted instantly. He grabbed the wheel, jamming it to the right, as proximity alarms screamed from all four corners of the car. We jerked, swerved hard onto the shoulder, Luka's body crushing mine into the car door with the force of his momentum.

"What the hell was that?" Emilio asked. He wasn't talking about Luka's driving.

Fiery debris littered the interstate. Most were small—the size of basketballs, maybe. But a piece of warped metal twice the size of our car had embedded itself into the asphalt, right in the middle of the lanes. The light traffic had come to a standstill; cars had skittered across the road like toys scattered by a child's tantrum.

At least one of the cars had been hit, a rock denting its hood. The owners stood safely outside, horror-struck and dazed.

Out, out, OUT, my brain chanted, my hands scrambling to free myself from my seat belt. Luka disentangled himself from me, following me out of the car seconds after. But our car was fine—we hadn't been hit. Luka had disengaged the auto-pilot and swerved us out of the way of the twisted metal sculpture that now protruded, smoking, from the asphalt.

Houston's skyline was no longer lit and glittering by the setting sun. It was shadowed by a mass of smoke, high in the atmosphere, like Houston had its own personal rain cloud.

Fire rained like falling stars for miles, streaks of orange trailed by smoke, like fireworks gone wrong. We were far enough away that we'd only gotten a minor drizzle of fire—the destruction was raining down for hundreds of miles. Something indescribably massive had exploded.

It's the end of the world, I thought, my insides quaking. Then—Skyfall. Had Crane already activated the device?

I wasn't aware Mitsuko and Emilio had joined us until she swore under her breath. "We're too late. That *damned idiot.*"

We were dead, then. I would never get to see my family again.

"No," Luka said. He was wincing as he stared at the destruction, as though it hurt his eyes. "I don't think this is the result of the Skyfall device. The smoke is dissipating. And look—the debris is scattered over a very large area. Most of the debris is very small. It will do damage, yes, but it is meant to appear as more of a threat than it is." He cocked his head as if a thought just occurred to him. "Get back in the car."

We piled in. My limbs felt jerky and uncoordinated, like I was operating them from a distance. Mitsuko started the car.

"Pull up the newsfeeds," Luka said.

We went silent as the car's windows lit with video clips, breaking news clips, firsthand accounts of witnesses live-tweeting and retweeting the events. Events, *plural.*

"This is happening all over the country," Emilio said, awestruck and full of dread.

"It looks like just in the major cities," I said. Something in my chest held taut. I scanned, gathering names. "Houston, Dallas, New York, Chicago, LA . . ." Nothing about Huntsville. We were small, compared to these places. My parents should be safe—for now. I *hoped.*

"Just the US?" Luka demanded. He flipped through the

increasingly panicked accounts—full of all caps and question marks and exclamation points. Most major outlets hadn't picked it up yet—these were raw feeds from people recording on their phones, going online with their panic and questions and reports, building on each other's info. "All I can see are American cities. Nowhere else?"

My eyes blurred.

"Nowhere in Japan are they talking about this," Mitsuko said, eyes roving over digital pages full of Japanese characters.

"This is not Skyfall," Luka said. "This is the work of my people."

We turned to stare at him.

"This is a provocation. This is to scare your country into a rash, violent reaction."

"They couldn't have picked a better country for *that*," Mitsuko muttered.

"Goading Crane into activating Skyfall when he otherwise wouldn't," Emilio said with a humorless laugh. "It's crudely brilliant."

"They'll make him use it," I said quietly. "The government will go to SEE for help. NASA's been using their technology for years, they don't have anything on their own to defend us from something like this, something from space. They're totally reliant on corporations like SEE for all their space tech. I bet the president has a direct line to Crane's office."

"Then our plans haven't changed," Mitsuko said as Luka put the car into gear and maneuvered it manually back onto the road, carefully navigating around the stopped cars, stunned pedestrians, and smoldering potholes. "Stop Crane. Stop the sky from falling."

The deeper we drove into Houston, the darker the sky grew. Sirens punctuated the air, and police were visible at every intersection, like they thought they should make an appearance but weren't sure exactly what to do about the cataclysm in the sky.

A few pieces of debris were still falling in smoking trails. There were ambulances, honking to get by in the crowded streets, blaring their emergencies. People were standing outside, looking stricken, looking up. Others were speeding out of the city as fast as their mph-controlled engines would take them.

We slowed to a crawl, unable to avoid seeing the damage: wrecked cars, cars pulled up on sidewalks, people sobbing openly, people on their phones, wandering the sidewalks, angling to get a better look at what had exploded over their heads.

"Fragmentation grenades," Luka murmured, as though to himself.

"What was that?" I asked.

"I was trying to figure out what was detonated. I thought perhaps a ship, but . . . we don't have enough of those to spare. And there would be more larger pieces, closer together. These seemed designed for massive smoke and fire, and just enough debris for light casualties."

"Light casualties?" I looked out the window at a bloody and

grim-faced family on the sidewalk, their apartment complex ablaze, four fire engines pouring water jets into the windows.

All this destruction, carefully cultivated. How *dare* they. How dare they calculate just how much damage and human hurt to inflict in order for us to meet *their goals.* How much we'd endure before fighting back. Use our fear to make us destroy ourselves.

But I kept those words inside. They weren't constructive, and they wouldn't help get us out of our current situation.

"When we finish here," I said under my breath, leaning in toward Luka's ear, "I'm going to need to discuss some things with these megobari commandos."

Luka's jaw clenched, and he did not answer.

When the streets grew so congested that people walking on the sidewalk were moving faster than us, we abandoned the SUV on a residential street and walked the last few blocks.

Though the smoke was too far above our heads to really cause any harm, the few people we passed had started wearing medical face masks. The last news report we'd heard on the radio had asked people to stay inside if at all possible. The air was acrid, bitter, thick with the scent of burning ash and saltpeter.

The crowds thinned to nothing the closer we came to downtown. People had either abandoned their workplaces or were sheltering in place. The towering headquarters of the Society for Extrasolar Exploration took up an entire desolate block.

"So . . . we just walk in?" Emilio said, his voice low.

"You two don't," I said. "Not with the guard on the door."

"I don't see a guard," Mitsuko said.

"On the other side of the glass. They'll be checking IDs, and I'm sure right now they've got some extra security."

"Then none of us are getting in," Mitsuko said. "None of us have badges."

"Hanna does." Emilio's eyes were set. He'd lost his humor on the burning interstate.

"And we're just gonna call her? We might as well call Crane and tell him to let us in."

"Why wouldn't he?" I asked. "He *is* looking for us."

"Then that's our in," Mitsuko said decisively. She grabbed my wrist. "Come on. Emilio, Luka, take the car back to my place. We can't have them grabbing Luka on top of all of this."

"No way are we hiding out at home," Emilio protested. "We'll lie low somewhere nearby, be your backup if something goes wrong."

"Fine." Mitsuko hadn't let go of my hand. She was dragging me away even as she spoke. "But if you don't hear from us by dark, get to my place and Michael will be able to help. This shit's bound to go sideways sooner rather than later."

I glanced at Luka one last time before Mitsuko was opening the glass door and pulling me into the air-conditioned lobby of SEE's headquarters.

It took a second for my eyes to adjust; the smoke outside had dimmed the daylight. My eyes barely took in the lobby, gathering only vague brushstrokes of marble, flowers in towering vases, swaths of slick architecture and modern, sparse furniture. The air smelled slightly of exotic perfume and lemon floor cleaner.

Immediately there were two men in black uniforms, side-arms holstered at their hips, blocking our way. "This building is currently closed to nonemployees. Please exit the building."

Mitsuko played the wide-eyed innocent act. "Look a little closer, buddy. This is Cassie Gupta. She's, like, turning herself in."

The man who'd spoken changed his expression only slightly—a single crease in the middle of his forehead. The other one gave me a quick, incredulous up-and-down. I was wearing jeans and a T-shirt. My hair was loose and tangled, and I'd just walked my way through a hot and humid city filled with smoke.

They didn't believe us. I could see it on their faces. I was so much thinner than in my old driver's license photograph, not to mention two years older. I'd changed my hair. I'd been through hell. I started to deflate, trying to come up with an alternate plan.

"Wait! Stop!" a loud feminine voice shouted from across the lobby.

"Ho-*ly*—" Mitsuko started.

Ms. Krieger, unmistakable blond hair in its high tease, was *click-clack*ing her way across the marble floor at double time, her narrow calves a blur. Everything about her was off-kilter: her hair frizzy and loose from its updo, long strands wafting near her face, eye makeup looking racoonish. Even her ruby-red lipstick had faded. "Don't let her go," she shouted. "Stop her!"

All four of us were stilled. And now that she actually wanted me, I was beginning to think the best thing for me to do was run.

But before I could, the guards each closed a hand around both my and Mitsuko's elbows, apparently not knowing which of us the female pronoun applied to.

As Ms. Krieger joined us, she huffed, "The Indian girl is the one we need. Take the other one outside."

Both of us bristled at that, but we didn't have time to call her out as the guard who held Mitsuko shoved her out into the smoky air. "Hey—!"

But her complaint was cut off as the guard closed the door on her.

And then I was alone, entombed within the walls of the Society for Extrasolar Exploration.

And trying hard to remember why this was, in fact, our end goal.

THIRTY-SIX

MS. KRIEGER TOOK me, along with a third guard who met us in the hall, up into an elevator that required an ID card to access. My heart was blinking rapidly in my chest, everything moving too quickly for me to hold out a hand to stop it.

But maybe I shouldn't stop it. This was what I'd come here for, wasn't it? My own safety versus the safety of the human race: it was no contest. And what was Crane going to do to me, anyway?

I tried to use that rationale to banish the fear. It didn't work.

Krieger took me into a room. Stark white. In the middle of the floor was a person reclined in a chair, helmet obscuring her head, wires connecting her to a computer. She didn't seem to be moving aside from slow, deep breaths.

The room was more sparsely populated than I'd expected.

Soldiers were stationed at intervals alongside men and women in white coats or polo shirts with IDs swinging on lanyards. No one seemed to be paying much attention to the human in the chair.

One entire wall was a screen. Nearly every face in the room was pointed at it. And nothing on it made sense to me. I couldn't even focus my eyes; I kept staring at the girl.

I didn't need to see her face to know that it was Hanna. Hanna, connected to Pinnacle. Hanna, awakening Skyfall, dooming us, killing us all.

I wondered if I could disconnect Hanna from Pinnacle without killing her. I wondered if I could even make it to the wires that connected her to Pinnacle before one of the soldiers in the room shot me.

I wondered if it was too late.

Someone was coming toward us. I tore my eyes from Hanna to see Crane, his age-spotted, crypt-keeper face even more deathly pale than usual. At his shoulder was a woman in a military dress uniform, four stars on her lapel, graying blond hair in a tight, low bun.

My limited time working at Marshall—having to show my ID badge every day to an armed guard at the gate, reading the local news, seeing soldiers in uniform at the weekly farmers' market in the parking lot—had given me basic working knowledge of military rank.

Four stars was the highest you'd get in peacetime. And this wasn't just any four-star.

This was the army chief of staff.

Crane didn't waste time with pleasantries. "You found her?"

"She came here," Krieger said. "Willingly."

Yep. Definitely a mistake.

Crane's gaze centered on me, questioning, suspicious, desperate. "You came because you knew we couldn't operate it?"

They couldn't? "I didn't know. Wait, what do you know about Skyfall?"

"Schulz showed up here out of the blue towing this alien relic, told us we could use it to fight back. This one," he said, jerking his thumb accusatorily back at Hanna, "thought she could control it. Now we can't get her, or the droneship, to respond." His eyes bored into mine like icicles, trying to read me.

"Where is it now?"

"On the helipad, on the roof," the general said, also eying me with suspicion. "What is Skyfall, exactly? What does it do?"

I groaned and exploded at Crane. "You're trying to turn it on without even knowing what it is?"

"She said she got it from you and that it was our only shot. Where the hell have you been, Gupta?"

So Crane hadn't sent Hanna to pick me up? She hadn't been working with him all along?

There was too much to explain and not enough time. "Across the galaxy and back," I said arrogantly. "We can't activate Skyfall. We're being set up—the vrag aren't attacking us, and the weapon isn't going to protect us."

That didn't have quite the effect I was hoping for. The four-star narrowed her dark eyes at me, and Crane hardly seemed to have heard.

I waved a hand in front of his face. "Hello? I'm telling you to stop this! Pull the plug! This thing is a bomb that we can't control, and it's going to blow up in our faces!"

That seemed to register. The four-star barked at a soldier stationed nearby. "Taylor! What's our threat status?"

He ran the short distance over to us. "The vrag ship is quiet, ma'am. We've been trying to trace the origin of the blast, but it's odd—we've been watching the ship in orbit nonstop, and our sensors didn't pick up any motion from it just before the blast."

"See?" My breath was coming hard. Maybe I could convince them. Maybe this would actually work, and nobody would have to get hurt after all.

"Means nothing," Crane said, dismissing me with a wave of his hand. "They could already be on the ground—they could have weapon capabilities that we don't have the technology to detect."

The soldier glanced nervously between the highest-ranking officer in the army and the old man. I couldn't read his rank, but he seemed out of his depth here.

"*Listen to me,*" I said. "You have no idea what's going on. You're playing with things that are way beyond you."

Crane's face morphed into a mask of outrage. I could almost hear him begin to say *now you look here, missy!*

Just then an alarm began to blare from a nearby computer, and the giant wall screen pulsed a flashing red "WARNING."

I was getting so *sick* of alarms.

"Damn it, what now?" the general snapped, pivoting on her heel. "Somebody tell me what the hell that alarm's for!"

The woman in front of the computer that was sending up the alarm leaned back in her chair, looking remarkably composed— only the wrinkle between her dark eyebrows betrayed her concern. "Massive energy output from the droneship. It appears to be preparing to launch."

Hanna had come through after all.

"You can't let that thing get off the ground!" I shouted at Crane. "Listen to me! The aliens who built that designed it to *destroy planets*. It's going to explode like a neutron star." I ran to Hanna's side before anyone could stop me. A jumble of thick cables connected the mask over her eyes to the floor. I scanned the setup, but didn't even know where to begin turning it off. This was nothing like what I'd trained on. "You have to get Hanna offline, *now!*"

There was suddenly a tech person at my shoulder—either there to help me or to stop me, I couldn't tell. "Can't," she said. "We don't know how enmeshed she is with the program at this point. Pinnacle may have taken over control of her breathing and heartbeat. If we pull the plug, she might die."

Exhales coming short and fast now. My eyes lingered on Hanna, a feeling of helpless necessity, of dreaded certainty, looming from some deep and terrible place inside me. She still hadn't moved.

My stomach was turning over, rebelling. But I couldn't listen to my fear.

"I can stop this," I said, forcing strength into my voice. "I mean—I can try."

Now there were several pairs of eyes on me. Crane advanced on me, eyes alight with curious intensity. "What are you talking about?"

Trying hard to escape the feeling that I was making a huge mistake, I spoke quickly. "I can do what Hanna's doing. Don't ask me to explain how. But I might actually be able to stop that thing. I mean, unless you have a better plan."

The chief of staff bounced her gaze back and forth between Crane and me. "Well, do you?"

He gave her a slight shake of his head. "Hanna was the only one sufficiently skilled. Gupta, you're sure you can control it? Pinnacle is—"

"I know." I nodded decisively, but every muscle trembled. If I was wrong, they wouldn't live long enough to realize it. "We can't let this thing activate."

The general must've bought my confident act. "Let's get her suited up, then!"

The minions in the room had already begun to follow the orders before they'd finished leaving her mouth. Suddenly I was pushed into a chair beside the motionless Hanna.

The tech that had been by my side earlier gently eased me into it, meeting my eyes briefly before lowering the mask over my face. I felt the slide of electrodes through my hair, and it brought back an unwelcome wave of déjà vu.

I'll shut it off, I told myself. *I'm in control. Not them, not the machine.*

Except something had happened to Hanna when they

connected her to the device. And with a nauseating swoop to my stomach, I remembered the fracturing of my mind the last time I'd been connected to Pinnacle.

I know what to expect this time. Everyone's counting on me. I'll be strong.

And then the wires touched my skin, and my thoughts scattered like leaves in the wind.

THIRTY-SEVEN

IT WAS LIKE being caught unawares by a rogue tidal wave. I was drowning, sinking, tumbling, falling.

Pinnacle was in my thoughts, scanning the data of my processors, learning, absorbing, cataloging. It was moving faster than I was even aware, multiple thought streams, memories, all replaying at once.

Me, age eight and onstage at my first piano recital, wearing a flouncy dress, my hair tied up with big red ribbons, still fuming at being dressed up like a doll—but my fingers flying, creating music that hushed the entire crowd. My family, huddled around a phone, crying behind a pane of glass. A classroom of hostile faces, dozens of eyes challenging me, just before I turned my back to them and felt smug as I wrote the correct answer on the board. Sitting alone at lunch in my school uniform, not making eye contact, and acting as though I couldn't care less.

I couldn't control it. Pinnacle had the reins.

Pinnacle wasn't used to me, though. It needed to sink into the sulci of my brain, send its electrical tendrils over the gyri, trace the neural connections. Every human brain was unique in its makeup, roots grown to suit the needs and habits of the tree. Pinnacle couldn't just move right in and take over everything at once.

I kept trying to tug the reins away, feebly. I knew I was supposed to be able to feel my body. There was a physical me, somewhere, but Pinnacle had stepped between my central nervous system and everything else. My body wasn't important to Pinnacle. I was just a set of electrodes.

It dragged me along, stumbling and falling, skinning my hands and knees as I tried to pull away long enough to have one original thought, to gain some kind of control.

More memories. Mr. Finley sitting across from me in his office. The blur of my selection process. Meeting God-Mother, pale and monstrous and massive, her mind touching mine as directly as Pinnacle was doing now.

But Pinnacle was not alive.

I struggled to keep hold of that thought. It seemed important.

If only I could—

It was like trying to concentrate in a room full of TVs, each playing a different channel, volume on full blast.

If only this noise would STOP!

I pushed back against Pinnacle with sheer, desperate will. I focused my concentration on a sole point, like burning a hole through paper by focusing sunlight through a magnifying glass.

The volume in my head lessened, just a little bit. I gained a bit of ground; I could string a coherent thought together. *You're not real. You're not alive.* I pushed back a little more, and Pinnacle retreated.

But it quickly recovered, redoubling its efforts to take over my brain, integrate my systems into itself as it was programmed to do.

No, no no! A living brain was unknowably complex. Surely a man-made computer program couldn't learn it so quickly, couldn't control it, take away autonomy and sentience just like that. This body was *mine.* I knew my own mind better than anyone or anything ever could. My dreams and hopes and wishes, they were mine alone.

Earth, floating in space. Luka, reaching across the car seat to take my hand. Mitsuko and Emilio, laughing, teasing.

These memories were *mine.* There were things I wanted for my future—people and places and experiences. A future I wouldn't let them take from me.

I gained more control. Tasted triumph.

For a moment, I had my hearing back—and then it was gone.

And then I realized my fatal error: Pinnacle was never going to tire.

I had a hard time keeping hold of my thoughts. They slithered like fish through my grasp, escaping back to Pinnacle's control.

Was that what happened to Hanna? Did she fight Pinnacle and lose, or was she still fighting it?

Hanna. HANNA!

I pushed Pinnacle back, hard, focusing my thoughts and energy past myself and into Pinnacle itself.

When God-Mother and I had touched, the communication had gone both ways. She'd obviously been in control of the interaction—it was her native language, she was far better at it—but there was give and take. If this technology was based on the vrag's communication abilities, maybe it would work both ways.

I gave up trying defense and went on the offensive, blasting my way into Pinnacle. *You're not in control here. You're mine. You're a machine, and you follow my orders.*

Show me Hanna.

Pinnacle wasn't human, but it wasn't like most computer programs, either. Pinnacle and Sunny were both designed to learn and adapt. I was banking on its adaptability as my only hope in overcoming it. If I was strong enough . . .

I didn't let up. I pushed my will into Pinnacle—like flexing all my muscles and holding my breath until Pinnacle seemed to let up, pause, reconsider.

Come on, you stupid machine. Do what I tell you. Listen to me.

And then I was pushing against nothing. Pinnacle had retreated, stopped trying to take over—for the moment.

I felt a tingling in my fingers. I felt my chest rise and fall.

The silence in my ears slowly gave way to sound. I didn't test my mobility—didn't want to draw a shred of attention away from my task.

Just like when I had been semiconscious on board *Odysseus*, I felt another heartbeat outside of my own. A slowly tapping rhythm echoing on the fringes of my awareness.

I reached my mind toward it and realized I was actually reaching *through* Pinnacle, to Hanna's brain—Pinnacle acting as a conduit between us instead of a wall.

This is wild.

Distantly, I felt Hanna twitch, as if she'd heard my thoughts.

As I eased my awareness further across the electrical bridge that linked us, exploring my limits, keeping Pinnacle at bay, I became more and more aware of Hanna, as if I were walking down a hall, hearing her voice grow stronger as I approached.

And then I realized Hanna was shouting at *me*, pushing back against *me*, because I was Pinnacle and that was all she knew.

Hanna had been fighting Pinnacle far longer, and Pinnacle had very nearly won. She was a small voice, guarding a small corner of her mind with trademark ferocity. But she was fading, and this inner voice was all she had left.

I was Pinnacle; I had it under my control and therefore also Hanna—not that I knew what to do with that information. I couldn't figure out a way to communicate this to her. So I reshaped our perception.

I formed a mental image that I knew would transmit to her

and make her believe it was truth: a visual representation of the two of us, alone in a quiet room.

It may have originated from my imagination, but divorced from our bodies, it was our reality—Hanna's especially.

I looked down at the mental image of my body, my hands. And then at Hanna. She sat curled in the corner, head ducked between her knees.

"Hanna? You're okay now. It's okay. It's Cass. Can you see me?"

Her head jerked up, strangely mechanical. Her pupils were fixed, eyes glazed. "What's going on? What . . . is this?"

"Something really weird." I tried to smile. "I . . . came to get you. They put you under with Pinnacle to activate Skyfall, but it didn't work."

"It was different than before," Hanna whispered, her eyes unfocused. "They've upgraded Pinnacle. He's different. Stronger. Trying to overpower me. He *did* . . . I couldn't move. I couldn't even feel . . ."

She looked down at her hands. "Is this real?" Then at the four white walls all around us—I had never paid much attention to setting. There wasn't even a door. "No. Not real."

"Pinnacle did the same thing to me. I just . . . yelled at it, I guess, until it listened to me. And then I used it to find you. I conjured this environment so we could communicate. Can you control it at all?"

Hanna held out a graceful hand, small and white and delicate. A cluster of sparkling, miniature stars exploded into being, floating over her palm. "Wild. This is . . . what I imagine a drug trip might be like."

My heart skipped a beat. This had gone from terrifying to amazing. I was still afraid I'd lose control at any moment, but it would be pretty incredible to explore what we could do with this—if we ever made it out.

"We can play around with this later," I told her. "They activated Skyfall. We have to stop it, Hanna, or it's going to kill us."

Her brow twisted in confusion, unusually slow to understand. "What?"

Perhaps mentioning it flagged some protocol in Pinnacle, because the white room and Hanna were suddenly gone, and I was thrown back across the bridge into my own mind, as Pinnacle rushed back into dominance.

I'd won some sort of permanent insight into Pinnacle. I knew it was now reaching out for Skyfall, linking, reigniting the launch procedures that had stalled when I was connected.

I knew it was holding Hanna out of the way, not letting her go, but otherwise leaving her alone. It was using me, instead, to unlock the doomsday device.

And it had already begun.

THIRTY-EIGHT

I WAS LOCKED out of communicating with Hanna. So I focused my energy on directing Pinnacle.

Abort! Abort countdown launch procedures!

Override, Pinnacle answered calmly.

Damn it, you stupid machine, I *am the human here. That means* I *am in charge of* you!

Pinnacle either didn't have any answer programmed, or didn't think that worth responding to.

Something. There must be something.

Plugged in to Pinnacle's network, I was also privy to its resources. While it was busy, I called up Sunny to help me access cameras and sensors. With her translating the data, I could see Skyfall powering up a few floors above.

I felt the network flowing through me, Pinnacle giving

Skyfall access to me, giving permissions on my behalf. My orders—my consent—weren't necessary. This was how they'd programmed this blasted computer.

They'd given Pinnacle so much power. They had so much faith in this computer, and so little faith in the brains of two teenage girls and our abilities to program not only these incredibly sophisticated computers but also our own brains.

Minutes. I only had minutes.

I tried once more. At each turn my attempts to access Skyfall directly were canceled, overridden, misdirected.

Minutes. MINUTES. Until the destruction of the Earth, unless I could figure this out and defeat this computer.

Wait. I still had access to my body, didn't I? I pressed my pinkie finger into my thigh, making the smallest possible gesture that wouldn't alert Pinnacle to my ability. I twitched one eyelid.

I had full control over my body. I could rip this mask off my face. Sever the connection. Would that work, now that Skyfall had been activated? Or would it just kill me? Render me brain-dead?

I pressed all five fingers into my thigh, five pressure points grounding me and reminding me I was real. They were watching this on the screens, I could hear. Someone was counting down the same numbers that were ticking through my brain.

No choice. My life versus the world? No comparison.

I pictured my parents. *I'm sorry*, I told their faces in my memory. *I'm doing this for you, too.*

I readied my hand.

Pinnacle reached out and stopped me. Took away my control over my hands.

"What are you doing? Are you crazy?" Hanna's voice fell in my ears as though she had actually spoken, though I knew she was still sitting a few feet away from me in the real world, unmoving. "Yeah, I figured out how to do this, too. Cool."

She'd crossed the bridge that Pinnacle made between us, same as I had.

"Let me go, Hanna! This thing is using me as a conduit to activate Skyfall."

"Then we'll override it. Both of us together should be able to make this damn computer listen to our commands."

The countdown. No choice. I didn't know what the hell I was doing—this was all happening inside my head like some kind of nightmare video game—but outside of us the consequences were deadly real.

But Hanna knew Pinnacle. Maybe she was the key. "Do it, then! Shut the damn thing off!"

Hanna's awareness shifted away from me, focused outward. I concentrated on finding my way through Pinnacle's sharp, cold logic, across lines of code crafted by the most brilliant minds Crane could afford.

And further, to the strangely alien, unknowable consciousness of Skyfall. Or at least the computer that housed it.

My consciousness could only circle around it, not touch it directly. But I saw it in my mind's eye, quietly menacing on the tarmac, a hum growing louder within. Powering up.

This thing that had destroyed two species. Two entire planets. Only seconds now separated us from the same fate. Seconds before a gamma-ray burst like a travel-sized supernova within our atmosphere and irradiated all life on Earth.

How did I shut it off? How did Crane plan to control it after launch—did he think he had any power over it at all? Or was that what Hanna had been for?

Those megobari commandos who had orchestrated this were probably watching from a safe distance and laughing to themselves about how easy the humans were to fool.

Wait. Where would they hide from a gamma-ray burst but be close enough to watch us?

"Hanna. Hanna!" I didn't know if I made any sound, or if it was all in my head, but I shouted anyway.

A few precious seconds ticked by before she responded. "I can't—I can't access this—Pinnacle is ignoring my commands. Cass!"

"If it launches, Hanna, can we direct its path? Can we send it into space?"

A quick pause. "Yes. I think so. Pinnacle has access to navigational systems, GPS . . . so we have access to it."

"Can you program it now?" My voice, even the one inside my head, was pitching toward hysteria. Seconds were in the double digits now and counting. "If you direct its path, I'll try to delay the activation of the gamma-ray burst until it's safe." *Try.* That was all I had.

We worked in silence for the tense few seconds we had left.

Then it was ten, nine, eight . . .

"Hanna?!"

Seven, six . . .

"Y-yes. I've got it. I think."

Five, four . . .

I tightened my tenuous grasp on Skyfall. Skyfall, an autonomous weapon designed to not be influenced by outside sources, to operate despite whatever chaos may be happening around it, created to resist the exact kind of tampering we were attempting.

Three, two . . .

Listen to me, damn you. This is not happening today. You will not end us.

One.

THIRTY-NINE

I FELT IT like it was happening to a detached limb. Skyfall lifted into the sky vertically, like a fly taking off, buzzing and humming with more energy than our sun would ever produce.

I immediately lost what little hold I had. "Hanna!"

"Got you." She somehow pulled the reins of Pinnacle back from my loosened grasp and we held them together, scrambling for purchase, for some sort of control. "I think I've charted its path, but it keeps fighting me."

I went silent, all my concentration focused as I searched for a weak point, an entry point. Changing tactics, I tried expanding my awareness, broadening it, using every output and input source Pinnacle had access to.

I dove deep into the network, like Pinnacle had attempted

to do to my brain. I wanted to control it like it would have controlled me: see with my eyes, hear with my ears, touch with my hands. I needed to *inhabit* the network.

For the briefest of seconds, I wished Luka had come. He might have been able to communicate better with Skyfall—it was his people's design, after all. But he was so changed from the form it was designed for . . . maybe it would have been useless, after all.

And then it hit me. Luka might not have been able to help me, but someone still could.

Skyfall continued to rise into the atmosphere, but its path curved. It was climbing over land, reaching the optimum altitude to disperse its payload. The explosion of gamma radiation that would sterilize Earth.

"No, no no no!" Hanna said, and went silent as I felt her working to correct its path. Skyfall stuttered, stilled in midair as they waged war for control.

I had to trust that she would win. I reached my consciousness out to its farthest borders—the GPS and communications satellites that Pinnacle had access to. And, as I had hoped, I felt God-Mother's curious and concerned awareness reaching out from the border of Earth's atmosphere.

God-Mother, help me save this place.

Once invited, I felt her swooping strength come into me, invading the network with such a furious strength it was as though she had been quietly tapping at the door this entire time. She was so very old and so very strong she didn't even need to be physically connected to us.

Her thoughts were radio waves. Her wireless hands touched our internet, our satellites, our computers. I saw glimpses of our world as she saw it: arcing rainbows of light across the surface of our world, each person connected to another and to machines through dozens of interlinked pathways. Trillions of connections. Our entire world was a neural network, a living organism, each human a neuron passing messages along endless dendrites.

Joined with her now on a common mission, I finally saw just how powerful she was. Why the megobari, though utterly misguided in their hate, had been willing to destroy themselves to rid the universe of these beings. How so very many of these God-Mothers working together would be a terrifying force.

It was God-Mother who found the weak point in Skyfall's firewall and dismantled it like a master locksmith. But it was Hanna and I, together with Pinnacle, who directed Skyfall to fly out of the atmosphere.

I closed my metaphorical hand around Skyfall and kept it from releasing into the open air.

"What should we do with it?" Hanna asked. "It's not able to be shut down once activated. We're just delaying it. As soon as we disconnect from Pinnacle, Skyfall will go back to autopilot and detonate."

"Detonate it on the far side of the moon," I suggested. *And if those megobari bastards are camped out there, serves them right.*

"But it's so close," Hanna said. "The moon *might* absorb it all. We don't know how big the explosion will be. The radiation burst might be so intense as to overcome the gravitational binding energy of the moon, and then we'd only succeed in breaking up the moon and causing it to rain down on Earth."

I swore. Repeatedly.

God-Mother made her presence known, unobtrusively, like raising a finger to gain our attention.

She had a solution.

FORTY

GOD-MOTHER WOULD TAKE Skyfall. She would take over the temporary stay Hanna and I had put into place on the detonator, and fly far from here. As far as possible, toward the interior of the galaxy, where there was naturally more radiation and less chance of impacting any galactic life. Once safely away, she would take her finger off the trigger and let it detonate, destroying the weapon for good.

We were silent. I sensed Hanna's utter bewilderment with what was going on and promised to catch her up later. If we had the time.

"Why would you do that?" I asked, half in awe, half suspicious of God-Mother's selflessness.

I am dying, she reminded me simply. *I would prefer this to the*

*alternative. And I will do whatever is necessary to protect my chil-
dren.*

She would leave them here, she said. They would survive
without her for a short time, though not for long—it would be
the equivalent of cutting out a majority of their brains. They
were only satellites orbiting her; without God-Mother, they
would eventually stop foraging for food and starve. They would
not know how to continue living.

But she had a plan for that, and as she explained, I saw the
elegance of it. She had come a long way, borne much pain and
many losses, to provide a future for her children. She needed my
help to complete the task. There was no way she could guarantee that I'd help her; she could only hope and trust. Trust a
member of another species like she'd sworn never to do again.

"I will help you," I promised. And I meant it with my whole
heart. "I won't take no for an answer."

God-Mother did not have a mouth, but I could feel her
smiling—or whatever emotion she exuded that was translated
by my brain as a smile.

"Can we trust this thing?" Hanna asked me, as privately
as was possible in this weird pseudoreality. "We're handing a
weapon that can cause mass extinction to an alien with questionable motives."

I felt that God-Mother heard her. But I was the one who
answered. "Her motive is to save her children. That's always
been her motive. Do you sense any dishonesty in her?"

It was possible that God-Mother was a master manipulator.

That she was expertly hiding her true thoughts and intentions behind a simplistic front. But I didn't think so.

"It's our best shot," I told Hanna. *And besides—I trusted you, and you betrayed me. An alien intelligence couldn't do worse.*

The thought escaped me without volition, and I realized as soon as it happened that Hanna would hear the words.

"Cass, I . . . I didn't know." I couldn't see her face, but Hanna's emotions came across. And it was perhaps the first time I'd ever heard her contrite. "I thought I was doing the right thing. Protecting . . . everyone."

"We all make mistakes," I said, still angry.

God-Mother worked with us to redirect Skyfall's path. We let her take control as it flew out of our atmosphere and into the open port of her ship. A few beats later, a small sliver of ship detached from the main body. God-Mother took her ship, took Skyfall, and directed her course.

I could sense her pain at leaving her children. Her determination to save them. Her hope for their future. *I'll keep my end of the deal. I promise.*

This weapon killed my sisters, she responded, already far away. *It is fitting I should join them this way. Ensure that it never happens again.*

The sole survivor of systematic slavery and genocide. The last survivor of this terrible weapon, volunteering to fall under the blade of her oppressors. I was under no illusion that this sacrifice was for us—for Earth, for humanity. We had done terrible things ourselves. Oppression and slavery and genocide were part of our DNA, too. We were no better. We hadn't yet destroyed an entire planet of rival aliens, but that was simply from lack of opportunity.

This was to save her children. This was a charge for us to *do better* for future generations.

And I was going to honor that sacrifice if it killed me.

With silent acknowledgment, God-Mother shouldered our burden and headed for the stars.

FORTY-ONE

I OPENED MY eyes to my mother's face.

I jumped. Or tried to. But my body wouldn't respond. I tried opening my mouth and that, too, wasn't working.

"Shh, shh, my love. You're all right." My mother's eyes were full of tears, but she was smiling, holding my hand tightly inside both of hers. I could feel her soft hands, her warmth. She'd been holding my hand a long time. My other hand was cold. "It's temporary. The paralysis, I mean. You were connected to that computer so long, they said . . ." She shook her head, confused. "They explained, but I didn't catch all of it. Your brain's neuroreceptors need to recover from all that stimulation. The important thing is you are okay, and you are safe, and I love you. You brave, brave girl." She kissed my forehead over and over, holding my face in her hands.

When she sat down again, my vision was blurred from tears. I didn't immediately notice the other figure in the room.

Hanna stood at the foot of my bed. "Yeah, it happened to me, too."

I blinked and the tears fell down my cheeks, clearing my eyes. Her arms were folded across her chest but she was smirking.

"Didn't last as long for me—I'd been training with Pinnacle for a lot longer. First time, I was out as long as you. Doctors say you'll get some locomotion back in a few hours. They can knock you out until then, if you want."

I tried shaking my head, couldn't. Blinked instead.

"I take that as a no." She came and sat on my other side. My mom didn't let go of my hand. "I just thought you might want to know what's up. You're at a hospital in Houston. They're giving you fluids and electrolytes and monitoring you. The government backed down after I explained what happened. I told them we neutralized the risk and they don't know enough to contradict me, just that there are no more explosions. Luka's apparently working to set up a meeting with his people, making sure I'm not a liar. He doesn't think that they'll . . . do what they did again, now that the main problem is gone."

She was being intentionally vague for my mother's sake. I'd have to tell her later how much I appreciated that.

"Anyway, the rest of your family is waiting outside. If you want them to come in, just blink."

I blinked.

She nodded and stood. "I'll leave you alone. There are more people waiting to talk to you when you're able to get up and around." She gave me a pointed look. "We have some loose ends."

That could wait. Other people could handle that. Luka could handle his people alone for a bit.

As the rest of my family poured into the room—not just my dad and my grandma and my uncle, but also my mom's sisters, my other grandma, all my cousins, and their kids, until the room was full to bursting—I just let myself be swallowed up in the suffocating, overwhelming, unconditional, complete love I had never fully appreciated until now.

"I do not know if they will agree to meet with you," Luka said.

I was perched on the edge of my bed, my balance still a little fragile, my legs contrasting darkly against the white hospital gown and bedding. I'd finally convinced my mom to go get some rest after she had been sure I could speak, sit up, and walk to the bathroom on my own.

There was an actual security guard at my door—hired by the hospital, my mom had told me, because apparently someone had leaked just enough information about what my role had been in "saving the world." Funny for a girl who had a bright red bumper sticker that said "FALL RISK" on my hospital room door.

I told the guard to let Luka in first, and wait a few minutes before bringing up Emilio and Mitsuko.

Luka had gone to embrace me, and then paused halfway, unsure. I laughed and told him he had better hug me. I was relaxed and happy, still drunk from all the love my family had heaped on me.

"I don't know how you did it. But thank you," he whispered in my ear.

"It wasn't all me." My arms were too tired to hold him long, but I didn't want him to let go. He'd held me tight until Emilio knocked.

I briefed them—*very* briefly. I didn't have time to field their shocked, outraged, and bewildered reactions, waving my hand for them to quiet down so I could talk.

"We're not out of the woods yet. There are still vrag in orbit; there are some rogue megobari commandos armed with, presumably, more explosives. We have a treaty to discuss."

Luka cocked his head at me.

"Your people are still heading here. God-Mother sacrificed herself because I promised to look after her children. I'm not going to let another war break out when they get here. I need to talk to your commandos."

"They're not *mine*," Luka said. "They don't report to me. I am no more important to them than a child to the FBI."

"But won't they at least *listen* to you?" Emilio asked.

"Don't tell them the reason for the meeting," Mitsuko suggested.

Emilio's eyes brightened, and he pointed at Mitsuko in agreement. "Yeah, do that."

Luka sat down beside me on the bed. Reached over and held my hand. Searched my eyes. "It's . . . I cannot guarantee this will go well."

"I'm not asking you to."

His face was beseeching. "Please . . . don't judge me based on their actions. We are not all the same."

I squeezed his hand weakly. "I know that."

"There is another thing." He took a long, steadying breath. "The threat is gone now. The original agreement between our people may have died with our crews. Would you wish to . . . should we . . . revive it?"

"I think . . . that's not a decision to make between you and me. This involves *everyone*. And I don't know how my country will feel about allying with aliens who just blew up shrapnel over all their major cities and tried to goad us into destroying ourselves."

He gave a nod, resigned.

"But I'm willing to use whatever influence I have—and that may be none, just so you know—to try to convince my people to say yes."

"Really?"

"Of course. What else are we going to do, turn you away to the cold darkness of space? You're refugees. We could help each other. You guys could make it up to us by teaching us how to NOT destroy Earth, so we could share it with you and future generations. And humanity has a pretty sucky history of generosity and overcoming our differences, but . . . I think there's a way we can move forward together. Become better together. Don't you?"

He smiled. "When do you want to do this?"

"As soon as possible. Now, if you can swing it."

And that was how we planned an impromptu intergalactic teleconference in my hospital room.

Mitsuko pulled the curtain over the window and told the security guard to let no one in under any circumstances.

Luka put in the call.

I sat in my hospital bed with my back to the wall, as straight as possible. Mitsuko had helped clean up my face and shape my hair in such a way that I didn't look like a wild animal anymore. But that was more for my confidence. We wouldn't be able to see each other with Luka's communication device; they had apparently left Earth when the whole thing with Skyfall had gone down, and were now too far away to be able to speak live on video.

Not that we'd be able to understand each other. Verbally, anyway—Luka advised us that the device would translate our speech into text both ways.

The wall flickered.

Luka spoke normally. "Thank you for speaking with us."

Text, in English, ran across the bottom of the rainbow display.

We are glad to see you yet survive, the one they call Luka. This planet came very close to annihilation.

Luka nodded as though these were typical pleasantries and

didn't mention that the only threat to Earth had come from them. "Is the fleet near? Has Tamaz joined you yet?"

The megobari seemed to think he wanted to jump ship with them. *He is with us. We await the fleet from the fifth planet of this system's star. We anticipate their arrival within one half of Earth's solar year.*

Six months. That might be enough time for us to prepare everyone on Earth for their arrival.

Text flashed again. *Do you wish to join us?*

Luka shook his head, though it looked like it pained him. "No, thank you. Earth is my home, and it always has been. I hope, in fact, it can become the home of all megobari."

And with that, he handed the device to me.

"Hello," I said, heart in my throat. "I'm Cassandra Gupta. I'm the one who saved this planet's ass," and then stopped and shook my head because that was not only stupidly phrased but also probably untranslatable. "I'm here to tell you that we, as humans, would welcome the megobari refugees to enter into negotiations for a plan that would allow long-term sanctuary on Earth for all megobari who desire it."

There was a long time before any response came through. I read that as shock. *You are the spokesperson for your species?*

"God, no," I said, and Emilio had to stifle a laugh. "There are so many of us, and none of us can ever agree on something for very long. I offer only the chance to negotiate. But before that can happen, I need something from you. I need the virus, or the technology that enables the creation of the virus, that allowed for Luka's family to adapt their forms to human."

The response was almost immediate. *No.*

"Yes," I replied. "First, because your biology isn't perfectly suited for this planet." That line had come from Luka. "And second, it may be a condition of the rest of my species to accept your living here. We have a hard enough time getting along with *each other*, with people who have the same DNA, but different skin colors or religions. At least at first, there's no way we can work together if we cannot even communicate face-to-face."

Acceptable, they finally said. *For the stated purposes only.*

"Actually, there was another thing. I need the virus now. And I need someone who can manipulate it."

Then I explained to them, patiently and calmly, that I had given Skyfall to the last remaining God-Mother, and if I was not given access to the virus that would allow the remaining vrag in orbit to change their DNA and live the rest of their natural lives on Earth in whatever form they chose, that I would call back God-Mother.

It was hard to tell, without seeing them, but I think it's safe to say they were furious. I'd given them no choice. Compliance or destruction.

Same as they had given the vrag.

The rest happened mostly without me. Luka oversaw the creation and exchange of the virus. A few weeks later, when I was fully functional again, Luka, Hanna, and I were brought aboard the vrag mother ship. The vrag were obviously bereft without

God-Mother; they floated aimlessly through their empty caverns, their colors muted and dull. Dying.

I picked out one of the larger ones, who approached me curiously, a friendly stray. I reached out my bare hand, covered with a shimmering electronic tattoo made of conductive gold leaf, that would act as a conduit and allow me to communicate—theoretically—without a direct neural link.

The air was chilly in here, like a basement in winter. My fingers slowly grew colder as the vrag reached a tentative arm toward my hand. "That's right," I encouraged it quietly. Luka and Hanna waited beside me with bated breath.

The moment its nerve endings touched my own amplified ones, the message we'd programmed—with help from a reluctant megobari commando—was transmitted.

It was a question. As simple as we could form it. We had no idea how much the individual vrag knew about what had happened, what they could comprehend or communicate, why their God-Mother had abandoned them, how much they could even understand about the world around them without God-Mother's influence.

It was an offering of peace, if they chose to accept it. Of freedom, albeit in a different sort of life.

We didn't know if they would even accept. They had never known "freedom." They had never known anything but life aboard this ship, and the directing of their daily lives. We didn't even know if they'd survive the procedure.

A tremor went through the vrag, and its arm wrapped

securely, though not painfully, around my wrist. With another yards-long arm, it reached out to one of its companions. The message traveled this way, through touch and through bright, arcing colors to those too far away to reach.

In moments, we had a unanimous response.

Yes.

FORTY-TWO

"WELL, CASS, YOU did it. Ended an intergalactic feud that destroyed two planets. Stopped the Earth from burning in the fire of a thousand suns. Brokered peace between the Capulets and the Montagues. Saved a dying species by giving them a new life on Earth. Well, maybe even *two* species, if we can all get our act together." Emilio was ticking them off on his fingers. "What *are* you going to do next? And don't say 'I'm going to Disney World,' because that's what EVERYONE picks."

I groaned, throwing myself back on the couch and closing my eyes. "Number one: eat popcorn. Number two: survive my birthday party. Number three: go back and finish my last year of high school so I can graduate, probably?"

"Holy shit, I forgot. You haven't even graduated yet.

Goddamn, you make me feel like I've done nothing with my life."

"Seriously, Cass? They're going to make you go back to high school? Can't they just retroactively award you valedictorian and mail you your diploma, with many apologies for being late and also a great big 'Thank you for saving our butts' bouquet made of money and/or chocolate strawberries?" Mitsuko plucked the bowl of popcorn from Emilio's lap and wordlessly shared it with Michael, who was sitting on her other side.

"If only. Anyway, I kind of like the idea of intimidating all my classmates and teachers with my heroic and godly presence." But also, I wanted to try to go back to that time when I was normal, and a nobody—even though I wasn't sure that would happen anytime soon. And I wanted to earn my diploma. Actually *earn* it. I'd already worked it out with my school to let me come back. Extenuating circumstances, after all. "Geez. It's so weird having all of you in my *house*. Where I *live*."

"Worlds colliding, huh?" Emilio grinned.

They were all here: Emilio, Mitsuko, Michael, Luka. All of us crammed onto the small couch in the same living room where I'd first pleaded my case to my parents to let me go try out for NASA. It seemed insane now that they'd let me go. They probably figured it was like a summer camp, that I'd be home in a week, two tops.

It had, in fact, taken almost a full year.

I'd gotten mostly back to normal, though I sometimes had nightmares where I was paralyzed in an HHM as the Earth blew up around me, leaving nothing intact except me.

Luka kept in regular communication with the megobari contingent on the moon, and they in turn had entered talks with receptive Earth governments. I hadn't communicated with them again. We hadn't ended on the best terms, after all. But they seemed to care about Luka and his well-being, and were actually considering our proposal. So that was something.

Luka was on my other side, holding my hand. He'd meant it when he'd told me he wouldn't leave. But he had no home left anymore. We'd had to petition the government, through Crane, to help craft him a new identity. His father had left him some money, and it hadn't taken long for him to find a job here at Marshall.

I also had a job waiting for me when I graduated. Pierce had called and offered it to me personally. I could have my pick of locations, he'd said. Pasadena, Houston, Florida. With all that was happening, Congress was falling all over themselves to throw money at NASA. They'd passed the biggest budgets since the Apollo programs.

My dad had laughed with joy when he'd heard how much his department was getting funded next year. "With this kind of money? We will catch up to your megobari friends in no time."

I'd told Pierce I wanted to stay at Marshall. Though I wanted to be in an engineering department this time.

Pierce told me not to worry about college. As long as I worked with NASA, they'd send me to school to learn whatever I wanted.

I hadn't told Mitsuko and Emilio that I wouldn't be going back to Houston with them. I'd lost a year with my family. I couldn't leave them again so soon.

Life was short. My family wouldn't be here forever. Dadi wouldn't be here forever.

She came through the doorway now, as full of life as ever, holding a massive tray of food. "What are you doing, silly girl, eating popcorn when I've slaved all day to provide this feast?"

"It's my birthday, Dadi!"

"Yes, yes, it's your birthday, but that does not give you the right to fill up on junk food! Have some respect for your elders!"

I jumped up off the couch and took the heavy tray from her hands, kissing her cheek. "I love you, Dadi. And I appreciate you cooking for me."

She rolled her eyes.

My uncle Guaresh's voice came from the open door to the backyard. "Where is the birthday girl? Everyone out here is hungry!"

"Coming, Chacha!" I called. I shot a glance at my friends on the couch and jerked my head toward the direction of the door. "Leave the popcorn!"

A cheer went up at the long picnic table my parents had set up in the backyard. It was August first and oppressively hot, but my entire extended family had gathered from across the country, and in some cases across the globe, to be here today, and we didn't all fit inside the house.

August first. On this day last year, I'd stepped into the

Johnson Space Center and my destiny. Now I was closing the chapter of my eighteenth year and . . . kind of had mixed feelings about it.

I'd lost half of that year asleep, hurtling through space. But I'd packed more than one lifetime in the remaining months.

Maybe I *had* peaked at eighteen.

My friends filed out behind me and were lost to the noise and chaos of my welcoming family members, who were now ignoring me in favor of these new people they could pester to death with questions.

I put the tray down on the table and sighed. Before this year was out, the megobari fleet would arrive. Would we have to do this all over again? Luka had sworn to me that his people would not risk a violent confrontation with humans. Most of us are not like that, he'd said. Desperate times, et cetera.

That remained to be seen. But it wasn't something to worry about now. There would be a place for me at the negotiation table; Luka had offered it to me, if I wanted it. I hadn't decided— not sure that I was the kind of person who needed to be in charge of such decisions. I'd made a lot of mistakes.

Or maybe I needed to be there, to help others keep from making similar mistakes.

I looked up at the Alabama sky, as blue as a blessing, immaculate. God-Mother had saved three peoples with her sacrifice: hers, ours, and her enemy's. And no one on Earth knew it. I'd have to do something about that.

The world was about to change wildly—and, hopefully, for the better.

"Looking up?" Luka came up behind me, close and safe and warm. He reached around me to show me his cell phone. It was open to a news site, a small article buried in the depths of the science section:

Scientists baffled by mysterious gamma-ray burst in Milky Way galaxy: Earth safely out of range

I smiled sadly up at him. "We owe her everything. You know that? She deserved more."

"You gave her what she wanted: all her children are now frolicking happily in Earth's oceans."

This was true. We'd allowed the vrag to each choose whatever animal, including human, they wanted to become in order to live on Earth. All of them had chosen the sea as their home. Most of them jellyfish, coral, or octopuses; it was a closer, more familiar form. "Yeah. To Earth's polluted, overfished ocean. Not much guarantee of a happy life."

"We'll change that. And there's never a guarantee of a happy life. We can only help others, and try to find happiness ourselves."

We still hadn't had that talk—about what this all meant for us. We were still just feeling our way. But I had told him that, even though I cared about him, I wasn't sure I'd ever be interested in doing much more than kissing. He'd been more supportive than I'd expected, promising we'd never go further than I wanted.

We'd been through a lot in a short period of time. We'd supported and relied on each other. And while the future wasn't certain, I was starting to wonder what it might be like to want

360

to do more. Maybe I'd come to feel differently a few years down the road, and maybe not. But right now, we were happy.

I squeezed his arms tighter around me, and hoped actions spoke louder than words.

I'd heard that they were recalibrating Pinnacle's programming under the direction of the FDA, so it couldn't be abused—a movement reportedly spurred on by very powerful female lobbyists, who were apparently appalled that their daughter was able to be rendered comatose and have her body taken out of her control by SEE's computer program.

Sunny, meanwhile, was a permanent fixture in my brain. I had been hearing her less and less, and was beginning to wonder if she was becoming part of me, or I was becoming a part of her. Hanna had sent me a message a few weeks ago, promising to keep in touch without Crane's influence, so we could help each other monitor the progression of our new . . . status. Pretty sure she was hoping to get some kind of new patent out of the deal. There weren't many like us, but there were a lot of people eager for technology like this to improve their lives, and willing to volunteer for trials.

Soon, there'd be a lot more people with implants like ours. Computers that would help physically disabled people communicate better with their robotic prostheses, or electrodes that could help reestablish communications between a paralyzed person's brain and body. It had been possible for a long time, but the technology had been in its infancy—and now was becoming an entirely new field. The fact that I was on the forefront, a prototype, was both exciting and a little nerve-racking.

Not only that, but with the coming megobari fleet, I was one of only a very small number of people who would be able to communicate with them, using Sunny as an intermediary. I'd already agreed to become one of America's translators, when the time came.

I'd heard that Hanna, using Pinnacle, was translating for the EU. Mitsuko was competing for the chance to be Japan's official spokesperson for their own seat at the discussion table, using their own computer program. I had hopes that we would all be there to help guide the future of human and megobari relations.

My mom was already fielding calls from researchers looking to include me in studies.

"Call back when she graduates high school," she always said before hanging up.

I hadn't expected Hanna to come. She hadn't RSVP'd to my invite or even spoken to me for weeks, beyond an occasional message asking me about how I was faring with Sunny. But then she was on my doorstep, an hour late to my birthday party, chagrined and cautious. She'd kept the darker brown color in her hair, just as I'd kept my short haircut, both of us choosing to own the ways we'd changed. It made her look older, and softened her a little.

"Can we talk?" she asked.

I stepped out onto the porch and closed the door behind me, muting the sounds of my little cousins chasing each other with lightsabers in the living room. "I didn't think you were coming."

She shrugged noncommittally. I waited a long moment for

her to speak, and then reached impatiently for the doorknob.

"I thought I was doing the right thing," Hanna blurted. She was facing the front yard, looking out over my street, as though she might leave at any moment. "Taking Skyfall to Crane. It was a mistake."

I crossed my arms over my chest. "How long did it take you to figure that out?"

"As soon as they hooked me up to it." She whirled on me, fists clenched at her sides. "I came really close to destroying everything. I stole Skyfall—"

"—and Mitsuko's rental car."

"And the rental," she added with some extra venom. "Things were looking bad. You and Luka, sacrificing yourselves. I thought giving the weapon to Crane was the one thing I could do. And, yeah, I thought it'd help smooth things over with him. I really did come on my own to help you, you know. But I didn't really trust Luka or your judgment, to be honest. So I took matters into my own hands. And I guess I . . . need to . . . apologize."

To her credit, she lifted her chin and met my gaze. And she wasn't cowed.

But she was sincere.

I raised my eyebrows. "Is this the first time you've ever apologized?"

She gave me a mocking look. "Shut up. I'm trying to make amends here. I realize I screwed up, okay? I can't stop thinking about how close we came."

"I know." I still had nightmares about the ways things might have gone. "But you're not the only one who screwed up. If we hadn't brought back the weapon. If Luka's family had told us the truth about it. If the megobari hadn't invented Skyfall in the first place. Long chain of screwups got us to this point. Mine still haunt me. Yours was hardly the worst of the bunch."

"Really?" Hanna looked incredulous. "Just like that?"

I shook my head, suddenly tired. "Life's too short, Hanna. We just can't make the same mistakes again."

She nodded slowly.

"Are we good now? Because I feel like we need to be good, you and me. We're not quite done yet." I held out my hand.

She bit her lip in a moment of hesitation, and then grasped my outstretched hand. "In the future, I'll call you out on your shit, if you call me out on mine."

I laughed. "Deal. Now get in here."

We went inside together and I wound my way back through the house, finding Luka on the way. Hanna went on to join the party without me, giving me one last nod.

"You okay?" he asked, reading my expression and watching Hanna walk away.

"Yeah." I smiled. "Let's eat."

The chairs at the table on the back porch were filling up. "We should probably find a place to sit down," I told him.

"No, no, no," my father said, taking hold of my shoulders. Dadi was with him. The four of us stood at the head of the table, and dozens of pairs of eyes were now looking at us. "You're the guest of honor—you'll stay right here!"

Luka, holding back his laughter and ignoring my silent pleas for help, left me to be the center of attention and took a seat at the table. He shunned the limelight as much as possible. Only a few people knew his true identity, or his actual role in everything that had happened.

Stragglers found their seats, and silence slowly descended over the backyard.

"Today," my father began, "my daughter turns nineteen. She has accomplished amazing things in those short years. She has become her own person. I remember when she was born, how small and helpless and beautiful she was. I was proud of her from her very first breath. Her every accomplishment has swelled my heart with pride, from the first moment she reached her hand out and grasped my own. The smallest thing, but it was the biggest thing imaginable. She has now gone further in her life than her mother and I could have ever imagined. She has shown that there is no limit to what she can accomplish. No matter what you do, my girl, you are the pride and the joy of my heart."

He kissed the top of my head, and my tears fell onto his plaid shirt. The table broke out into cheers and whoops, and I recognized the voices of my friends.

"Can I say something?" I asked, struggling to clear the tears from my eyes and voice.

"Oh, fine. But keep it short, people are hungry!" Dadi said, giving me a sly smile.

I was overwhelmed. Words weren't fitting together quite right. The smiling, expectant faces before me kept blurring.

"Just that . . . I'm here because of all of you. Thank you for your support. Okay, I sound like a politician, but . . . really. I wouldn't be here without all of you. And I wouldn't want to be. So, thank you all for coming so far just to celebrate my birthday with me." Luka had cleverly dodged the spotlight by maneuvering around the table. He now stood at the edge of the patio. I met his eyes. "And . . . I love you."

His face broke into a wide, radiant grin.

Everyone else clapped and clamored for food, but Dadi held up a hand to silence them. "We don't always bless our food before eating it in this family," she said, with a pointed look at her oldest son. "But we will tonight. Tonight we have many people of different beliefs. But we are all gathered around the same table, and we are all blessed with our lives, our health, and our homes. And we will give thanks for these blessings. Yes, Gauresh, that means you, too! Bow your heads!"

And she spoke a prayer she must have worked on with my mother, as it was a strange and beautiful mix of Christian and Hindu and a little she might have made up on the fly. "Let us always look up to the stars with wonder in our hearts. Let us look into the eyes of another and find those same stars. Let us have gratitude. Let us live joyfully with one another."

As everyone grew distracted with eating and the passing of plates, I met Mitsuko's eye and slipped around the side of the house where darkness would shield me. The din of the crowd faded.

Moments later, my friends joined me, the shadows shifting

to close around them like a protective curtain. I saw the white flash of Mitsuko's grin as she reached out and squeezed my hand, Michael coming right behind her. Emilio was all shadows and movement. Hanna's dark hair gleamed as she trailed behind them both.

Luka arrived last. He came to my side, and in the privacy of darkness, I pressed my fingers into his palm. I was too over-come with emotion to speak.

Luckily, Emilio never had that problem. "You guys, we're missing out on the food!"

"Do you ever think about anything beyond your stomach?" Hanna asked.

"Yes," he said defensively. "Just not right now. There is *so much Indian food.*"

"If you kids can't get along, I will turn this thing around," Mitsuko said.

"Already such a good mother," said her husband, resting his chin on her shoulder.

"I just wanted to talk to you guys all at once," I began. "I wanted to tell you . . . if it wasn't for you, we wouldn't be here celebrating my birthday today. And I—"

Mitsuko cut me off by wrapping her arms around my shoulders. "As if you needed to say anything, Cass."

Emilio followed, engulfing the both of us. Michael, Hanna, and Luka circled the three of us like Saturn with its rings.

I looked up at the bright stars in the blue-black sky, shim-mering from behind the tears in my eyes, and knew without a doubt that I would see the stars again.

"So are we going, or what?" Emilio asked.

"Going?" I repeated, puzzled.

"You know how we've been jealous of you going on this interstellar mission without us, Cass?" Mitsuko asked.

"Yeah, it's not fair," Emilio said. "So we kind of asked—"

"—*bribed*—"

"—Luka into setting up a little surprise for your birthday."

I gave Luka a quizzical look.

His eyes glittered in amusement, a mischievous expression I'd never seen him wear before. "I brought *Penelope* here. God-Mother had sent it back to the desert. It's hidden out in the trees behind your house. I thought we could introduce your friends to the stars. If that sounds good to you."

Laughter burst out of me. "You people are ridiculous. Here? Now? Go to *space*?"

Luka was still smiling at me, eyebrows raised in challenge. "Why not? It's only about sixty-two miles straight up. *Penelope* can run pretty quiet when she wants to. We can just go as far as low Earth orbit, take a quick look around. We can be back in twenty minutes."

Incredulous, I turned to Hanna. "You're okay with this?"

"Luka assured me that megobari ships are much roomier than ours. And if I didn't want to go into space, I wouldn't have been in that competition to begin with."

I shook my head at them, now all grinning like fools at me, and knew there was no dissuading them. Not that I wanted to.

Why not indeed? We had the technology now. This was

just a glimpse of our future: safe, casual, even *easy* spaceflight. Maybe humans would have their own designs in production before long, but it'd take a few years, at least.

We might have just been a handful of above-average kids making a series of questionable choices, but right now we were the only ones on Earth who had that technology all to ourselves.

It'd be a waste not to use it. Right?

Space would never be without danger, but at least here, and now, there was nothing standing in our way. I had once thought that if only I could go to space, just once, I could die happy.

Now I knew that once would never be enough.

"Okay," I said, and my friends cheered. "Let's go to space."

ACKNOWLEDGMENTS

IT'S SUCH A strange thing to be writing acknowledgments for this book—one that I wasn't sure I'd ever get to even write. Thank you, readers, for following Cassie's journey to its end.

Thank you to everyone at Harper who worked on this duology: my editors, Jen Klonsky and Catherine Wallace, and especially to the copyeditors who saved me: thank you for helping me discover that I apparently like to rhyme subconsciously. Thank you also to production editors Alexandra Rakaczki and Gwen Morton; Sarah Kaufman and Alison Klapthor, who made the most beautiful cover I could ever have hoped for; and Allison Brown, Bess Braswell, and Sabrina Abballe, for all your hard work.

Thank you to my audiobook narrator, Soneela Nankani, who

did such an incredible job narrating *Dare Mighty Things*, and did fantastically with made-up words and lots of people with accents.

To my agent, Kristin Nelson, who never wavers in her support, and helped whip this book into shape with her keen editorial eye: a million thank-yous are never enough.

A special shout-out to JJ DeBenedictis, who helped me describe as best I could what space might actually look like while traveling faster than light.

Thank you to my critique partners, Alexa Donne and Emily Neal, who held my hand during the rough ride that is writing a sequel, and to Elly Blake, who could also totally sympathize. Thanks to S.F. Henson, Alex White, and Beck McDowell, for being such great local author friends, and making sure my first-ever bookstore event was well attended. To my debut author friends—thank you for being such a supportive group and for always being there to answer questions! To my library patrons, some of whom I've literally watched grow up: it's been such a pleasure serving you. Thank you for supporting me in return.

Last time, I thanked my library ladies, but now I need to update that list with a couple more names. Elaine, my self-proclaimed publicist, who never passed up an opportunity to shove my book into someone's hands and surrounds every-one she meets with love: a big hug and thank you! Keshia and Hwoak, thank you for being so awesome at your jobs that I don't have to worry when I'm not there, and especially for cov-ering for me during all those times I needed to take off for one thing or another! Balancing a day job, parenting a small child, and managing a writing career can take a lot out of a person, but you all helped me make it possible.

A huge thank-you to the subscription boxes that included *Dare Mighty Things* in their book boxes: Once Upon a Book Club and The Bookie Box. That was a dream that I never even knew was possible until you made it happen.

Thank you from the bottom of my heart to everyone who shouted about *Dare Mighty Things* online, took beautiful Instagram pictures, wrote reviews, interviewed me for blogs, preordered my books, invited me to come speak to your groups, recommended my book to someone else, or just sent me nice messages. You are literally the reason authors do what they do.

To my husband, who is always game to field my questions about what's feasible in physics, logic, and engineering: I'm so glad to have had you beside me these past thirteen years. To my daughter, for being my motivation to succeed, for helping me learn time management skills, for sitting still long enough to give me a few minutes at the computer here and there, and for being just so darn cute. I love you both.

And most of all, to my parents. You shaped me, gave me the tools to become a fully functional adult (most of the time), pushed me to accomplish more than you yourselves had, and never failed to provide unconditional love and support all my life. I quite literally would not be where I am, or be the person I am, without your years of hard work, dedication, and sacrifices. Love always, and forever.